AWARDS AND HONORS FOR
Symptoms of Being Human

A Lambda Literary Award finalist

An ALA Top Ten Quick Pick for Reluctant Young Adult Readers

ALA Best Fiction for Young Adults

A Rainbow Book List selection

Goodreads Choice Award Young Adult Fiction nominee

A CCBC Choices Pick

Chicago Public Library's Best Teen Fiction

A Bank Street College of Education Best Book of the Year

Bank Street College of Education's "From Refugees to Voting
Rights, Books to Inspire a Just, Inclusive Society" list

"Riley is a smart, funny, sharp-eyed force."
—*Publishers Weekly* (starred review)

"One of the first YA books to deal
with the complex issue of gender fluidity."
—ALA *Booklist* (starred review)

SYMPTOMS
OF
BEING
HUMAN

JEFF GARVIN

Balzer + Bray
An Imprint of HarperCollinsPublishers

Some of the websites mentioned in this book are fictional. For real life LGBTQ support and information, please see the Resources section at the end of this book.

 HarperCollins
PUBLISHERS
Since 1817

Balzer + Bray is an imprint of HarperCollins Publishers.

Symptoms of Being Human
Copyright © 2016 by Jeff Garvin
All rights reserved. Printed in the United States of America.
No part of this book may be used or reproduced in any manner whatsoever without written permission except in the case of brief quotations embodied in critical articles and reviews. For information address HarperCollins Children's Books, a division of HarperCollins Publishers, 195 Broadway, New York, NY 10007.
www.epicreads.com

Library of Congress Cataloging-in-Publication Data
Garvin, Jeff.
  Symptoms of being human / Jeff Garvin. — First edition.
    pages cm
  Summary: "A gender-fluid teenager who struggles with identity creates a blog on the topic that goes viral, and faces ridicule at the hands of fellow students"— Provided by publisher.
  ISBN 978-0-06-238287-0
  [1. Identity—Fiction. 2. Gender identity—Fiction. 3. Sex role—Fiction. 4. Bullying—Fiction. 5. Blogs—Fiction. 6. High schools—Fiction. 7. Schools—Fiction.] I. Title.
PZ7.1.G377Sy 2016   2015015403
[Fic]—dc23   CIP
                                                                                  AC

17 18 19 20 21   PC/LSCH   10 9 8 7 6 5 4 3 2 1
❖

First paperback edition, 2017

To my parents,
who told me I could be whatever I wanted when I grew up.
Sorry I kept you waiting.

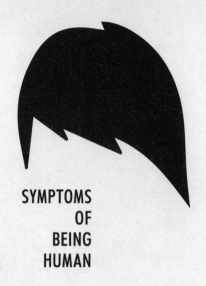

SYMPTOMS
OF
BEING
HUMAN

CHAPTER 1

NEW POST: ONE OR THE OTHER

OCTOBER 1, 6:55 AM

The first thing you're going to want to know about me is: Am I a boy, or am I a girl?

I STOP TYPING AND STARE at the cursor, which flashes at me incessantly, as if mocking my inability to write one stupid post.

"Riley!" It's my mom, calling me from downstairs in her singsongy voice. "If you still want to be early, you'd better come down for breakfast!"

I glance at the clock. I'm not really running *that* late—but I want to get the lay of the land while the campus is still mostly empty. "I'll be down in a minute!" I say, then click Delete, slam my laptop shut, and slide off my bed.

At least I can tell Doctor Ann I tried.

I stop in front of the mirror to examine myself. I don't know if this look will help me blend in at my new school, but it definitely exudes a sort of existential punk vibe, like, "I care so much, I don't care," that feels distinctly *me*. As a last touch, I mash down my bangs so they hide as much of my face as possible. It'll have to do.

Downstairs, my mother gives me a wide smile. "First day!" she says.

I manage to smile in return, and then I grab a box of cereal from the pantry and sit down at the table across from my dad.

"Ready to conquer Park Hills High?" he says. Then he looks up from his tablet, and his smile wilts as he notices my outfit.

I'm wearing a pair of jeans and my dad's old Ramones T-shirt, which I've modified to fit my smaller frame. Black Doc Martens—synthetic ones, no cows were harmed in the making of my shoes—round out the ensemble. I'm grateful that I don't have to wear a uniform anymore—I remember how suffocating it was to be confined to the same identity day after day, regardless of how I felt inside.

But the truth is, it still doesn't matter how I feel—because however I show up today, people will expect me to look the same tomorrow. Including my parents.

So my only choice is to go neutral.

"Is that my Ramones shirt?" Dad says.

"Once upon a time," I say.

He clears his throat. "Riley, are you sure that's how you want to present yourself on your first day?"

I open my mouth, then close it without saying anything.

Dad gestures at me with his grapefruit spoon. "You only

get one chance at a first impression."

I want to scream: *Like I don't know that!* But instead, I say, "I guess I'm hedging my bets. I want to see how the kids dress at public school. Don't want to overdo it and end up looking stupid." Dad seems to consider, then nods his head approvingly. By appealing to his sense of strategy, I've averted the Inquisition.

For now.

Ten minutes later, the three of us pile into Mom's minivan. I've agreed to let both parents escort me on my first day, but only on the condition that we *not* take the black Lincoln. I don't want anyone to see Dad's government license plates and connect Riley Cavanaugh with *Congressman* Cavanaugh. Maybe I'm being paranoid, but that kind of notoriety is the last thing I need on top of . . . well, on top of everything else.

We turn out of our gated community and onto Imperial Highway. The closer we get to the school, the more butterflies flap around in my stomach; I don't know what to expect. At Immaculate Heart, it was impossible for someone like me to avoid being singled out; the school was just too small and too conservative. Maybe the people here will be more open-minded. Or, at the very least, maybe I'll be able to blend in.

Finally, we reach the top of Lions Ridge, and Park Hills High School comes into view. It's a massive, U-shaped, concrete abomination, surrounded by wrought-iron gates encrusted with ten years of accumulated green paint.

"Hey," I say. "You can just pull over and drop me off here."

"It's a steep walk, honey," Mom says. "We'll drop you at the front."

"Mom, we talked about the 'honey' thing."

"Right," she says. "Sorry."

"Please, you guys, I just want to walk in."

"You mean you want to make an entrance," Dad says, a smile turning up one corner of his mouth.

I blink at him. He couldn't misunderstand me more if he actively tried. But if believing that will keep him from making a scene out of my arrival, I'll fake it.

"Yeah," I say. "I guess I do."

Mom glances at me in the rearview, her eyes narrowed, and I get the feeling she sees through my lie. She starts to say something, then seems to change her mind and just presses her lips together instead. Dad pulls to the curb and turns to face me.

"You're smart and resourceful, Riley," he says. "Put yourself out there, and you'll be an asset to this campus."

But I don't want to be an asset; I want to be invisible.

As they pull away, Mom gives me an ironic princess wave, and Dad makes devil horns with one hand. I roll my eyes, wait impatiently for the van to turn the corner, and then look around to get my bearings.

I'm about fifty yards from the school entrance, where a few clusters of students are beginning to form. I let out a long, slow breath and start toward the gates.

A green SUV pulls into the circular drive, and a blond girl in a short skirt climbs out. As she approaches her friends, she walks past a circle of guys passing around a basketball. One of them wolf-whistles at her, and she gives him the finger.

Then it's my turn to walk past them. My heart beats faster as I get close; I keep my head down and try to blend in with the concrete. To my relief, no one says anything to me; I've dodged the first bullet.

I'm only a few yards away from the big green gates now. All I have to do is make it past the group of girls, and then I'll be on campus, where I can disappear into a crowd.

But as I draw closer, two of the girls look up and notice me. I glance away, but I feel their eyes on me, scrutinizing, categorizing. I've been through this before, and it shouldn't get to me—but today, it does. My skin breaks out in goose bumps, and I wrap my arms around myself and walk faster.

"Oh my God," one of the girls says, and my head involuntarily turns to look at her. She's got long brunette hair and a small, perfect nose. "Holy shit, you guys." She lowers her voice to a stage whisper, but I can still hear what she says:

"Is that a girl, or a guy?"

A fit of giggles erupts from the group around her. My face goes hot. I walk faster, trying to escape the whispers.

"No," another girl says. "That has to be a . . ."

"Yeah, but look what it's wearing."

It. She called me *it*.

CHAPTER 2

THE FIRST DOOR I COME to is a restroom, and I burst in and lock myself in a stall. For a moment, I just lean against the cold metal door, staring at a patch of discolored grout on the tile wall.

It.

I've been called worse—much worse—but somehow this comment stings more than the rest. I haven't been here five minutes, and the harassment has already started. I even made an effort to dress as neutrally as I could stand—but it doesn't matter. My *differentness* is impossible to conceal. I feel a familiar heat behind my eyes and the beginning of a quiver in my bottom lip, but I bite down on it. I can't give in this easily. I can't let one bad moment ruin my chance at a fresh start. I close my eyes and take three long, deep breaths. Slowly, my heartbeat returns to normal.

I pull out my class schedule and check the map on the

back: my first class—AP English/Room 207—is on the other end of the campus. Class starts in fifteen minutes; if I want to avoid the rush, I'd better go now.

The quad at Park Hills High is approximately nine hundred miles from end to end and feels just like "the yard" in some old prison movie. I entertain a brief escape fantasy in which I'm shanked from behind and bleed out before the first bell rings so I don't have to face the rest of the day. No such luck—but I make it across without incident, push open the door to the language arts wing, and start down the hallway. I stop outside room 207 and peer in through the window, one of those tall, narrow ones with chicken wire between the panes. I can't see anyone inside, so I open the door and enter.

The empty desks are arranged in a grid, and I take a moment to consider my options. The front rows are no good, because I'd be on display for everyone as they come in—and, after the morning I've had, I'd rather avoid the scrutiny. But the last few rows are out, too, because teachers love to call on kids who sit in the back.

I choose a desk in the center of the room, drop my bag next to it, and slide into the chair. It's new; there's hardly any graffiti at all, only the word "penis" etched in one corner. Briefly, I consider inscribing "vagina" on the opposite side, just to balance it out.

Then the door bangs open and a huge guy lumbers into the room. He's at least six feet tall, probably over three hundred pounds, and he's wearing a black T-shirt depicting Darth Vader clutching an ice-cream cone. His nest of messy black hair is clamped under a pair of red headphones, and he appears to be playing an air guitar solo as he walks down the aisle, eyes closed, face contorting in an apoplexy of rage or ecstasy—it's hard to tell which. He goes up on tiptoe, pinwheels one arm to strike a triumphant chord on his imaginary ax, then falls to his knees and throws his hands up like he's taking in the applause of a stadium crowd.

After a long, gasping moment, he gets to his feet, slides into a desk right across the aisle from mine, and begins rummaging through his dilapidated backpack. I clear my throat to get his attention, but he doesn't respond; he probably can't hear me with those headphones on.

Finally, he turns his head to crack his neck. He opens his eyes, sees me—and flinches in surprise, knocking his backpack off the desk. His belongings spill into the aisle between us: books, papers, a Yoda pencil case, and an avalanche of small pink candies.

We stare at each other in wide-eyed silence for a long moment. And then the guy speaks, his voice about forty decibels louder than necessary.

"Jesus Christ on a cupcake! You scared the crap out of me!"

I gesture for him to take off his headphones.

"Oh yeah," he says too loudly. When he pulls them off his head, his hair springs up, giving him an electrocuted look. He stands and retrieves his backpack, while I slide out of my chair to help collect his belongings.

The candies turn out to be strawberry Starbursts, dozens of them. When I've picked up the last one, I drop the pile onto his desk and meet his gaze. His eyes are large and dark, and he stares at me for a long time, not saying anything. Part of me wants to turn away, to pull out a book and bury my face in it—but there's something about his presence, a gentle goofiness, that makes me take a chance.

Tentatively, I break the silence. "I'm Riley."

He blinks. "Solo."

I raise my eyebrows.

"That's what people call me," he says. "Short for Jason Solomona."

Solo snatches one of the Starbursts from his desk, unwraps it deftly, and crams it into his mouth. After a few hearty chews, he says thickly, "Want one?" I don't, but I feel like telling him no would be tantamount to refusing a peace offering from a foreign diplomat.

"Yeah, thanks," I say, and take one. It's sweet, and immediately adheres itself to one of my back molars like quick-dry cement. Solo stares at me for a moment, his eyebrows drawn together. He starts to speak, but hesitates.

My heart sinks; here we go. Come on. Let's get it out of the way.

Finally, he seems to make a decision, and says, "You're new."

"Yeah," I say, relieved.

"Where are you from? Wait," he interrupts himself, "don't tell me." He glances at my shirt, then leans into the aisle to look at something on the ground. My shoes? He straightens. "Midwest," he says.

Half amused and half confused, I tilt my head to one side. "Why the Midwest?"

He points to my Doc Martens. "Boots, not very practical for Southern California."

I start to retort, but he's already moved on.

"Authentic vintage Ramones shirt, not something you can just pick up at Hot Topic." He inclines his head as if waiting for confirmation.

My heart gives a pleasant twinge; the guy doesn't seem put off by my appearance at all; in fact, he seems genuinely interested. "Go on," I say.

"Unusual haircut. Rebellious air about you."

"Why does that make you think I'm from the Midwest?"

Solo shrugs. "Where else could you develop such contempt for traditional American values?"

That makes me smile. He smiles back.

"Now," he continues, putting a finger to his lips in a cartoonish imitation of a TV detective, "your vampiric Irish pallor suggests north of Indianapolis." He sits back in his chair and folds his enormous hands. "Chicago. Am I right?"

"Not quite," I say.

"Detroit!" he replies.

"Nope."

"Madison?"

I shake my head.

He throws up his hands. "I give up. Where?"

"Park Hills. About a mile from here."

He sags back into his seat, deflating like an enormous car dealership balloon that's been punctured by a sharp rock.

"Damn," he says. "I thought I had you pegged."

I shrug. "Sorry to disappoint."

He laughs. "Not disappointed, just surprised. You look . . ."

He pauses midsentence, and my heart sinks again. All the

words I'm afraid he might say rush in to fill the gap in his speech: Weird. Freakish.

Wrong.

But then he does speak, and he doesn't say any of those things. He says, "You look . . . too *exotic* for Park Hills."

Something inside me seems to swell and grow warmer, and I'm surprised when a weird laugh escapes me—something between a bark and a giggle. At the sound of it, Solo laughs, too. Caught up in the moment, I sort of flip my bangs back and say in a low voice, "Exotic, am I?"

Solo's smile falters, and the silence that ensues is so awkward that I want to climb under my desk and die. Solo flushes a deep brown, and I drop my gaze to my lap.

Stupid, stupid, stupid. I'm so desperate to make a friend that the second I get comfortable with someone, what do I do? I make some weird, embarrassing joke, and he interprets it as flirting. Ugh! It was the wrong thing, the wrong energy to send out in that moment. And despite my feeling neutral today, this guy clearly sees me as a guy; I can tell by his uncomfortable reaction to my unintended flirting. Now, there's a palpable weirdness between us, and I desperately wish I could take back that stupid hair flip and just keep my mouth shut.

Much to my relief, Solo starts speaking again as though nothing happened. "If you're from Park Hills, why am I seeing you for the first time a month into junior year?"

Eager not to make an ass of myself again, I execute the most nonchalant shrug in the history of shrugging. "I transferred from Immaculate Heart," I say. As soon as the words are out of my mouth, I wish I hadn't said them. If he asks why, what am I going to say? That I'm my father's political pawn? Or that I was trying to escape from a place where I was harassed and bullied on a daily basis? Charming small talk for a first conversation.

But Solo doesn't ask—he just glances down at my boots, then up at my hair, and says, "Catholic school. Of course. That would give anyone contempt for traditional American values."

I smile. "You were right about the Irish part, though." That seems to cheer him up.

The classroom door opens and two girls enter. I recognize the shorter one: she's the brunette with the perfect nose who speculated about my gender when I walked on campus. The one who called me "it." Hastily, I lean over to pretend I'm pulling another book out of my bag, surfacing only after the girl and her friend have taken their seats. As the classroom fills up, Solo sets about putting the Starbursts back into his backpack and stowing his headphones, and I bury my head in my AP English textbook.

I actually enjoy my first class. Miss Crane has a round, pleasant face, and turns out to be a total book geek; she makes multiple Harry Potter references and takes note of who gets them. She catches me snorting at one in which she speculates how an appearance by Ginny Weasley might have altered the plot of *Sense and Sensibility*. When the bell rings, I take my time packing up; I'm not eager to leave Solo or Miss Crane's Sanctuary for Geeks. I'm relieved when Solo tells me he has AP Government second period—because I do, too—and we head to class together. Or, more accurately, I follow him through the halls, walking in his considerable wake.

After the *it* incident this morning, I've braced myself to

be gawked at, even openly mocked in the halls—but mostly, the other students walk right past me like I'm anyone else. I do draw a few looks, though; a blond girl in a pretty lavender dress gives me a friendly smile as we pass each other. I smile back.

Then, just as I'm starting to believe I might actually fit in here, a short guy in a blue baseball cap looks me up and down. At first I think he's checking me out—but when we make eye contact, he shakes his head, frowning like he's disgusted. I pick up my pace as I walk past him and follow Solo up the stairs to our next class.

Mr. Brennan, the Government teacher, has an enormous Chuck Norris mustache and assigns desks by alphabetical order—so I'm forced to take my place in the middle of the second row, while Solo ends up one row over. When Brennan starts his lecture, I'm not listening; I'm replaying the whispers from this morning, and the disgusted look from the guy in the hallway.

At some point, I look up to find Mr. Brennan standing directly in front of my row.

"Anybody want to hazard a guess?" Brennan says, referring to a question I apparently didn't hear. "This is the US House of Representatives, people. The YOU-nited States. The country in which most of you were born." I look down at my desk, praying he doesn't call on me.

"Riley Cavanaugh," he says.

I open my mouth, intending to reply, but nothing comes out. After a moment, the guy in front of me—slight-framed, with dark hair to his shoulders and a black peacoat I kind of want to steal—speaks up in a voice that sounds like it hasn't changed yet: "Fifty?"

Brennan turns his gaze on him. "Incorrect. You might be thinking of the Senate, which comprises two representatives from each of the fifty states, for a total of one hundred."

The guy shrugs.

"Ah. Well, close, but no cigar. But, in any case, DeLucca, I didn't call on you." He turns to face me again. "Cavanaugh? Care to take your shot?"

The entire class is looking at me now, and the sides of my face instantly get hot. When I blush—which I do with pathological frequency—it's not like a subtle change in skin tone; it's more like a new paint job. Warning thoughts flash through my head: *Play dumb! Give the wrong answer!* But habit wins over caution, and I reply.

"Four hundred thirty-five," I say. My face basically bursts into flame, and I look down at my desk.

"Correct," Mr. Brennan replies, turning to pace the center aisle. "It appears that only two of us in this room stand between our fragile republic and the clandestine oligarchy. Let's see if we can't increase our numbers this year, shall we?" With that, he resumes his lecture, and I zone out for the rest of the period.

When the bell rings, everyone explodes out of their desks and stampedes toward the door; I get the impression that Mr. Brennan is not in the running for Park Hills High School's Most Popular Teacher. I follow Solo into the hall. It's less crowded now, and I can actually walk next to him without being shunted aside.

"What's next for you?" I ask.

"*Español*, then Algebra I."

"You're still taking Algebra I?"

"I hate sequels," he says.

I laugh. "Which period do you have lunch?"

Solo is about to answer when a tall guy slams into me, knocking me sideways. He's broad-shouldered, with a mop of sun-bleached hair, and his left arm is encased in a yellow fiberglass cast. In his good hand, he's clutching an iPad. As he blows past, he turns his head and looks at me. I catch that familiar flicker of uncertainty as he tries to figure me out. He gives up more quickly than most, and just says, "Watch where you're walking, bitch." He shoots Solo a reproachful glance, then continues down the hall. A younger kid chases after him, shouting, "Give it back, man!"

Solo steadies me with one big hand. "You okay?"

"Yeah," I say, regaining my balance. "Thanks. Who was that?"

"Jim Vickers," Solo says, frowning as the chase proceeds around the corner. "Prank enthusiast-slash-running back. But he's out for the season."

"Running back? As in football?"

Solo shakes his head. "Chess."

I snort. "Is he always such an asshole?"

But Solo doesn't seem to hear me as we round the corner and push through the double doors that lead out to the quad. It's a bright day, already approaching the mideighties. The sun feels good, and I stand up a little taller.

"You know where you're going next?" Solo says.

I dig into my bag and pull out my schedule. "Precalc, then French, then lunch."

"Well," Solo says, "then we part ways." He puts his palms together and makes a mock bow. "May you survive your first day." I feel slightly nauseated at the thought of being on my own again; even though it's only been two hours, I was getting used to having a massive bodyguard. I turn and mirror his mock bow.

"May you endure the horrors of Algebra," I reply.

Solo smiles.

"So, see you at lunch?"

At that, Solo's eyes drift to something in the distance behind me.

"Yeah," he says. "Maybe."

CHAPTER 3

IT TAKES ME FOUR TRIES to get the combination right when I stop by my locker before third period because I can't shake the feeling that I'm being watched. I glance to my left and catch the brunette girl with the perfect nose staring at me from her own locker about ten rows away. I expect a glare—but her look shows more curiosity than contempt, as though she's observing some fascinating animal at the zoo. When our eyes meet, her expression doesn't change—and then, after a moment, she walks away. Feeling unsettled, I unload the books I don't need and set off for Precalc.

Mr. Hibbard is ancient and mind-numbingly dull. The only redeeming quality of his class is that he's so old-school he's brought in actual blackboards. The smell and the clicking of chalk on board are comforting, but I still hold out little hope of getting an A.

In French, I sit behind a blond girl named Casey Reese who notices the stitching on my Ramones shirt and asks where I got it. Feeling slightly suspicious of her motives, I tell her I bought it online and then pretend to look for something in my bag.

At first, I like Madame Bordelon—she's French-Canadian, and her accent sounds exotic and sophisticated. But halfway through the period, she realizes I'm the only student who hasn't chosen a French alias—and then she asks me to pick one in front of the whole class. When I respond with stunned silence, she quickly refers me to a list in the textbook, and then moves on with her lesson.

I avoid further interaction by pretending to study this ridiculous list, which contains a blue column for boys' names and a pink column for girls'. I glance up only to check the clock; on one hand, I can't wait to get out of this room. On the other, I'm dreading the arrival of lunch.

Park Hills High is big; there must be four thousand students here. The thought of being seen by even a quarter of those people at once in a single, massive room makes my heart contract. A low buzzing starts up in the back of my head, as if wasps have begun building a nest inside my skull. It's the beginning of an anxiety attack—and I can't have one now. Not on my first day.

I close my eyes and take three slow, deep Doctor Ann breaths. My heart palpitates one more time, then settles back into its normal rhythm. I've delayed the attack for now, and maybe I can fight it off indefinitely—or, at the very least, until I've made it through lunch.

At Immaculate Heart, I avoided the cafeteria at all costs. During the first week of my sophomore year, Ben Haskell slapped my tray when no teachers were looking, splattering my uniform with tomato soup and showering me in Diet Mountain Dew. Two days later, Patricia Shea tripped me as I was walking past her table. I landed on my wrist, and it swelled to the size of a softball. After that, I never went back to the cafeteria again. I would have lunch in Miss Kerns's English classroom—but then she moved to Arizona, and I had to eat on the stoop behind the art supply room.

When the bell rings at the end of French, I'm the last one out of the classroom. The quad is already crawling with students, all of them swarming toward the outdoor eating area like ants descending on the remains of a discarded Popsicle. Maybe I don't have to do this; maybe Miss Crane will let me eat in her room. I turn and start in that direction—and then I stop. I told myself it was going to be different here. I told myself *I* was going to be different. That I was going to blend in, to find my place. And I don't want that place to be hiding in a teacher's room every day at lunch. Not again.

I turn and start across the quad, not stopping until I reach the top of the stairs that lead down to the lunch area. From here, I can see everything. The "cafeteria" at Park Hills High is actually an enormous covered patio, half the size of a Costco and twice as ugly. The gray concrete wall is punctuated by three takeout windows and a giant graffiti-style mural reading "Roar, Lions!" In the open area, students sit crammed shoulder to shoulder at green fiberglass picnic tables arranged in seven long rows with a wide aisle down the center.

I stand at the top of the stairs, observing the arrangement of all the cliques, trying to find a safe place to sit. The table in the back-left corner has been claimed by a congregation of guys, and a few girls, with Seven Seize and Bleeding Out Slow T-shirts, prominent piercings, and dyed hair. If I don't manage to spot Solo in the crowd, this table might be my best option. To their right, there's a group of students mostly dressed in thrift-shop chic. No way I'd blend in with them. The other two corners are occupied by, respectively, band people, as distinguished by their bulky instrument cases, and a group of what looks like senior AP students studying while they inhale their pizza pockets and pudding cups.

The center of the room is dominated by a swath of green and gold, students in various team shirts and jerseys: the student government people, the cheerleaders, and members of the football team. To get to the food line, I'm going to have to walk down that center aisle, a gauntlet of Park Hills High's social elite. Before I make my approach, I scan the room one more time, trying to locate Solo. He's twice the size of the average student, so I figure he won't be hard to spot—but I don't see him anywhere. It's okay; I've already made my plan B. I'll grab some food and head straight for the pierced and dyed contingent, who I've affectionately nicknamed "the Hardcores." There are quite a few open spots at their table, and my Ramones-T-shirt-and-Doc-Martens ensemble might grant me some cred.

But first, the Gauntlet.

Halfway down the stairs, I notice how tightly I'm grasping the rail. I relax my grip and try to control my breathing—but when I make it to the bottom, I can't help walking faster.

The comments start halfway down the aisle.

"Nice hair, bro."

"Dude, that's a chick."

"Oh shit, sorry, bro!" A burst of laughter.

I can't tell who's saying what, because I'm not looking—but it doesn't matter. If this is as bad as it gets, I can handle it. I just lock my eyes on the menu board above the café line and keep moving. To either side of me, whispers persist, but after a few moments, it appears that I've survived the worst of it. And then:

"Dude. Is that the new tranny?"

It's like someone pours a bucket of ice water directly into my stomach, freezing my guts. My head jerks in the direction of the voice.

I immediately recognize the blond guy with his arm in a cast, the one who practically bowled me over in the hallway: Jim Vickers. He regards me with sharp contempt, and I'm unsurprised to see that the brunette hanging all over him is the same one who called me "it." Seated on either side of the couple are a thick-necked, stringy-haired guy with the name "Cole" printed across the back of his jersey and another, smaller guy with red hair and wire-rim glasses.

Finally, I locate Solo. He's sitting across from Vickers, staring down at his tray in silence. I don't know how I missed his big form, stuffed in between two guys in football jerseys. And then I notice that his Darth Vader T-shirt is gone—Solo is wearing a jersey, too. I stop in the aisle.

Solo's on the football team?

At first I reject the idea—but I quickly reconsider. He's certainly built like a football player. And back in the hallway, he not only knew Vickers's name, but his position on the team. I should have realized it then.

As if he can hear my thoughts, Solo looks up and makes eye contact with me. He shakes his head once, then looks back down at his tray like he's trying to find a hair in his mashed potatoes. The ice water feeling spreads to my chest, and I turn and start walking again, as fast as I can. Somebody shouts, but I can't make out the words over the sound of blood pumping through my ears.

I walk past the lunch line and turn left. Just beyond the Hardcores' table, I see an outdoor hallway that leads away from the cafeteria and bends left behind the auditorium. I head for it; only a few more yards to go. Tears build up behind my eyes, and this time I'm powerless to stop them leaking down my cheeks.

As I'm passing the Hardcores, I notice a guy in a black peacoat sitting at the table—the one who sits in front of me in Government. He's pale, with a long, narrow nose and a ring in his bottom lip, and he's locked in heated conversation with another boy. But, as I walk by, he cocks his head and gazes at me with intense blue eyes. He turns to watch as I pass, but if he says something to me, I can't hear it; I've already lowered my head and started to run.

CHAPTER 4

I TAKE THE BUS HOME, riding with my face pressed against the window and my eyes closed so I don't have to see anyone looking at me.

I'm grateful to find the house empty; Dad is speaking at the groundbreaking ceremony for a new elementary school in Acacia Heights, and Mom is taking the day off from teaching to be with him. I suspect my mom hates being in the public eye as much as I do, because on days when she makes appearances with Dad, she gets this hollow look on her face and compulsively chews cherry-flavored antacids. I don't understand how she maintains her sense of humor under all the pressure and attention that comes with being a congressman's wife; I get only a fraction of the torrent she has to endure, and I can barely cope with it.

I guess that's why, since my little meltdown over the summer, they haven't asked me to attend any events. But after my six-week stint of "recovery" at Pineview—which sounds like a quaint hotel in the mountains, but is, in fact, a psych hospital about an hour away—my weekly follow-ups with Doctor Ann, and my carefully administered cocktail of antidepressant and antianxiety meds, I'm supposed to be better now. I'm supposed to be able to function. So I know it's only a matter of time before they ask again.

Dad got home from Washington late last night after being in session for a month, and Mom has a special family dinner planned for tonight, just the three of us. I don't even want to think about the first-day-of-school cross-examination I'll be facing in just a few hours.

Closing the door to my room behind me, I cross to my record player—a vintage Marantz turntable my dad got me last Christmas—and pull out an appropriately angst-riddled Police album from 1978. I revel in the hiss and crackle as the needle rides the groove into the song I've chosen, "So Lonely." I lie back on my bed and stare up at the ceiling, letting the thumping, jangling rhythm wash over me. The lyrics, at once desperate and determined, bounce around inside my head, and I'm overcome with a sudden pang of doubt: *Am* I alone? I try to think of who I might call if I wanted to go out and do something—like, I don't know, browse records at Stray Cat, maybe—but I can't come up with a single name. For a moment this morning, I let myself hope that Solo might fill that role—but his behavior at lunch ruled out that possibility.

The doubt seems to congeal in my throat, sticking there like a half-swallowed pill, and I try to think of *one person* I can call my friend. The only one I come up with is my old wardmate from Pineview, but somehow, remembering Murph brings me no comfort. I think back to last year. Who would I have called then?

There was Derek Yu, my one and only real friend from Immaculate Heart. Before he moved away, he would eat lunch with me behind the art supply room. Sometimes we'd sneak cigarettes. A couple of times, when his dad wasn't home, I went over to their McMansion in Acacia Heights and we went swimming in their Olympic-sized pool. Derek was a serious swimmer, the only sophomore on the varsity water polo team, but he was never cruel to me like his teammates were.

He had these amazing lat muscles; they were like wings. I remember the way the water would bead up and roll off his skin when he got out of the pool. It was beautiful.

Sometime during the summer, Derek stopped asking me to come over. His replies to my texts became colder, more infrequent. I felt him detaching, but I didn't know why. Then, during the last week of July, he failed to reply to six texts in a row, and I threw my phone at the kitchen tile as hard as I could. How could he drop me like that? What gave him the right to just cut me off with no explanation? I didn't know how, but I knew I'd driven him away.

I pull my phone out of my pocket now and run my thumb over the screen, feeling the nicks and indentations in the spider-webbed glass. Remembering that moment stirs something inside—anger, at first, and then a deep, hollow sadness that ripples through me in its own spiderweb pattern.

A few days after the phone-throwing incident, I went to

Pineview, and I figured I'd never hear from Derek again. But then, to my surprise, he showed up during my third week. He had this look on his face when he walked into the visitors' lounge, like he was afraid he might catch whatever I had. After a few minutes of uncomfortable small talk, Derek told me his dad's company was relocating them to India, and that he was leaving the next day.

I wished there had been a pool we could swim in—but, you know, mental patients and deep bodies of water, not so much. That was the last time we talked.

I bring up a picture of Derek. Looking at his face on the cracked screen rekindles my old anger; he shouldn't have dropped me like that. I shouldn't have let those girls get to me this morning. And Solo should have stood up for me at lunch.

The thoughts ricochet frantically off the edges of my mind. The buzz of anxiety grows louder now, making my head hum like an electrified fence, threatening to break out and return in full force.

I close my eyes and focus on the big three—the coping mechanisms Doctor Ann says I'm supposed to employ when I start to feel out of control. One: breathe. This part I seem to have mastered. I take a long, deep breath and let it out slowly. It helps, a little. Two: practice acceptance. This seems impossible after the day I've had. Who am I supposed to accept—the girl who called me "it"? Jim Vickers, who referred to me as a "tranny"? Or Solo, who sat by and watched it happen? No. I don't think I can accept any of them just now.

That leaves number three, the one I've been resisting since Doctor Ann insisted I start a journal blog, way back when I was still at Pineview: *share*. She told me that, in the old days, she made her patients keep journals; but for me, she prescribed an anonymous blog so I could interact with "people like me" in a "risk-free" way.

So, when I got out of Pineview in the middle of September, I started a Bloglr account under the username "Alix," which I picked at random from a baby name website, altering the spelling to make it more ambiguous. Over the past month, I've read and "liked" and reblogged dozens of posts by "people like me" all over the country. But I have yet to attract any followers, and the closest I've come to posting a single word of my own was this morning's aborted attempt.

But lying here, listening to the frenetic, unapologetic wailing emanating from my speakers, I figure desperate times call for desperate measures.

Miss Kerns always told me she liked my compositions; she said it was a gift to be able to work things out with words the way I did. So maybe I can work this out. It's not like anyone is going to read it.

I sit up, pull my laptop toward me, and open the Bloglr log-in screen. The green frog logo blinks at me as I enter my password, and then I open a new post and begin to type.

NEW POST: BOTH AND NEITHER
OCTOBER 1, 4:45 PM

My name is Alix. And the first thing you're going to want to know about me is: Am I a boy, or am I a girl?

Don't worry. I'm used to it; it's the first thing everyone wants to know—even when I'm standing right in front of them. And, even if they don't come right out and ask, I can tell they're thinking it, because they narrow their eyes or tilt their heads slightly to one side. At best, it's invasive curiosity; at worst, open condemnation. Either way, they want an answer: Girl. Or. Boy.

I look up from the keyboard and read what I've typed out so far. It sounds sort of defensive, almost like I'm pissed off at my imaginary reader—but at the same time, it feels good to get it out.

Anyway, it's not that simple. The world isn't binary. Everything isn't black or white, yes or no. Sometimes it's not a switch, it's a dial. And it's not even a dial you can get your hands on; it turns without your permission or approval.

"Okay," people say, "but you were born one way or the other. Like, biologically. Anatomically."

As if they have a right to know! As if, since I've so rudely failed to make it obvious, I ought to wear a sign.

Well, it's none of their damn business.

You think I'm unaware that my gender isn't immediately apparent to you? You think I didn't choose these clothes and this haircut specifically to avoid being stuffed into one pigeonhole or another?

I'm gender fluid. Not stupid.

/rant

Okay. I'm sorry. I don't actually want to antagonize you, imaginary reader. It's just hard to explain—but I'll try.

Ugh. How do I describe this without sounding like a Wikipedia entry? I've read dozens of posts on Bloglr and sites like QueerAlliance, but none of them get it quite right—at least, not right for me.

I walk over to the turntable and put on a new record, something a little rawer, and then sit back down at the keyboard.

⊙ NOW PLAYING: "Where Is My Mind?" by the Pixies

The truth is, some days I wake up feeling more "boy" and some days I wake up feeling more "girl." And some days, I wake up feeling somewhere in between. It's like I have a compass in my chest, but instead of north and south, the needle moves between masculine and feminine. I know it's not like that for all gender fluid people—but that's the best way I can describe how it is for me.

But no matter where my internal compass points, my body remains the same. And some days—maybe half the time—I feel alien inside it. Like the curves and angles are in all the wrong places. Like I was born with the wrong parts. It's a heavy, suffocating feeling—my doctor calls it dysphoria—and it makes concentrating in class (not to mention surviving in the halls) nearly impossible.

On days when it's really bad, dressing in a way that fits how I feel inside—a way that matches the direction my masculine/feminine compass is pointing—seems like the only thing that might relieve the dysphoria. But I can't always present myself how I want to. If I show up feminine on day one, people will assume I'm always a girl.

Then, if I show up the next day dressed like a guy, they'll react: taunts, ridicule, even violence. I've seen it happen. Because I live in the most gender binary place in the known universe: Park Hills, California.

And let's not forget my parents. If I were to start ping-ponging all over the gendersphere, my dad's blood pressure would skyrocket, and my mother would chew off her fingers—because I haven't told them yet.

I'm just not ready.

So I have to settle for looking "neutral." My safe zone is in the middle of the masculine-feminine continuum, somewhere between a tomboy and a feminine-looking guy; which means I always feel slightly fake, like I'm in costume. I can't remember the last time I felt comfortable in my own skin.

And, okay, I get it; it's confusing. I understand why people wonder, and why they give me weird looks and ask me invasive questions. But the thing is, they do a whole lot more than just wonder and ask questions. People can be cruel.

People can be very cruel.

So, imaginary reader, while I'm certain that you're a unique unicorn, you are not the first person to wonder what's between my legs. And maybe this blog can be a place where I don't have to address that particular issue. A place where my identity is not constrained by my anatomy, or by the gender binary confines of my concrete-and-stucco suburban prison. A place where I'm free to be what I am.

Whatever that is.

#firstpost #genderfluid #GenderFluidProblems

I sit there for a minute with my finger hovering over the trackpad. My mouth is suddenly dry. Sure, I've disguised my identity by making up a fake username and choosing a vintage photo of David Bowie as my avatar, but suddenly, it feels like clicking Post is the equivalent of outing myself to school, Mom, Dad, and the entire US House of Representatives. I scroll up, delete "Park Hills, California," and replace it with "Stucco Town, USA."

I click Post.

Then I stare at the wall for a long moment, feeling something between excitement and terror. I don't know whether to fall onto my bed and bury my face in my pillow or jump around the room, squealing like a guinea pig on meth. On the one hand, it feels good to have said it "out loud." On the other hand, I feel exposed. Like I've just broadcast my darkest secret over the school PA system. It's true, no one reads my blog. But they *could*. It's out there now.

I exhale a long breath and reach for the keyboard to log out, when I notice that there's a little blinking icon in the upper right-hand corner of the screen. The text hovering next to it reads:

yell0wbedwetter is now following you

I feel a smile of satisfaction spread across my face—and that's when I notice that the buzzing feeling has receded way into the background. It's almost gone.

Son of a bitch; blogging *is* therapeutic.

I log out and close my laptop. I'm reaching for my French textbook when my mom suddenly calls up from downstairs.

"Riley!"

I flinch in surprise and drop my book. I didn't even know she was home.

"Are you going to hide up there all night, or would you like to come down and have dinner with your family?"

I glance at my phone: it's past seven o'clock. I was so involved in writing that blog post that I didn't even hear the garage door. So much for homework. I call down to her, "I'll be right there." Then I flip off the light and head downstairs.

The table is ridiculously packed with dishes—and, upon seeing my incredulous expression, Mom says, "Don't judge me, it's a special occasion." No kidding, she gestures to the food on the table like the hostess from one of those blender info-mercials, giving me a goofy smile. I sit down, and she sets a gargantuan plate of pasta in front of me.

"Vegan cashew-cream ravioli!" she says, her voice pitched high with enthusiasm.

I take a bite, and my eyes roll back in their sockets. "Oh my God, Mom, this is so good!" I say it with my mouth full, and it's true. My father tears into his bloody steak and grunts appreciatively. Mom, having received unanimous approval, takes her place at the table.

I sense an electric charge in the air, like the way it feels before a thunderstorm—an area of low pressure. Eager to forestall first-day-of-school questions, I turn to my dad and execute evasive maneuvers.

"So," I say, "how did the session wrap up?"

My mother shoots me a disapproving frown—she's seen through my tactic—but it works on my dad, who promptly sets down his fork and clears his throat.

"It was infuriating," he says. "The committee seems intent on stripping my bill of any real punch before it goes to the House. Or, they're stalling because they think it's a reelection tactic."

"That must be so frustrating," Mom says. She's doing her best to sound involved without stirring the pot.

"I just hope they pull their heads out long enough to prevent the collapse of public education," Dad says, gesturing emphatically with his fork. "I doubt anyone in their families has attended a public school for four generations."

I bite back a comment about how I hadn't, either—right up until five weeks before the election. Opponents of Dad's bill made a huge deal about my transfer, calling it "political maneuvering." It's not a fair judgment, though. Not that I haven't been used as a pawn in Dad's campaign before—photo ops with his sullen teen make him seem more "real" to the voters—but in this case, I was as eager to leave Immaculate Heart as Dad's consultants were to get me enrolled at a public school. I wanted out because of the way the other students were treating me— so I agreed to do it, on the condition that they waive my PE requirement. So, as my dad would say, it was a win-win.

Except it's turning out to be no different than Immaculate Heart. I guess it was naive to think that kids at Park Hills would somehow be more open-minded just because it's a public school.

"But enough shop talk," Dad continues, turning to me. "How was your first day?"

And, the questions begin. As practiced, I execute my casual shrug and say, "Fairly consistent with the impending collapse of public education."

Dad smiles. "I see they haven't managed to tame the Cavanaugh sass."

I shake my head. "Not yet."

He picks up his fork and knife again. "Make any new friends?"

I glance up at him, watching the perfectly congressional patches of gray hair on his temples twitch as he chews—and I'm struck by a sudden urge to stand up and start spilling my guts. To tell them everything: my morning bout of dysphoria. Being called *it* the moment I set foot on campus. The lunchroom Gauntlet, Solo's betrayal, the boy with the lip ring and the bright-blue eyes.

But I won't. It would be what my mom calls "opening a can of worms." Inviting a conversation I'm not ready to have. Because after what happened today, I don't know what I would do if my parents rejected me, too. So I just shrug, look down at my plate, and poke at the now-congealing cashew cream with my fork.

"Well," Dad says. "Taking your time isn't a bad strategy. I did the same thing when I got to Congress."

I don't reply, and the quiet stretches out for a long moment. Finally, Mom can't stand it anymore.

"So," she says, turning to my father, "has Shelly finalized the seating chart for Thursday?" The question sounds rehearsed; something's up.

"What's Thursday?" I ask.

Dad clears his throat. "It's one of our last big dinners at the Grand Lido."

My heart twinges. They're going to ask me to go. I know they are.

I *hate* fund-raisers. Between the noise and the crowd and the clothes I have to wear, I feel like an animal on display at the zoo. And the last time they asked me to attend one of these dinners, I couldn't handle the pressure, and I ended up riding to Park Hills Community Hospital in the back of an ambulance.

"Riley," Dad says. He doesn't use his congressman voice; but that's probably a calculated choice. All of his choices are calculated. "I know these events aren't your favorite part of the process."

"But you've been doing great," Mom says. "We think you're ready."

Dad nods. "This is a big one, Riley. We need you there."

I don't look directly at either of them; instead, I let my gaze linger in the space between, and my eyes drift out of focus.

"Okay," I say.

Dad nods and pats Mom's hand before taking up his fork and knife again. "This will all be over in five weeks."

I try to smile, but I can't seem to fake it.

When I'm finished eating, I retreat to the kitchen, thinking I'll drop my plate in the sink and escape to my room—but Mom follows me in. It's an ambush. I give her a quick smile and try to move past her—one last attempt to avoid further questions—but she stops me with a hand on my shoulder.

"Hang on a second," she says. "I want to talk to you."

I stop and look at her. "Okay. About what?"

Mom sighs and reaches up to push my bangs out of my eyes. "I know how you must be feeling," she says.

"Really?" I say, raising my eyebrows. "How is that?" I don't mean for it to come out sounding angry, but it does.

Mom opens her mouth, then closes it, then opens it again. She looks ridiculous, like a spilled goldfish gasping for oxygen— and then I realize that *I* do the same thing when I'm at a loss for words, and my anger flares even hotter.

Mom shrinks back at the look on my face, and I'm immediately ashamed. The snarky retort I had on deck dies before it reaches my lips. She drops her eyes. "You're right. I probably don't know. I went to high school in another century." She looks up at me. "Was it a really bad first day?"

"It was fine," I say. I can tell she's not buying it, so I go on. "It's just . . . normal stuff. New-school jitters. That's all."

Mom frowns; she knows there's more to it, but she doesn't know what or how much. I consider making up a story— some uncontroversial bad-day scenario that will alleviate her concern—but something in her look stops me. There's confusion on her face, but there's tenderness, too. My heart seems to swell, and I wonder if there's a way she could understand. If I just tell the truth.

But I'm pretty sure the truth would break her heart, and my father's, too.

I'm their only kid, and sometimes I feel guilty for being how I am. I think maybe they would have been happier with a son who would play football like Dad did. Or, maybe Mom might have preferred a daughter she could paint her toenails with and take to ballet lessons. But instead, they got me—something they don't quite understand and tend to handle alternately like a glass figurine and a feral cat.

No, I can't tell her what's really going on. But I have to tell her something.

"It's . . ." My voice trails off. I don't know what to say.

Mom finishes the sentence for me. "The other kids?" she says, pretty much hitting the bull's-eye. But I don't want to go there, so I deflect.

"It's the campaign, you know. All the attention. I'm not . . . I just really want to blend in here." This last part sort of slips out without my permission. I didn't intend to be so honest, and now there's a lump in my throat.

"Well," she says, tilting her head to one side as she takes in my appearance. "Maybe 'blending in' is overrated."

CHAPTER 5

I TRY TO SLEEP, but little snippets of the day's events keep playing over and over in my head, like the looping DVD menu
sequence of some bad high school movie. After staring at the
ceiling for I don't know how long, I sit up and turn on my
computer.

NEW POST: GENDER FLUID DYSPHORIA BLUES
OCTOBER 2, 1:04 AM
   Dear Follower (singular),
   I can't sleep. Right now, I'm sitting on my bed, hating
my body. My arms feel wrong. They're not soft or sup-
ple, but they're not firm or muscular, either. My chest is,
like . . . too slender to be masculine, but too angular to
be feminine. I don't feel "girl" or "boy" right now, I just
feel . . . other. I feel wrong. Sometimes this happens after

a long day of dressing neutrally; it's like I need to press Reset or something. I wish I knew how.

I need something loud to drown out this feeling, so I get up, plug my headphones into my record player, and drop the needle. And then I sit back down on my bed and start to type again. I read what I've written, decide that it's a load of self-pitying drivel, and almost delete it—but then I think about Doctor Ann, and how she says complaining isn't therapeutic, but *sharing* is. Fine, then. I'll "share."

⊙ *NOW PLAYING: "Transgender Dysphoria Blues" by Against Me!*

I remember the exact moment I realized I was different.

It was my sixth birthday, and my dad took me to Toys"R"Us to pick out my own present. I was allowed to choose one thing, and I walked the aisles for what felt like hours to my six-year-old self. Finally, I narrowed it down to two possibilities. The first was a blue Power Ranger—I remember I wanted it because it had a shield that lit up when you pushed a button on his belt. The second was a Bratz doll. She had enormous brown eyes and long, dark hair with a purple streak running down one side. I was totally fascinated by that purple streak.

I held the two packages side by side, looking from one to the other, unable to decide. When I glanced up at my dad for help, his expression was . . . weird. I knew something was wrong, that for some reason, he didn't approve of my choices—but I didn't know why.

So I put down both toys and walked on to the next aisle.

Looking back, it probably wouldn't have been that big of a deal if I'd chosen one or the other. But that uncertain look in my dad's face—that was the moment I knew there was something different about me.

We ended up getting some stupid Pirates of the Caribbean board game; I was disappointed, but I could tell from my dad's body language that it was a safe choice. And that's what I've been trying to make my whole life.

Safe choices.

Until I turned fifteen. There was a local news story about a transgender girl who sued her school district for the right to use the girls' locker room. I must have read the story on five different news sites, and then I voraciously inhaled every blog post and YouTube response I could get my eyes on. At some point during my research, I came across the term "gender fluid." Reading those words was a revelation. It was like someone tore a layer of gauze off the mirror, and I could see myself clearly for the first time. There was a name for what I was. It was a thing. Gender fluid.

Sitting there in front of my computer—like I am right now—I knew I would never be the same. I could never go back to seeing it the old way; I could never go back to not knowing what I was.

But did that glorious moment of revelation really change anything? I don't know. Sometimes, I don't think so. I may have a name for what I am now—but I'm just as confused and out of place as I was before. And if today is any indication, I'm still playing out that scene in the toy store—trying to pick the thing that will cause the least amount of drama. And not having much success. Which leaves me with this question:

What would it take to change something?

I rub my burning eyes and stare at the question I just typed out. As I read, the words seem to lose their meaning. I glance at the clock.

Holy crap, single follower, it's almost two a.m. I guess we'll have to wait for an answer to that question.

Good night, Bloglr.

#genderfluid   #GenderFluidProblems   #Gender-Dysphoria #AgainstMe!

I click Post and lean back against the wall. I haven't thought about that day in the toy store since I was a kid. I'm not even sure I remembered it until I typed it out—but now, the details hover, fresh and vivid in my memory: the rough denim of my dad's jeans against my cheek as I clutched his leg. The dark lines that formed between his eyebrows as I looked up from the toy packages, seeking his approval. That sensation of compression, of being trapped, of knowing there was something wrong with what I wanted, and that I had to hide it from everyone—especially my dad.

And then, sitting there on my bed, remembering—it's like a dam breaks, and a dozen other memories flood my mind at once: staring at my reflection in one of those angled shoe-store mirrors when I was six or seven, thinking there was something wrong with my body. Glancing up to gauge my dad's expression as we picked out books in the children's section at Barnes & Noble. Riding home from the salon with my mom, hating my new haircut. Sorting through paint swatches the summer we moved here, watching her face for that smile of validation as I picked out colors for my room. Struggling to choose the "right" eighth-grade elective. Shopping for clothes. All the decisions I made to hide the feelings I didn't understand—and every single choice altered by the fear that I would choose wrong, and that my parents, or my teachers, or the people at my school would reject me. My whole life, designed around hiding.

But today, even with all my careful forethought, I couldn't hide. People at school still knew something was different.

I grab my phone and turn on the selfie camera so I can look at myself. I run a hand through my messy hair, brushing my bangs out of my eyes and watching them fall right back into place. A cracked image stares back at me, and it doesn't look anything like I feel.

The clock on my laptop changes from 1:59 to 2:00, and I decide I'd better try to get some sleep unless I want to wake up tomorrow looking like an androgynous harbinger of the zombie apocalypse. I'm about to log out of Bloglr when a little red envelope icon appears in the upper right-hand corner of my screen, indicating I have a new message. I click it, and a new window pops up.

Anonymous: your a fag

And suddenly, I feel very awake.

Alix: Dear Anonymous, while I'm eager to illustrate for you the difference between sexual orientation and gender identity, I think we had better start with a more fundamental concept:

Apostrophes.

What you meant was, "You're a fag." "Your," sans apostrophe, is possessive, as in "your devastating lack of creativity," while "you're" is a contraction of you + are, as in "you're a homophobic asshole." I hope this sheds some light on the misery that is your life.

Love,

Alix

#genderfluid #homophobia #grammarpolicearrestthisperson

I could reply privately—but I decide that this particular anon would benefit from a little public smackdown. So, with a rush of righteous triumph, I click Post. I watch the screen for a solid minute, waiting for a snarky reply to pop up, but nothing happens. Apparently, even the trolls have gone to bed, and so should I. Like leprechaun gold, the triumph is fleeting, and now exhaustion takes its place. I close my laptop, drop my head to the pillow, and fall asleep.

CHAPTER 6

I DREAM ABOUT CHOOSING THE Bratz doll and awake with a nearly irresistible compulsion to put a purple streak in my hair. I'm feeling absurdly feminine—like the compass needle is all the way on F—so pulling on my neutral/ambiguous jeans-and-tee combination feels particularly wrong, because what I really want to do is put on a dress.

The dysphoria is going to be rough this morning; I can already feel the buzz in the back of my head. Crossing the quad feels like one of those dreams where you go to school naked—I keep imagining that the people around me can *see* how wrong I feel in these neutral clothes. I get to Miss Crane's classroom early and apply a coat of lip balm, a trick I learned from another gender fluid blogger. It feels enough like gloss to give me a small sense of outward femininity without spoiling my neutral look—and no one else can tell. It helps, a little. That buzz—anxiety or dysphoria, I'm not sure which—recedes slightly, but it doesn't quite disappear.

I feel Solo's eyes on me as he walks into AP English, but I don't meet them. Why did he bother pretending to be nice to me yesterday, only to ignore me in front of his friends? I avoid looking at him for the duration of the class—and when the bell rings, I'm the first one out the door.

Ten minutes into AP Government, the buzzing sensation starts to intensify. My arms feel particularly wrong—too skinny and angular for how feminine I'm feeling—so I pull my hoodie out of my bag and put it on, tugging down the sleeves. It doesn't make much difference. I cross my legs at the knee— sometimes a shift in posture helps—but today, it's not bringing any relief.

French passes in a blur. All I can think about is trying to cross the quad feeling like this—or worse, walking the Gauntlet. My heart is beating in my throat now, and a numb tingling blossoms in my cheeks and the tips of my fingers.

It's starting.

But I know what I'm supposed to do. I'm supposed to close my eyes and picture the whiteboard. I'm supposed to paint it black with my mind until there's nothing left but a calm, quiet void.

I close my eyes. I dip my imaginary paintbrush into the surrounding blackness and begin to paint the board with long, slow strokes. Long, slow strokes. I'm three-quarters of the way to the right edge, almost done, when a patch of white appears on the left border. The black is dripping away, revealing more and more of the whiteboard beneath.

This always happens; I've never once succeeded in painting the whole board black. Sometimes the exercise manages to calm me anyway—but this time, it's not working.

My face is completely numb now, and the tingling has spread through my hands all the way up to the wrists. My shortness of breath must be audible, because the pretty girl with long blond hair who sits in front of me, Casey Reese, keeps looking over her shoulder at me.

As I pass her on my way out of class, she asks, *"Ça va?"*

"Yeah, thanks," I reply.

But I'm not okay.

My vision is starting to tunnel. I'm not thinking, just putting one foot in front of the other—and before I know it, I'm halfway down the stairs to the cafeteria. When I realize where I am, ten yards from the Gauntlet, part of me wants to turn and run; but I don't. I continue forward, eyes on the ground, drawing my shoulders up toward my ears as if I'm bracing for impact.

I've covered most of the distance to the cafeteria line, and there have been no taunts yet, nothing thrown; maybe the novelty of harassing the new kid has worn off. As I pass Solo's table, I'm tempted to glance over and see if he's watching, but I keep my head down instead; it's not much farther. My heart thuds against my rib cage.

And then I'm through. I make it to the outdoor hallway and break into a run. The concrete wall of the auditorium blurs past as I round the corner. Just ahead, there's a wheelchair ramp by the side stage door. It's protected by a low wall about two feet high—just enough to conceal me if I lie flat on my back.

Finally, I make it, Doc Martens squeaking as I come to a stop on the smooth concrete. I bend over, chest heaving, hands gripping the aluminum safety rail. I try to slow my breathing.

But then a hand touches my shoulder, and I flinch hard.

"Take it easy," a voice says.

My eyes are blurred with tears, and I draw one still-numb hand across them to clear my vision: the figure standing before me is the pale boy from Government I saw sitting with the Hardcores yesterday—the one with the long nose and the lip ring. He's standing on the ramp, hands up in a gesture of surrender. Despite the heat, he's wearing that same black coat. Circular sunglasses with mirrored lenses obscure the blue eyes I remember from yesterday, and I can't tell if the look on his face is more surprised or amused. There's something soft about the curve of his jaw, and the neck of his T-shirt is cut low to reveal—

And that's when I realize: He's not a boy. He's a girl.

"I'm sorry," she says, lowering her hands slowly, "but you've discovered my secret lair." She gestures at the ramp. "And now, I'm afraid, you'll have to pay the toll."

I stare at her, speechless, gasping for breath.

"I accept juice boxes, Amazon gift cards, and narcotics," she says. Then, in response to my blank look, she adds, "For the toll."

I recognize that it's a joke, but I don't manage to laugh. My face is still numb, and my heart is beating a frantic tattoo against my breastbone.

The girl seems to realize something is wrong, because her expression softens. "Hey," she says, pulling down her sunglasses to regard me with those bright-blue eyes. "Hey, sit down." She moves to help me sit on the ramp—well, it's more like I fall and she catches me—and then she pulls off her backpack and produces a juice box. "Here, drink this." She punches in the straw and hands it to me, and I drink. My heartbeat slows. The tingling recedes a little.

She sits there, watching me patiently. I expect to find her gaze invasive—but there's no threat in her eyes, just curiosity, and . . . something else. Something strangely comforting.

Her voice is high-pitched and doesn't match her punk-boy wardrobe, but despite my initial mistake, I'm certain she identifies as a girl. Maybe it's the confident way she wears her low-cut shirt, or the angle of her neck as she cocks her head at me—but beneath these superficial observations, there's just a strong intuition.

What I'm not certain about is how she views me. When a girl sees me as a guy, I usually feel dismissed as unworthy or, at best, as nonthreatening. When a girl thinks I'm a *girl*, I get the feeling she's comparing and judging me. But *this* girl isn't doing any of those things. Her posture is open, her body relaxed. And even though her eyes are hidden behind mirrored lenses, there's an intimacy about her expression that penetrates my wall of anxiety and sends a shiver through me—but a shiver of what? I don't know.

"Are you diabetic?" she says.

I shake my head. She frowns.

"Are you having a psychic vision?"

I shake my head again, feeling the hint of a smile curl the corners of my mouth. "I can wait," she says, glancing at her wrist in a gesture of feigned impatience.

A slurping sound informs me that I have finished this juice box, which is odd, because I don't remember tasting it at all. The girl pulls another out of her backpack and offers it to me. I reach for it, but she pulls it back.

"I require a name," she says.

I smile. "Your parents didn't give you one?"

She opens her mouth in mock surprise and leaps to her feet.

"The creature speaks!" she says, standing and shouting down at the parking lot below. "I hath revived it with mine purple potion!"

I glance up nervously, checking to see if anyone's looking at us. Is this girl making fun of me? I can't tell. But the last thing I want, the last thing I can *handle* right now, is more attention.

"Listen," I say. "Please don't—"

But Lip Ring Girl is now making a four-point bow, blowing kisses to an imaginary audience. "I'd like to thank the Academy, my fans, my team at Minute Maid who—"

At this point I reach up, grab her by the sleeve, and yank her back down onto the ramp. "Riley," I say, exasperated. "My name is Riley. Please, just don't attract any more attention."

"Right," she says, straightening her collar. "Riley Cavanaugh."

She knows my name, too?

At the look on my face, the girl puts up her hands again. "I'm not a stalker. Brennan said your name in Government yesterday." She leans in. "He called on you, and I tried to bail you out, remember?"

I nod. "Yeah. Thanks."

"Then you pulled that obscure factoid out of thin air. Maybe I ought to make you tutor me, as partial payment." She tilts her head and squints like she's examining me. After a moment, she nods. "I'm Bec."

I blink at her. "Short for Rebecca?"

She closes her eyes for a moment and lets out an exasperated sigh. "*Le bec*," she says, "is French for 'beak.'" She gestures to her face. "I have a large nose. Beak-like, one might say. Therefore, *Bec*."

I frown. "Who could've possibly given you that name? Some mean French kid?"

"Absolutely not," she says. "I gave it to myself."

I shake my head, incredulous.

"Not everyone is born a *Riley*," she says. And then her thin lips form a delightfully crooked smile. It's contagious. She offers me the second juice box, and I take it.

"Did you . . . follow me behind the building?"

"Yes, I did," she says, sounding completely unperturbed.

I take a long sip through the straw. "Why?"

"After yesterday, I didn't think you'd come anywhere near the caf again. I told myself that, if you did, then you were the kind of person I wanted to meet." She inclines her head like a Renaissance courtier. "Well met, Riley Cavanaugh."

She noticed me? Two days in a row? I gape at her, then realize what I'm doing and clamp my jaw shut.

"So," she says, glossing over my awkwardness as though this sort of thing happens to her all the time. "You're a transfer?"

"Yeah."

"Where from?"

I hesitate, then say, "Immaculate Heart."

Bec starts to laugh, something between a giggle and a chuckle. I feel myself blush. I start to get up, but she grabs my hand. Her fingers are cold, her palm smooth, and her touch sends goose bumps up my arm.

"I wasn't laughing at you, I promise. Look." She pulls open her peacoat, revealing the graphic on her T-shirt: a large black cross inside a red circle with a diagonal line running through it. Above that, the caption reads: BAD RELIGION. "I was laughing at the irony," she says, "that I'm welcoming your defection from Catholic school wearing a Bad Religion shirt."

"Oh, right," I say, relieved, "the band." When she lets go of my hand, I feel a pang of disappointment. She pats the ground next to her, and I sit. "I thought maybe you were referring to my school's unfortunate nickname."

Bec leans in. "You realize you're going to tell me, right?"

I sigh. Of course I am. "Instead of Immaculate Heart, they called it 'I Masturbate Hard.'"

Bec laughs. It starts out as that low chuckle, but quickly becomes a full-on guffaw. Now, I start laughing, too.

"Sounds like my kind of place," Bec says, finally regaining her breath. When I realize what she's implying, I feel myself blush for the nine thousandth time in two days. Our laughter fades, and I notice that, though my heart is still beating harder than usual, the tingling in my hands and face is almost gone.

"What's your real name?" I ask.

But Bec speaks right on the heels of my last word, as if she didn't hear me.

"So, you're not diabetic," she says. "Were you, like, about to have a seizure? Is it epilepsy?"

I open my mouth to reply, and then the bell rings, a long, ugly wail. It's how I imagine the lights-out buzzer sounds at Folsom Prison.

Bec gets to her feet and offers me a hand. I take it. She pulls me up and we just stand there, looking at each other. Finally, I can't take the silence anymore. "Saved by the bell," I say.

She blinks. "You're better than a cliché."

My stomach does a flip. I almost ask her, *How do you know?* But at the thought of saying the words, my face goes hot as a match head. Unable to meet her gaze any longer, I glance down at the unopened juice box in my hand, and offer it back to her.

"Keep it," she says, then turns and walks down the ramp.

CHAPTER 7

MOM'S SCHOOL HAD AN EARLY-OUT day, so I'm not surprised to find her minivan already in the driveway when I get home, but what I don't expect to see is the unfamiliar red Mercedes that's parked next to it. If Mom's having some kind of campaign-related meeting, I don't want to get drawn into it, so I enter the house as quietly as I can. I hear voices drifting up from the kitchen; she's definitely not alone. I turn to head upstairs to my room—and then the door to the downstairs bathroom opens.

A short girl about my age with long brown hair steps out. She looks up, and my mouth drops open slightly in surprise— it's the girl who called me *it*. Hastily, she tugs down her sleeves and folds her arms—and then she appears to recognize me, too.

"Hi," she says, but it sounds more like a threat than a greeting.

"Hi," I reply.

I'm about to ask what she's doing in my house when a voice calls from the kitchen, "Sierra, come in here. I want you to show Mrs. Cavanaugh how the tea tree oil cleared up those blemishes."

The girl—Sierra—closes her eyes, shakes her head, then turns and walks back toward the kitchen. I'm already heading for the stairs when my mom calls me.

"Riley? Did I hear you come in?"

I grip the banister. I don't want to go in there—but now I don't really have a choice. "Yeah, Mom."

"Come in and say hello."

Cautiously, I approach and peek around the corner.

With her tight red dress and long, shiny hair, Sierra's mom looks more like an older sister. She's seated across from my mother at the table with a case of little glass bottles between them. The kitchen smells like a potpourri factory.

"Look at the size of these blemishes," she says, swiping through photos on her phone. Mom is trying to be polite, but I can see that she's embarrassed. Sierra's mom continues enthusiastically. "You know teenagers, they eat junk all day and refuse to take care of their skin. But this stuff works like a miracle. Sierra, turn around, show her what it looks like now."

"Mom—" Sierra starts to protest, but her mother flaps an impatient hand at her. Reluctantly, Sierra turns and her mother lifts up the back of her shirt. Now *I'm* embarrassed, and I start to retreat into the hallway, but it's too late—Sierra makes eye contact with me. I expect her to shoot me a dirty look, but she just grits her teeth and looks away. When her mother finally lets her sit down, I take a half step into the room, trying to act as if I haven't been watching the whole time.

My mom makes the introductions, which I acknowledge from the archway.

"Sierra runs the peer tutoring program," my mother says. "Maybe you could join."

I try to hide my revulsion at the thought of working alongside this girl who so obviously loathes me—but Mom seems to read my thoughts, because she shoots me an apologetic look. I glance at Sierra to gauge her reaction, but she's too busy glaring at her mother.

Sierra's mom—Mrs. Wells—ignores her, turning her attention to me. "Riley," she says, "you have such fair skin. Are you using a chemical-free sunscreen?" She reaches for one of the bottles. I open my mouth to say something, I'm not sure what—but my mother intervenes.

"I know you'd love to stay and socialize, honey," she says, "but you still have a month's worth of homework to catch up on. Better get to it."

And then, I swear to God, she winks at me. I suppress a smile. My mother just came to my rescue. I forgive the "honey" immediately. In fact, I kind of want to run into the room and hug her, but instead, I turn and head upstairs.

I know I should feel bad for Sierra—clearly her mom makes her life a nightmare—but I can't forget how she treated me yesterday, and it's obvious she doesn't feel bad for me. I pull my copy of *The Crucible* out of my bag, flop on my bed, and read until dinner.

☊

Mom excuses me from dish duty so I can log more time catching up on homework—but my brain is already fried from two hours of Arthur Miller, so I decide to click around Bloglr instead. When my dash comes up, I frown at the numbers.

MESSAGES: 1

FOLLOWERS: 58

That can't be right; when I wrote my first post yesterday, I had precisely one follower. How could that jump to almost sixty overnight?

I click on the activity icon. My original post, "Both and Neither," which I put up only yesterday, has been liked, commented on, or reblogged over a hundred times. Beneath the hashtags is a stream of comments:

BPButtercup: Wow. Just Wow.

IrishPaulie: ^ ^ This.

phoebe98: I feel u Alix!!

I have to scroll down to read them all.

I click on Followers, and a list appears. There's Queer-Boi1996, MiMi_Q, gowestyounglady, and more than fifty others. All of them are Bloglr users who read my first post and decided to follow me.

I sit back and stare at the screen as my skepticism gives way to surprised acceptance. I know how they found me—the same way I discovered there was a name for what I was feeling—by searching the internet. Browsing hashtags. And honestly, it wouldn't have surprised me if a few dozen people had found my first post at random and liked it—but over a *hundred*? In one day?

I lean in and move my pointer down to my second-ever Bloglr message. I consider clicking Delete without opening it; I don't want to spoil my good mood with a repeat of "your a fag." But, after a moment, I can't stand not knowing what it says, and I click the message.

> yell0wbedwetter: You are #@%^& hilarious and super helpful. Please post more!!

I want to reply, but I don't know what to say. Finally, I just type "thanks ☺" and click Send.

I'm oddly touched that some random stranger wrote to me. The idea that my writing actually helped someone else makes me want to do more—so I decide to take yell0wbed-wetter's advice. I open a new post and start to write.

NEW POST: MY RAGING HYPOCRISY. ALSO, LIGHT-SABERS.
OCTOBER 2, 9:47 PM

Today, I met a boy.

Well . . . I thought I met a boy. Actually, I met a girl. That's right: I got all prematurely gender-assigny . . . and I was WRONG.

In my defense, I was in the middle of a fairly epic anxiety episode, and she—whom I thought was a he—has these unsettlingly gorgeous blue eyes. NO ONE could be expected to maintain objectivity while under the gaze of those eyes. They were, like, lightsaber blue. My guts have turned to Jell-O just replaying the scene in my head.

Oh, and did I mention the lip ring? HOT.

⊙ *NOW PLAYING: "There She Goes" by the La's*

Okay. Given the fact that even I am capable of making premature assumptions about someone's gender, I will attempt to explain this with less than my usual dose of Gender Fluid Rage™. (Which, by the way, is the name of my new punk band.) The point here is that somebody's gender expression—in this case, Lip Ring Girl's goth-boy vibe— doesn't necessarily indicate their gender identity. There are dudes who like to cross-dress (expression), but are still 100% comfortable being dudes (identity), and vice versa. So, even if you had X-ray vision and could see through my jeans, what you'd see there—or not see—does not determine my gender identity. Gender identity is not external. It isn't dictated by your anatomy. It's internal. It's something you feel, not something you see—and it can be way more complicated than just male or female. Some people, like me, slide on a continuum between the two. Others, as I've learned via my pathological blog-reading obsession, feel like neither, or like a third, unnamed gender.

I can't blame you for trying to categorize me. It's a human instinct. It's why scientists are, to this day, completely flabbergasted by the duck-billed platypus: it's furry like a mammal, but lays eggs like a bird. It defies conventional classification.

I AM THE PLATYPUS. (Coo coo ka-choo.)

We're all taught from a young age that there are only two choices: pink or blue, Bratz or Power Rangers, cheer-leading or football. We see gender in two dimensions because that's what society has taught us from birth. But, are you ready for a shocking revelation?

SOCIETY NEEDS TO CHANGE.

#genderfluid #crushinghard #lightsaberblue

When I'm done, I obsessively reread, tweak, delete, and rewrite. I want it to be funny—but more than that, I want it to be true. By the time I click Post, it's well past midnight. I ought to be exhausted from staying up so late last night, but I'm not. Reliving my encounter with Bec has my mind awake and racing. So instead of going to sleep, I click around Bloglr for more than three hours. At first, I intend to do some heavy reading on gender issues—but that rapidly devolves into watching funny cat videos and reblogging Harry Potter gifs. By quarter to two, my eyes start to droop—and then, at some point later, still curled up with my laptop, I fall asleep.

When I wake up on Wednesday morning, I'm certain it's going to be a girl day. But then, halfway through English, I feel a pang of dysphoria—a sort of plasticky sensation, this time in my hips—and I start to squirm in my chair. I've been sitting up straight with my legs crossed, but now I put both feet on the floor and slump down in my desk a little. I even let my left foot stick out into the aisle. It feels better.

Solo pretty much ignores me the whole period. I'm still pissed at him, definitely—but underneath, I think I'm more disappointed. He glances up at me once, but I can't read his expression; and when class ends, he slips out before I do.

On my way to Government, I notice I'm feeling edgy; that low-grade anxiety is starting to buzz in my head. The plasticky feeling comes back, and suddenly my walk feels artificial and stiff. It takes me a second to realize what's happening: I'm fluctuating. The needle on my internal compass is inching away from feminine toward the opposite pole—and I've been struggling to compensate with the way I move. Rather than try to fight it with deep breaths or Dr. Ann's whiteboard exercise, I decide to "go with the flow." I reach into my bag and pull out the beanie I keep in case of bad hair days. I put it on, hook my thumbs into the pockets of my jeans, and lean into my walk a little. I start to feel better on the inside—but I wonder what the people around me think, or whether they even notice.

And then I walk into Brennan's class and see Bec, and all my concerns are obliterated by her bright-blue eyes, cryptic and curious as a cat's as they flick up to meet mine. A hint of that crooked smile plays across her lips, and I feel a flutter in my chest. It's a pleasant feeling, but totally disconcerting. I try to smile back, but I'm afraid it comes out wrong on my face.

I drop my bag and slide into the plastic chair behind her. I want to lean forward, to say something to her, but before I can, she turns to face me instead.

"Riley Cavanaugh," she says.

It's like a purr, the way she wraps her voice around my name, and suddenly I can't catch my breath.

"B-Hi," I reply, and feel my face turn purple. I started to say her name, but changed my mind too late and ended up sounding like a complete idiot; but Bec goes on as if she didn't even notice.

"Thursday," she says. "Seven o'clock."

I blink. "What?"

"Come to my house at seven o'clock on Thursday," she says.

I feel the blood slowly draining from my face. Is she asking me out?

Without breaking eye contact, Bec gestures over her shoulder at the whiteboard. Written in red dry-erase marker are the words "QUIZ FRIDAY."

"You help me ace this quiz," Bec says, "and maybe we can forget about your toll."

The pleasant fluttering stops abruptly. Bec doesn't want a date; she wants a study partner. A pet nerd.

"I can't," I say, suddenly remembering Dad's fund-raiser. "I have a thing on Thursday."

"Oh," she says, raising her eyebrows. "Okay." For a second, I detect genuine disappointment—like "I just got turned down for a date" disappointment, not like "I'm going to fail this quiz" disappointment. And now I wonder if I've made a mistake. I open my mouth to say something—but at that moment, Brennan clears his throat and calls for quiet. As Bec turns to face the front of the classroom again, I catch the scent of something sweet—vanilla shampoo?—and all my neurons seem to fire at once, obliterating any further rational thoughts. Brennan begins his lecture, but I'm far, far away. I'm at Bec's house on Thursday night, trying to figure out if I'm her date or her tutor, and discovering that I wouldn't mind being either.

Right before class ends, while Brennan is gesturing emphatically at a diagram of the three branches of government, Bec reaches behind her and drops a folded piece of notebook paper onto my desk. Just as I'm about to unfold it, the bell rings.

CHAPTER 8

BEC ISN'T AT HER USUAL table at lunch, and on Thursday morning, she doesn't show up for school at all; she must have come down with a cold or something. Sitting alone on the ramp, I unfold and read her note for the zillionth time. It's just the words "In case you reconsider," and a phone number.

In case I reconsider what—a date, or a tutoring appointment? I can't tell if she's being mysterious on purpose, or if she's already given me some obvious sign that I'm just too socially inept to recognize. I pull out my phone, thinking I'll send her a text to say "hi" or "feel better soon," but my thumbs just hover helplessly over the screen. What do I say? And, what if I sound too desperate, and she's repulsed?

This is why I'm not popular; I can't decode the subtleties of text message etiquette, let alone figure out how to act around live people. My thoughts drift to Solo, who appears to have given up trying to talk to me. Apparently, I misjudged him like I seem to misjudge everyone. And instead of keeping my guard up, I've allowed myself to hope that this place would be different. But so far, the only difference between Park Hills High and Immaculate Heart is the clothes.

I click off my phone, refold the note, and stuff it into my back pocket.

When I get home from school, I drop onto my bed, not even bothering to open my laptop, and fall asleep.

The muffled sound of my phone's air raid siren alarm tone wakes me. It's six p.m.; my parents will be home to pick me up for the fund-raiser in less than an hour. I drag myself out of bed and cross to my closet.

I stand there, staring at the outfit I have to wear tonight, which is still wrapped in plastic from the dry cleaner's. It's the most gendered thing I own, and I hate it.

I hate it.

I call it my "campaign costume." It's a stupid name, but it helps me to think of it like that because that's how my *body* feels when I wear it—like a cheap Halloween costume that somebody else chose.

Putting it on is like a suicide ritual; as I dress, I'm killing any possibility of expressing my other, less acceptable self. Just standing here looking at it triggers a powerful wave of dysphoria. My arms feel like plastic. Like mannequin limbs. The tingling starts up again in my cheeks and the tips of my fingers. I've got to get this over with.

I take down the hanger and lay it on the bed. I tug off my

jeans and T-shirt, rip open the cellophane bag, and begin to dress. The material feels suffocating against my skin. I picture myself walking into the hotel ballroom with my parents, deafened by applause and blinded by camera flashes. I put my arms through the sleeves; my hands are shaking. Another flash goes off, and I can't tell if it's real or imagined. I pull fabric over my head, and it seems to rush in at me, clinging to my face like the plastic from the cleaner's, covering my nose, my mouth. I can't breathe.

I can't do this.

Piece by piece, I tear off the clothes and hurl them against the closet door. I stand there, chest heaving, staring at the heap, my breath coming in gasps. And that's when it hits me: This is what I wore the night I went to the hospital.

There was supposed to be a fund-raiser that night, but Dad had to cancel it—because of me. I remember I kept apologizing to him in the ambulance, and his cornflower-blue tie got tangled in the IV tube as he leaned down to tell me it was okay. I spent the night at Park Hills Community Hospital, and the next day, my parents drove me to Pineview.

I fall back on my bed and stare up at the ceiling. I haven't thought about that night in a long time.

Pineview was terrible—but it was also kind of . . . *easy*. I felt like the healthiest person there, as opposed to how I felt at Immaculate Heart, like I was the only one who was broken. It feels good to be the normal one for a change, but it's awful to be surrounded by sick and hopeless people. Like being in a room full of the worst possible versions of yourself, surrounded by reminders of what you'll become if you don't get better. If you don't fix yourself. And, in those moments when you're sure you never will, it feels like there's a rope winding around your body, tightening every time you exhale. And after a while, you can't even breathe.

I feel that way now, like there's something heavy sitting on my chest, squeezing the air out of me. I stand and pace my room, clenching and unclenching my fists, trying to catch my breath, trying to stave off the tingling already making its way up my arms. I can't let this happen, not before a fund-raiser. Not again. I can't do this.

I can't do this.

My dad's ringtone cuts through the air, and I jump. The phone rings again, and I grab for my jeans, which are still crumpled on the floor next to the bed. As I pull my phone out of the back pocket, a slip of paper drops to the floor.

I answer the call, and my mother's voice says, "Riley?"

But I don't reply immediately; I'm still trying to catch my breath. I can tell I'm on speakerphone in the Lincoln because I hear my father berating another driver in the background. Somehow, that grounds me.

"Honey, are you there?"

"Yeah, Mom. Hi."

"We're on our way. Are you dressed?"

"Almost." I glance at the clothes piled against the closet door, then look down at the piece of paper that fluttered to the floor. Bec's note.

"Well, you better hustle. We'll be there in fifteen minutes and we can*not* be late. Your father . . ."

I put Mom on speaker, then set the phone on my bed

and bend over to pick up the paper. Mom rambles on in her wife-of-congressman voice, but I've checked out.

In case you reconsider.

"Mom," I say, attempting to interrupt her stream of nervous chatter. "Mom!"

"Yes, Riley, what is it?"

"I can't go."

"What?"

"I can't go to the fund-raiser tonight."

There's a long pause on the other end. Finally, Mom speaks. "Is it . . . are you . . ." She thinks I'm having another episode—which I sort of am, but she doesn't need to know that.

"No, Mom, it's nothing like that. I kind of . . . made plans."

No one says anything for a good ten seconds. I hear the traffic on the freeway. I hear keys clicking against the dash panel. And then my dad's voice erupts from the speaker: "You made *plans?*" I can almost *hear* him throwing up his hands. "Unacceptable, Riley. The election is five weeks away. Family matters to these people. We have a respons—"

"I have a study date." I blurt the words without thinking.

"A date?" he says.

I smack my palm against my forehead. Of course that's what he'd react to. I shouldn't have used that word. Why did I use that word?

"No, no. It's not a date. I don't know why I said that. It's just . . . studying."

I hear my parents whispering to each other, but I can't make out the words. Then Dad says, "Studying for what?"

"I have an AP Government test." Technically, I'm telling

my parents the truth. It feels odd.

"When?" Dad says. He's asking for details. That means he's considering letting me off the hook. He's actually considering it.

"Tomorrow, second period," I say, and then words start to spew out of my mouth like noodles from my mom's pasta maker. "Brennan's really tough, Dad. He's not cutting me any slack even though I transferred. Also, I think he recognized my name. I'll feel like an idiot if the congressman's kid doesn't ace the first test."

More whispering.

"Where are you going?" Dad asks. "Will there be parental superv—" I hear a *thwack* on the other end. "Ow. What, Sharon?"

"Riley?"

"Yeah, Mom."

"You can go on your study date."

"It's not a date, Mom."

"Okay, it's not a date. Your father and I think it's great that you're making friends."

"Who is it?" Dad asks.

"Just someone from my Government class."

"Boy or g—"

"*Sean!*"

"All right, all right!"

Mom clears her throat, then says, "Study hard and we'll see you after the event."

"Home by ten," Dad says.

"Okay," I say.

"Bye, honey."

"Bye." The call ends, and I stare at my phone in fascination and disbelief. It actually worked. I don't have to go to the event.

Overcome with relief, I collapse onto my bed. I play back the phone call in my head and decide it was probably the most normal conversation I've had with my parents in years.

Except for one part: *Boy or girl?* My dad was about to ask before Mom cut him off.

Boy or girl?

The question rings in my head, the implications echoing around the inside of my skull like a ricocheting bullet. Dad was probably asking because he suspects I'm gay. That's not so bad, especially since he seems open to talking about it. But then, Mom cut him off before he could ask; why? Is it because *she's* not okay with it? Or because she suspects something more, and didn't want to open a can of worms right before an event?

A bark of laughter escapes me. I don't know why, but just now, the thought that my parents are trying to figure me out strikes me funny. They have no idea what's actually going on with me. And, for now, that's how I want it.

I unfold the note and read it again. Bec's writing is nearly illegible, a tangled scrawl of black letters.

In case you reconsider.

She wrote it, so she must have wanted me to come over. But then she went AWOL. She might be sick, or out of town— or, she might be home, waiting for me to call. Just the thought of it heats up my cheeks.

I turn my head to glance at my laptop. I could just stay here, reread the chapter summaries, and then burn five hours on Bloglr and tell my parents the studying went well. They'd never know the difference. But then I remember Bec's bright-blue eyes and the cold, smooth touch of her hand on mine.

I take a deep breath and punch in the number.

The phone rings. It rings again. I end the call. Apparently I can't do *this*, either.

I stare up at the screen, trying to decide if I should call again—and then the phone surprises me by ringing in my hand, and I drop it on my face. It glances off my chin, bounces on the mattress, slides across the carpet, and comes to rest under my dresser. It rings three more times as I scramble off the bed and drop to my knees to retrieve it. It's way in the back, by the wall, and I have to press the side of my face to the dresser to reach it. Finally, I lay a finger on the phone, ease it out from its hiding place, and answer it on the fifth ring.

"Hello?" I say, slightly out of breath.

"You called right on time."

At the sound of Bec's voice, my face splits in a grin. "How did you know it was me?"

"This is Sam, right?"

My heart leaps into my mouth. "Sam? Who—"

"I'm kidding, Riley."

My heart slides back down my throat and into its usual place in my chest.

"I knew you would call," she says.

"Really?"

"Mmm-hmm. I spiked those juice boxes with an addictive chemical. I knew you could only withstand the cravings for so long." Even though I'm alone in my room, my whole body heats up. It's like a fever chill.

"Earth to Riley," Bec says.

"Yeah, I'm here."

"I thought you had a thing."

"I did. I mean, I do. I mean, I'm not going. So." I bury my face in my pillow. Please kill me now. I do not know how to speak English to the human people.

Bec says, "You . . . still want to study for Brennan?" The way she stretches out the word "you" makes it sound almost like a panther growl.

"Sure," I say, trying not to sound eager, and failing miserably.

"I'll text you my address."

CHAPTER 9

BEC LIVES ON THE OLDER SIDE of town, in a neighborhood separated from the more upscale part of Park Hills by Banyan Road, a wide, diagonal street marred by potholes and a defunct train track running down the center. Most of the streetlights on her block are out, and I have to click on my high beams to read the fading addresses painted on the curb. I spot her street number and pull over, suddenly self-conscious about the shiny newness of my mom's minivan in contrast to the peeling paint on Bec's old, one-story house. I get out, walk up the crumbling concrete steps, and knock on the door. There's no answer. I see light from a TV flickering through the thin curtains, so I ring the doorbell.

Heavy footsteps approach, and the door opens. A tall, extremely overweight boy with a shaved head looks down at me from behind the screen door. He's wearing a sweaty gray

T-shirt and has a video game controller clutched in one hand. His breath comes in wheezes.

"Hi," I say. "Is Bec—"

The boy cuts me off. "Shh! My mom's resting." I start to reply, but then he pushes open the warped screen door, and I take a step back instead. The boy squints down at me. It's the look that precedes the Question, or the taunt, or whatever is coming. I brace myself for it—and then, to my relief, Bec appears in the doorway.

"Thanks, Erik," she says. "I'll take it from here."

But Erik pays her no attention; his eyes are still on me.

"Are you—" he starts, but Bec cuts him off.

"Erik. Game. Go."

He shoots Bec a death glare, but she doesn't look away. After a moment, his eyes flick back toward me. "Have fun studying," he says, then retreats into the living room.

Bec watches him go, then turns to me and says in a hushed voice, "Come on in."

An ancient square TV dominates one side of the family room. Somebody, probably Erik, has dragged an old blue couch and a mangy beige recliner off to one side to make room for a white plastic mat, which lies in the center of the patchy rug. Erik steps onto it and unpauses his game. It's on mute, but the screen flashes as he drops clumsily to his knees and starts doing what my father would refer to as "girl push-ups." It's some kind of workout game; on screen, a beefy dude in a muscle shirt makes encouraging gestures as Erik matches his avatar push-up for push-up.

"My room's back here," Bec whispers, then leads me

through the family room and into the hall. We come to a room at the back of the house, and Bec pauses outside the door.

"Sorry about Erik being a dick," she says.

"It's okay."

"He's had a rough week. Some guy on the football team is yanking his chain."

Immediately, I think of Jim Vickers. "Who?"

"I don't know, some meathead douchebag. He's fooled Erik into believing he's got a chance to make the team if he loses weight and does a few 'favors.' Which probably means pulling pranks that could get him kicked out of school, or God knows what else." Bec glances back toward the family room, a tender expression on her face. "I tried to tell him they're just making fun of him, but he won't listen." She shrugs. "Anyway." With a smile and a flourish, Bec opens the door and motions me in. "Welcome to my humble abode," she says, closing the door behind us.

This is clearly the master bedroom, but it's tiny—smaller than my room at home. I look around, trying to hide my confusion, because the layout doesn't make sense at all. The room is split down the middle, with a twin bed resting against each of the long walls. One side of the room has been painted dark gray, while the other side is a painfully bright shade of yellow. Unframed charcoal drawings adorn the walls on the yellow side, and in a corner against one of the gray walls, a battered electric guitar leans against an old schoolhouse desk. At first, I wonder if this bipolar arrangement is a manifestation of some hidden mental illness, but after a few seconds, I realize it's more likely that two people share this room. Across the sliding closet door—also half gray and half yellow—someone has applied an enormous rainbow decal that seems to bridge the two halves of the room. I can't imagine Bec putting up a sticker like that.

"I had a sister," Bec says, and I jump. I had almost forgotten she was in the room with me.

"Oh," I say.

"She died a while back. I keep it like this to remember her. I hope that doesn't freak you out."

"No," I say. "Not at all." But it kind of does.

Bec is looking at one of the charcoal drawings, a portrait of a horse standing behind a split-rail fence. In the background, heavy storm clouds gather.

"Are these yours?" I ask.

"Oh, God, no. I can't even draw stick figures." She turns, smiles at me.

I set my bag down on the desk chair and gesture at the guitar. "Do you play?"

"Yeah. Not great, but good enough for rock and roll." A sudden image of Bec on stage, thrashing away at this red-and-black duct-taped guitar, sends a wave of heat through my midsection. My eyes lock with hers, and for an unknown interval of time, I'm lost in bright blue.

Finally, Bec breaks the spell. "I guess we ought to study, huh?"

I look away. "Yeah. Totally," I say, reaching into my bag to get my laptop.

"So, did I miss anything while I was out?"

"Not much." I set my computer on the desk and push the power button. "Actually, I don't know. I've sort of had a hard time paying attention in class. There's a lot going on."

"I know what you mean," Bec says.

"So, how come you weren't at school the past few days?"

Bec looks away. "My dad travels a lot for work," she says. "Sometimes I get to go with him."

"Oh. Is he still traveling?"

"He doesn't live with us," she says, crossing to push in an open drawer hanging out of her dresser. She lingers there for a second with her back to me, and I decide to change the subject.

"Do you have Wi-Fi?" I ask. And then I think about the old square TV and the crumbling steps out front, and I'm suddenly embarrassed that I brought my brand-new Mac.

But Bec is unfazed. "Erik hacks it from our neighbor. He's a savant with computers." She holds out her hands for the laptop. "He has to tweak your settings."

Reluctantly, I hand it over.

While Bec is out of the room, I resist the temptation to do any serious snooping. I do, however, glance at her extensive and scattered book collection, and I'm delighted to find two of my favorites, *Catcher in the Rye* and *Bridge to Terabithia*, among the more worn-looking paperbacks.

A few minutes later, she returns with my computer, and we're connected. She stretches out on her bed, resting her chin on her palms, while I sit at the desk and open a browser window. I go to the school website and click on Mr. Brennan's page.

"So," I say, "according to the syllabus: 'This quiz will consist of five essay questions about how online dialogue shapes the American political climate.'"

Bec groans. "Kill me now. Essay questions? On a quiz?"

I scroll down. "We're supposed to click through this list of links in preparation."

"Well," she says, sliding off the bed, "I'm going to need a drink, you want something?"

"What do you have?"

She ticks the options off on her fingers. "RC Cola, juice boxes, cooking sherry, drain cleaner. I'm probably going for drain cleaner."

I laugh. "I'll have one of those addictive juice boxes. You know, to prevent withdrawal."

Bec smiles. "Good thinking. I'll be right back."

Bec returns with two juice boxes. She hands me one, pops the straw into her own, and then raises it in a toast. "To Mr. Brennan."

"And our fragile republic," I reply, and we click our juice boxes together.

Bec leans back, eyeing me. "You're funny," she says.

"Defense mechanism," I reply. "Like how sea cucumbers vomit their guts at you when they feel threatened."

"Do they actually do that?"

"I don't know. But I choose to believe it because it's an exceptional metaphor."

Bec takes a pull on her straw, swallows. "So, you feel threatened?"

I blush, immediately and completely.

"Hey," she says, scooting toward me on the bed. "I'm sorry. I do that sometimes. I push people's buttons." And then, she puts her hand on my knee. It's an innocent enough gesture . . .

or is it? I feel the heat in my face intensify.

"I'm—it's fine," I say. "I just have a blushing thing. It's a—"

"Defense mechanism?" Bec offers.

"Something like that."

"Well, that's more sanitary than vomiting your guts out," she says. I laugh. Then she sort of pats me on the leg. It's a weirdly maternal gesture, and it immediately douses the fire that had begun to spread through my body with a flood of disappointment. For a moment, when she put her hand on my leg, I thought she was . . . I don't know, hitting on me. But then it became this weird leg-patting thing, and the energy changed. Ugh. It's so frustrating being totally incapable of interpreting signals—and on top of that, I still don't know how she views me. If she sees me as a girl, am I just, like, a friend? Or, is she *into* girls? Or, if she gets more of a guy vibe from me, am I her type? Or am I just some nerd she can flirt with to get tutoring?

If Bec notices my reaction, she doesn't show it. She sits back against the wall and says, "All right. Teach me stuff about things."

We spend the next hour clicking through the links on Brennan's syllabus. Half of them lead to clean, white, extremely boring government websites, but the other half link to pages run by various fringe political groups and conspiracy theorists. Most of these are wildly colorful, poorly formatted blogs that look like they were designed roughly the same year *Titanic* won Best Picture—but the content is fascinating.

One guy's blog consists entirely of videos of him ranting about how the Patriot Act was a direct violation of the Bill of Rights. Another guy—who my father would term a "nut job"—blathers on and on about how there's actually no law that requires American citizens to pay income tax.

"What's the point of all this?" Bec says, gesturing at the screen with her drink box straw, which she has chewed into a knot. "Half of them seem legit, but the other half look like they're run by the tinfoil-hat brigade."

"Which is the name of my new rock band," I say.

"Huh?"

"Tinfoil Hat Brigade."

Bec rolls her eyes, and I feel my face start to heat up again. If she thought I was even vaguely appealing before, I'm doing an excellent job of changing her mind.

In an effort to divert attention away from my apparently repulsive nerdiness, I return my focus to the screen. "We only have a couple more sites to go."

The next link leads to the home page of a democratic congresswoman from Texas. Below her bio, there's a grid of icons, all of them logos of associations that have endorsed her for reelection. One of them is a sparkling, animated rainbow.

"What's the rainbow?" Bec asks.

So I click it.

A clean, well-formatted page comes up. At the top, there's the rainbow logo again, and the masthead reads:

QueerAlliance.org
LGBTQ Resources

"Pretty controversial endorsement for a Texan," Bec says.

"Yeah, right?" I'm doing my best to keep my face impassive; I know this site. I've never been to the home page, but I've clicked through links on Bloglr and read a few articles on it. Mostly, QueerAlliance.org consists of posts by gay and trans community leaders—but I did find one by a gender fluid writer in San Francisco that helped me a lot, back when I was still trying to figure out what was going with me. In any case, I never expected it to show up on a homework assignment.

Below the menu, there's a square photo of a professional-looking woman with a broad smile and short wavy hair, captioned "Mike/Michelle Weston." Next to that is a calendar of events, including several pride festivals and the annual Transgender Day of Remembrance in November. I scroll down.

In a section called "What's New," there's a list of "Featured Blogs" with photos, short descriptions, and links to each site. I scan through them.

When I see my David Bowie avatar, I almost drop my juice box.

The description reads:

Hiding and Other Social Skills

Alix's online diary communicates the experience of being young and gender fluid with personal stories and humorous rants

Hastily, I click the Back button, silently praying Bec wasn't paying attention. How did my blog end up on this website?

"I should get home," I say, powering down my Mac.

"What? Now?" Bec says. She sits up on the bed. "Is everything okay?"

"Yeah," I say, stuffing the laptop into my bag. "It's just getting late."

Bec glances at her watch. "It's, like, eight fifteen."

"On school nights I'm supposed to be home by eight

thirty." It's a lie, but it comes easily enough.

"Okay, well, I'll walk you out."

My head is spinning as I drive away from her house, thoughts going back and forth in my mind: What are the odds my blog would turn up on Brennan's homework assignment? Did Bec notice my panicked reaction? And then I think about the awkward knee-patting incident, and I want to bury my face in a pillow until I suffocate. Was she flirting, or am I deluding myself?

The thoughts rush in like that, one after the other, disconnected and out of order. I wonder if I ought to pull over until I calm down, but I can't seem to change course. Finally, I get home, close the garage, and head straight up to my room.

Dad has laid out my meds for me. I swallow my pills, brush my teeth, and crawl into bed. I try to do the whiteboard exercise, but fail before I get halfway through. Somehow, I still manage to drift toward sleep. My last thought is of Bec's hand on my knee, and the radiant heat that spread out from it.

I have a mixture of strange and pleasant dreams.

CHAPTER 10

ON FRIDAY MORNING, MOM TAKES me to school early so she can get to her parent-teacher conferences on time, and when she drops me off, the campus seems empty. But as I'm approaching the gates, movement on the athletic field below catches my eye. I squint: it's Bec's brother, Erik, standing on the otherwise deserted football field with Jim Vickers.

At first, I'm not sure what they're doing. Vickers stands close behind him with his hands on Erik's hips, almost like a dance instructor. He adjusts Erik's stance, then positions his arms, and I realize he's holding a football. At Vickers's nod, Erik hurls the ball, and it sails about twenty yards before falling back to the turf. Vickers says something, and Erik tries again. This time the ball goes farther. They talk for a moment, and then Erik reaches into his pocket and hands Vickers something—a piece of gum or candy, maybe; it's hard to tell at this distance.

Then the two of them walk out of sight behind the gym.

I stand there for a minute, wondering why the hell the two of them were down there together. It looked like Vickers was teaching him how to throw—but why? Bec did say that Erik wanted to make the team, and I suppose it's possible that Vickers is trying to help—but somehow, I don't buy that. Not from him. Then again, Erik handed him something; maybe it was a trade for the lesson. Either way, it's probably none of my business—so I turn and make my way across the quad.

Solo is waiting for me outside AP English. We haven't spoken for days—not since he denied me at lunch. At the sight of him, anger flares up in my chest.

"Hey," he says.

I walk right past him and into Miss Crane's empty classroom; he follows. Picking a desk in the middle of the room, I slump down in the chair, drag my English textbook out of my bag, and pretend to start reading.

Solo drops into the desk next to mine. "How long are you planning to ignore me?"

I turn the page.

"A rough estimate is cool," he continues. "I just want to be able to plan my route to class so I can avoid the Medusa death glare you keep giving me."

"I don't know," I say, my eyes still on my book. "How long are you planning to pretend you don't know me when I walk into the cafeteria?"

Solo lets out an exasperated sigh. "Oh, please. Don't be such a drama queen."

"I'm not being a drama queen. You completely ignored me!"

"I did not ignore you. I gave you a cautionary glance, indicating that that particular table would not be a good choice for you."

"A cautionary glance?"

"I was trying to help."

I shake my head and look back down at my book.

"Oh, come on," Solo says. "We all do what we have to do to get along. Don't pretend you didn't stand at the top of those stairs and look at every single table and think, 'I don't want to sit with those people. Ew, I don't want to sit with *those* people, either. Oh, look, those people like sports! They'll *never* understand my existential crisis.'"

I snap my book shut and glare at him. "That's easy for you to say. No one messes with you. You don't look—like I look."

Solo bursts out of his desk.

"I look like *this*!" he says, gesturing first at his face, then at his enormous frame. "You don't think I had a rough time the first week I came here?"

I'm breathing hard and fast through my nose, like my dad does when he's angry.

Solo points a thick finger at me. "You walk around here like you're better than everyone. Like you're surrounded by a bunch of shallow, bigoted assholes."

I open my mouth to reply, but at that moment, the door opens and two girls walk in. One of them is Sierra; I steel myself for her glare, but she doesn't even look at me as she takes a seat near the front. I'm relieved. I glance at Solo, and we make a silent agreement: to be continued.

We don't speak on the way to Government, but I don't try

to avoid him, either; I just walk behind him. It's much easier to navigate the halls in his wake.

And then I walk into Brennan's classroom and see the word "QUIZ" on the whiteboard, and everything that happened last night comes rushing back to me: My study session with Bec. The awkward sexual tension. Finding my blog listed on that LGBTQ website.

Just as the bell rings, Bec walks in, looking frazzled. Her hair is tucked up into a newsboy cap, and I notice dark circles under her eyes. As she slips into the desk in front of mine, I want to say something to her—but what? Twice while Brennan drones on about his grading system, I almost tap her on the shoulder, but I pull my hand back at the last minute.

Finally, Brennan starts handing out quizzes. When Bec turns to pass them on, she mouths, "Good luck," and then smiles at me, causing my stomach to squirm pleasantly.

When the bell rings at the end of class, she's the first one out of her seat. She drops her quiz on Brennan's desk and gives me a weird little wave as she walks out of the classroom. I consider going after her, but what would I say? "Hey, thanks for the studying, want to make out later?" Just the thought makes me blush.

In Precalc I pay precisely zero attention; my thoughts have turned to the bigger issues plaguing me. Why did Bec leave class in such a hurry—is she avoiding me? Is it because of the weirdness during our study date, which may or may not have been an *actual* date? And, as if this train of thought isn't distracting enough, Solo's indictment keeps replaying in my head.

"You walk around here like you're better than everyone. Like

you're surrounded by a bunch of shallow, bigoted assholes."

But the thing is—I *am* surrounded by shallow, bigoted assholes. Within one minute of setting foot on this campus, I was called "it." Later that same day, my gender was called into question in the middle of the cafeteria by half the Park Hills football team. Even the anonymous visitor to my own freaking blog called me "fag." How does that fail to qualify as being surrounded by shallow, bigoted assholes?

By the time French is over, I'm seething. I'm going to find Solo, and we're going to have this out.

From my vantage point at the top of the stairs, I spot Solo seated at his usual table. Cole is there, his long, stringy hair pulled back into a ponytail, and so is the redheaded kid with glasses who always seems to be hanging around.

Jim Vickers sits facing Solo, his bulging shoulders stretching the fabric of a Park Hills Lions T-shirt. Sierra is practically in his lap. Solo makes a comment, and Vickers responds by throwing a ketchup-soaked french fry at him; it splats on Solo's chest and sticks there. Sierra throws back her head and laughs. Solo peels the fry off his shirt and starts to dab at the red stain with a paper napkin. I don't understand why he tolerates this treatment—I only know *I* won't. I clench my jaw and start down the stairs, taking two at a time.

And then I'm in the Gauntlet.

But this time I'm not trying to sneak past unseen; my head is high and my shoulders are set. Solo looks up as if he intends to say something to Vickers, but when he sees me, his eyes go wide and he shakes his head. Sierra notices and turns to look in my direction. When she recognizes me, she smiles and says something to the group that I can't hear.

Ignoring them, I walk up to the table and face Solo—but before I can address him, Vickers interrupts.

"Hey, Solo, it's your boyfriend." He looks me up and down. "Oh, sorry. Girlfriend?"

Vickers and Cole laugh, and Sierra leans toward me.

"Seriously, it's hard to tell," she says. "Are you, like, an effeminate dude, or just an ugly chick?"

More laughter. I feel my face turning red.

Vickers says, "What she's trying to ask is, are you a *dyke* or are you a *faggot*?"

With heat rising in my cheeks, I ignore him and turn to Solo. "Can I talk to you for a minute?"

But Solo is frozen, glaring at Vickers.

"That's not really it, babe," Sierra says to Vickers, her voice dripping with artificial sweetness. "What I want to know is"— she turns toward me, gestures at my crotch—"is there, like, a dick in there? Or a vag?"

"Oh, damn!" Vickers says. Cole snorts.

It takes me a moment to react; I'm honestly surprised. It's one thing to whisper about me to her friends, or to laugh when her boyfriend taunts me—but I didn't expect Sierra to be openly aggressive.

Slowly, I turn and look her in the eye. "That's none of your business," I say. "And, while I'm flattered by your interest, you're really not my type."

The redheaded kid howls with laughter and claps his hands. Vickers smacks him on the arm, and he shuts up.

Sierra's face is white with rage. I feel a rush of triumph—

but underneath it, my adrenaline is surging.

Then, slowly, Vickers stands, and the group goes quiet.

"You want to repeat what you just said to my girlfriend, faggot?"

The blood drains from my face. I take a step backward.

And then Solo is on his feet, his imposing frame towering over the table. He reaches out a massive hand and claps Vickers on the shoulder.

"Sit down, bro," he says. "You're being an ass."

Cole's eyes widen in surprise, and the redheaded kid shrinks back in his seat. Vickers glares at Solo—and for a moment, I think he's going to hit him. But after a few seconds, Sierra reaches up and touches Vickers's arm, and he shakes his head and sits down.

Solo blinks, grabs his backpack, and starts up the aisle without further hesitation.

He doesn't say a word as I follow him through the outdoor hallway and around the back of the auditorium. I think he'll turn left and head toward the ramp, but instead, he plunges down the slope toward the parking lot, and I hurry after him.

His car is an ancient, peeling, silver Toyota hatchback. The back window is plastered to the point of opacity with decals; featured prominently among them are a vintage KROQ FM bumper sticker and a Rebel Alliance logo.

"Lift up the door when you open it, or it'll fall off," he says.

"Where are we going?" I ask.

"We're ditching."

CHAPTER 11

TEN MINUTES LATER WE'RE SPEEDING down the freeway, Solo's hatchback shuddering like a porta-potty in a 5.0 magnitude earthquake.

"Where are we going?" I yell.

Yelling is necessary because the radiator in Solo's car is shot, so he keeps the heater on full blast to prevent the car from overheating, which means all four windows have to be rolled down or else the car becomes a pizza oven.

He replies, but I think I mishear him, because it sounds like he says, "The Reagan Years."

But then we get off the freeway in downtown Fullerton, and sure enough, there it is, lodged between a tiny sushi restaurant and a hair salon: the Reagan Years. Solo pushes open the door and we step inside.

It's an authentic eighties video arcade, packed wall-to-wall with old-school stand-up games like *Galaga* and *Dig Dug* and *Donkey Kong*. An old Oingo Boingo song blares from tinny speakers, and two square TVs mounted overhead show crackly, low-resolution MTV videos.

"This place is awesome," I say.

"Wait till you see the back."

We walk around a big partition, and there's a full-blown fifties soda fountain, complete with checkered linoleum flooring and red vinyl bar stools. The guy behind the counter is even wearing one of those little paper hats.

"When I get pissed," Solo says, "I play *Ms. Pac-Man*."

He produces a roll of quarters from his backpack, and I follow him to one of the sit-down table games. He squeezes into a tiny chair, plugs two quarters into the machine, and starts to play, yanking on the joystick as though his physical strength might somehow make the cheesy 8-bit graphics move faster. I watch him play for a while, noticing the way he presses his lips together like a trumpet player when he concentrates. It's kind of adorable.

"I'll get drinks," I say.

"Chocolate malted," he replies without looking up. Something about the way he says it—even though we haven't begun to work things out yet—gives me a sense of relief, as though it's already understood that we're going to move past this and be friends.

He's not paying attention to me, but I smile at him anyway. "Coming right up."

When I return with the drinks, Solo is just finishing a game. He stands, pumps a fist, and extends both middle fingers to the screen.

"Eat that, machine!" he yells. "I ain't afraid of no ghosts!"

I set his malted on the game table and unscrew the cap on my water bottle.

"You don't like malteds?" Solo says, leaning over to take a long drink from his straw.

For a moment, I consider launching into the whole vegan thing, but just the thought of it exhausts me, so I shake my head instead.

Solo shrugs. "More for me. Did you order fries?"

I nod. "Can I ask you a question?"

"Shoot."

"Do you really think I walk around acting like I'm better than everyone else?"

Solo takes another long pull on his malted. "I think you assume everyone is going to be your enemy. And by doing that, you sort of make it come true."

"So you think I made Jim Vickers call me 'dyke' and 'faggot'?"

Solo shakes his head. "No, of course you didn't *make* him. You maybe *invited* him to."

"*Invited* him to? Please tell me how I invited someone to attack and humiliate me in front of the entire cafeteria."

"See, this is what I'm talking about."

"What?"

"I met you four days ago. Today, I abandoned my teammates of three *years* to ditch school and take you to the largest fifties soda fountain-slash-eighties video arcade in the western hemisphere—but are you grateful? No. You want to fight with me."

I glare at him.

"You invite it," he says, "because you dress in a way that makes it nearly impossible for people to tell if you're a boy or a girl."

"It's none of their business," I reply.

Solo sighs, then leans across the table. "How much do you think I weigh?"

"What?"

"How much do you think I weigh?"

I shake my head. "I have no idea."

"Look me in the eye and tell me you haven't guessed a number."

I hold his gaze but say nothing.

"I'll bet it was the first thing you thought about when you saw me. Maybe the second, after trying to figure out what race I am."

I look down. Solo sits back.

"I can't dress like a skinny person," he says. "Or a white person. I am what I am. And people are going to react."

"That's different," I say.

"I'm sure it is," Solo says. "But the point is, if I walked around waiting for people to call me 'fat boy' so that I could get into a fight about it, I'd *always* be in a fight." He leans over and finishes his malted with one final slurp, then pushes the glass away.

I look at him. He smiles, and his enormous cheeks sort of fold up and hide his ears.

"People really messed with you your first week?" I ask.

"Yeah," Solo says.

"But you're huge. You'd think they'd know better."

Solo throws up his hands. "Right?"

"What did they say?"

"The usual. Remarks about my weight. Wetback jokes."

"Long swim from Samoa," I say.

Solo wags his finger at me. "Nothing pisses me off more than an improperly applied racial epithet. Know your minorities, people. They should make a pamphlet."

I laugh.

Solo says, "My first day in PE, Coach Terrance pulled me aside and asked if I was interested in being on the offensive line. I didn't know what the hell he was talking about. Then he asked me if I liked video games. I thought he was making fun of me—but when I said yes, he told me to go buy *Madden NFL* and play it for a week."

"The football coach told you to buy a video game?"

"Crazy, right? But I did. And I totally fell in love with football."

"What is there to love about *football*?"

"Well, it's like . . . ," he begins, sheepishly. "You've read Harry Potter, right?"

"Seven times all the way through."

"Okay. Well, I'm sitting there playing *Madden* on my PlayStation, and it occurs to me that football is basically Wizard's Chess."

I cock my head.

"You call your play, you line up your guys, and you let them fight. That's a down. Sometimes you gain ground, sometimes you lose it. It's not just a bunch of sweaty jocks out there banging into each other. You have to know your opponent. You have to think ten moves ahead."

The guy from the counter shows up with our fries. "Enjoy," he says, and then walks off.

I reach for a fry, and Solo continues.

"Anyway, when I came back the next week, Coach asked me what I thought about *Madden*, and I just started jabbering at him, telling him what I liked about the game. You should have seen the smile on his face. You'd have thought he just won the lottery."

"So you joined the team."

Solo shakes his head, frowning. When he replies, his voice is low and flat. "What I did was go to the gym every day for two weeks, and eat nothing but baked potatoes and boiled chicken breasts. Then I went to the tryouts—and practically got laughed off the field."

"They laughed at you? And you still wanted to join the team?"

"They knew me as the three-hundred-pound brown kid with the furry Chewbacca backpack. I didn't fit in yet. I hadn't passed the test." He reaches for a handful of fries. "And yes, I *did* still want to join the team. I wanted to play."

"So what happened at tryouts?"

He answers with his mouth full. "I tackled Vickers in the first drill. Laid him out flat."

"Was he pissed?"

Solo shakes his head, swallows. "Nope. He was impressed. Grudgingly, but still. That's how I earned my way in. By proving myself on the field." He looks at me. "That, and I had to lose the Chewbacca backpack."

"You did not."

He shrugs. "It took a long time to lose the nickname Chewie. But eventually, I became Solo. I like that a lot better."

"Wow," I say. "So you gave up something you really loved just to fit in with a bunch of guys who laughed at you and called you fat."

Solo folds his arms. "I didn't stop liking *Star Wars*, or even talking about it. I just stopped wearing the furry backpack to school. You'd have done the same thing."

I look at Solo, then down at my lap. "I think this is where the analogy breaks down for me."

"Explain."

"I can't just stop wearing a backpack."

Solo raises his eyebrows. "Care to elaborate?"

I open my mouth, then shut it. Is this the person I want to come out to? And, if he is, what will I say?

Solo leans in. "Look. I don't expect you to spill your guts to me. Your business is your business. Dress how you want to dress. Let people wonder. Fuck 'em."

I smile.

Solo raises a finger. "But you've got to stop looking for a fight every time someone makes a comment. High school sucks for everyone."

I feel my smile fade, and I sit back in the chair. "It kind of feels like you're defending those guys."

Solo shrugs. "There will always be guys like Jim Vickers. But I'm not going to let them stop me from doing what I want. And neither should you."

CHAPTER 12

WE PULL OFF THE FREEWAY, and the wind rushing past the window fades to a gentle breeze. It's the first cool evening of fall, and the air on my face is exhilarating. It feels good to be driving on a Friday night with the windows down after ditching school for video games and french fries, and I look over at Solo and feel a sudden rush of affection for him.

"Thanks for standing up for me today," I say.

He nods. "You needed it."

"So." I glance out the window, then back at Solo. "What happens on Monday?"

We turn onto my street.

"You could come sit with us," he says.

"And get verbally abused by the entire football team? No thanks." I expect him to reply, maybe even get defensive, but he just pulls up in front of my house and sets the parking brake.

And then we're quiet for a while, listening to the irregular idle of the old car.

"Are you going to get it for ditching?" Solo asks.

"Probably. You?"

He shrugs. "Half the time my mom yells at me, I can't understand what she's saying. Plus, I have a really good shame face." He tilts his head toward me and his massive cheeks fall forward. He looks like an enormous sad bulldog.

"That *is* a really good shame face."

I glance out the window at my house; if the attendance office called my parents, I'm probably in for a talk when they get home. In the meantime, I feel . . . good. Maybe for the first time since I started at Park Hills.

After a moment, I get out of the car.

"Have a good weekend," I say, carefully closing the rickety door.

Solo bows. "May the Force be with you."

My parents won't be home for another hour and a half, so I sequester myself in my room, fire up my laptop, and log in to Bloglr. When my dash appears, I lean back in my chair and stare at the numbers on the screen:

MESSAGES: 27
FOLLOWERS: 568

Five hundred sixty-eight followers? Last time I checked, it was fifty something—and it's been less than a week! I click Refresh, but the numbers remain the same. How did I gain so many followers so quickly?

I start clicking on their avatars and browsing through their profiles, paying particular attention to the connections we have in common. When I notice that the first dozen or so also follow QueerAlliance's Bloglr feed, things start to make sense. QueerAlliance is a popular site; it probably gets thousands of hits every day. All these people must have found me because I was featured in the "What's New" section on the home page.

I run my fingers through my hair. These five hundred new followers—these strangers—have read my most personal thoughts. My most embarrassing feelings. My secrets. All at once, I feel naked. I know it's practically impossible . . . but what if someone reads this and knows it's me? I glance at the window to make sure my curtains are closed. They are. Then a nervous laugh escapes me, and I shake my head; I'm just being paranoid. Bloglr is anonymous. There's nothing anyone could use to connect Alix the blogger with Riley the congressman's kid. I let out a long breath, and then I scroll through the comments.

People appear to actually like what I've shared. More than that, they seem to take comfort or inspiration from it, and that makes me feel . . . I don't know. Like I matter. Like maybe I'm not so alone after all.

I click on Messages and start reading.

> Anonymous: Love ur blog! XD
> yell0wbedwetter: Moar pleez!
> Anonymous: OMG. Thank. U. So. Much. I came out to my mom over the weekend & she cried & couldn't understand. Kept asking if I was trans, and I couldn't explain.

After I read ur post I told her your line "it's not a switch it's a dial." I think she finally got it! U have no idea. Thank u!!!!

MiMi_Q: Oh, Alix, I don't envy where you are, but you will make it. You are an inspiration. Keep writing.

I scroll down. There are more messages like the ones above. I start replying, thanking the senders, and welcoming my new followers. And then, after about twenty minutes, I come to a more substantial message, and I start to read:

Anonymous: Hi Alix. I totally started crying when I read ur story about being in the toy store with ur dad. That is what I've been feeling my whole life. Exactly that. Anyway thank u so much. I want to come out to my sister but I don't know what to say. Any advice?

I reread the message. My heart physically aches at the thought that something I wrote helped this stranger figure out what they're going through. I start to type out a reply, tentatively at first, but with increasing velocity. Soon, my hands are flying over the keyboard; I'm surprised how much I have to say.

And then, just as I'm about to click Post, I hesitate. Because the message is anonymous, I can't reply privately; anyone who follows my blog will be able see this. I reread what I've written. It all sounds . . . wrong. False. Arrogant. Who am I to give this person advice? For one thing, I don't know *anything* about coming out. I'm still in the closet myself. How am I remotely qualified to advise this stranger on something so big?

I delete my reply and type a new one.

> Alix: Hi, Anonymous. I wish I could give you advice, but the truth is, I'm just a big fat coward. The only person I've come out to is my therapist, who is oath-bound not to judge me and required by law to keep my secrets. In my own searching, I've come across a couple sites that might help: try Bloglr.com/genderbender, and also QueerAlliance.org. Sorry I couldn't be more helpful.

I reread my response, consider deleting it again, and then finally click Post. I sit back in my chair and frown at the screen. I feel unsatisfied, like I just brushed someone off. I find myself second-guessing myself, wishing I had shared my original response after all.

My thoughts are interrupted by the sound of the garage door.

My parents are home.

They're waiting for me in the living room when I come downstairs. My mother is stationed on the long sofa, her face tight with worry, her arms and legs crossed as though she's trying to tie her whole body in a knot. Dad paces in front of the coffee table, stopping when I enter.

"Riley," he says. "We need to talk to you. Sit down."

His voice is even, but I can tell by the set of his jaw that he's really angry. I approach and sit in a chair facing them.

"We got a call from school," Dad says. "They said you weren't in class after lunch."

I nod.

"You want to tell us where you were?"

"I ditched with a friend. We went to Fullerton."

"Were you drinking?" my mother asks.

"What? No. I had water. We were just talking."

Dad moves toward me. "Let me smell your breath."

And just like that, we backslide. The trust I've worked so hard to rebuild over the last month is gone in one afternoon. And the stupid part is, I was never even into drinking—it was just that one time. *The* time. But even after six weeks in Pineview, they've never forgiven me, and they've never forgotten.

Dad leans forward, and I exhale in his face. He nods, satisfied, and moves to sit next to my mother.

"I'm sorry," I say. "I know I shouldn't have ditched. But I needed to get out of there."

"We're going to need more of an explanation than that," Dad says.

I look down at my lap. "I was having a bad day."

Dad exhales through his nose. "You can't walk out of school just because you're 'having a bad day.' You have to—"

But Mom lays a hand on his knee to cut him off. "Tell us what happened, honey."

I think about Vickers demanding to know whether I was a dyke or a faggot, but I can't tell them that. So, I say, "Some kids were making me fun of me."

Dad throws up his hands. "And?" His face is the color of beets, and I feel myself shrink from him. At my reaction, he folds his hands and softens his voice. "Riley, listen. Words can hurt. I get it. Jesus, right now, there are consultants being paid thousands of dollars to write bad things about me. But you can't just walk out. You have to keep your chin up."

I feel tears stinging my eyes, and I clench my jaw. I don't want to cry. I don't want to break down in front of them.

"What did they say to you?" Mom asks.

I shift in my seat. I have to tell them something. "They were making fun of the way I dress."

Dad shakes his head and looks up at the ceiling. Mom reaches out to put a hand on his knee again, then thinks better of it and folds her hands in her lap. "We're just concerned," she says. "You spend all your time shut up in your room on your computer. And . . ." She looks me up and down, and I just know she's about to make a comment about my clothes. "When you were at Immaculate Heart, we thought . . ." She glances at Dad. "I mean, we thought you were just rebelling against all that structure. The uniform, and the strict rules, and everything."

"But now we don't know what it is," Dad says.

I hear Doctor Ann's voice in my head, telling me to take a slow, deep breath. I try, but find that I can't; my chest is too tight. My fingertips are beginning to tingle.

Mom picks nervously at her cuticles. "You know," she says, "not having a uniform can be really liberating. It's a great opportunity to wear what you want. To stand out from the crowd."

I want to scream: That's exactly what I *don't* want to do.

Dad gets up, thrusts his hands into his pockets, and starts pacing again. "We're not dinosaurs, Riley. We remember what high school is like."

He has no idea what it's like.

"And I know you think this is superficial," he says, "but the fact is: appearance matters. People *do* judge books by their covers; it's human nature. They react to the way you look before they hear a single word that comes out of your mouth."

I don't respond. The tingling spreads to my face.

"If you don't like the outfits I bought you," Mom says, "we could go shopping together. We could make a day out of it." She smiles, but it withers when she sees the look on my face.

"You think I wouldn't rather lounge around in sweats all day?" Dad says. "Believe me, I would. But you have to dress for the life you *want*. Is this how you want to live?" He stops, pulls a hand out of his pocket, and makes a dismissive gesture at me. "Is this who you are?"

My vision starts to tunnel. I grip the arm of the chair and stand.

"I need to go lie down," I say. My voice sounds distant.

"We're not through talking."

"I can't—I can't talk about this."

"You can, and you will."

"Riley—" Mom begins, but now it's Dad who interrupts.

"Let me handle this, Sharon." He turns toward me. "Don't pretend we're the bad guys here. You want to dress this way? Fine. But don't use other people's reactions as an excuse to walk out on your obligations." He holds up a finger. "First, you cancel last-minute on a very important fund-raiser. And we supported you, because we want you to have friends. We really do. But the very next day, you turn around and ditch class?"

"Please stop," I say.

"Sean—" Mom says, but Dad cuts her off.

"I'm trying to run a very public campaign about education reform. You don't think the media will hear about it if my kid starts racking up truancies? How do you think this reflects on me?"

And then, it's as though a dam breaks in my head, and the tingling floods through me. I feel like I'm in someone else's body. My father is still talking, gesturing emphatically, but his voice and his movements seem far away.

"Stop," I say, covering my ears with my tingling hands, holding my head so it doesn't fall apart. My voice sounds like it's coming from someone else. Someone talking in another room. "Stop talking," I say, more loudly. "Just—please, shut up."

"Do *not* speak to me—"

"SHUT UP!" I scream.

Mom's face goes white. My father's mouth falls open, and suddenly he looks like a little boy. I can't stand to look at him.

I feel my body turn and move toward the stairs. And then I'm in my room, and I feel the comforter on my face, and the tingling is everywhere. I bury my face in the pillow, and I scream.

And I scream.

When I come back to myself, I'm lying on my side in bed, facing the wall. I can hear my parents talking softly behind me. I start to roll over. Mom senses me moving and lifts the cold cloth from my neck.

"It's okay, honey," she says. I blink up at her.

Dad moves to stand in the doorway. "You have your regular appointment with Doctor Ann tomorrow." He's still angry, but the heat is gone from his voice. "In the meantime, you're grounded." He holds up my laptop.

I want to yell and punch the wall. I want to scream again, and say I'm sorry, and cry and push my mother away. I want to do all these things, but instead, I roll over and press my face into the comforter. After a moment, I hear the door close.

CHAPTER 13

THERE ISN'T EVEN A COUCH in Doctor Ann's office; just a big Pottery Barn desk and two ugly leather armchairs that always make me feel like I'm sitting on a dead cow.

Doctor Ann sits across from me wearing a blue dress, one leg crossed elegantly over the other. She doesn't use a notebook or anything during our sessions, which somehow makes me feel even more scrutinized, because her eyes never leave me. But all I can think about as I stare at the pale-green wallpaper is my dad's blank look when I screamed at him to shut up, and my mother shrinking into the couch.

"What's going on over there?" Doctor Ann asks. "Are you replaying the confrontation from last night?"

I stare at her. "How did you know?"

Doctor Ann nods toward the wall of diplomas behind her desk. "I have very expensive degrees," she says.

I laugh, then run a hand through my hair. "I didn't mean to yell at them. It was like . . . someone else was using my mouth to do the yelling."

She nods.

"My face was doing the tingling thing, and I couldn't breathe."

"Has that been happening a lot?"

"I guess. I mean, it's been worse since I started school."

"Are you taking your meds?"

I scrub at the carpet with one foot. "Yeah. Dad's doling them out."

Doctor Ann steeples her hands and touches her two index fingers to her lips. "Why don't you tell me something *good* that happened this week?"

"Something good?"

"Yes."

I think for a minute, and then I just start to babble. I share about meeting Solo and our subsequent fight. I describe my fluctuation episode in the hall, my panic attack the next day, and finally conquering the Gauntlet. I tell her about ditching the fund-raiser to study with Bec, and how I thought there was sexual tension, but it was probably all in my head. I tell her about going to the Reagan Years with Solo and making up. When I finally glance at the clock above the door, I've been talking for almost thirty minutes straight, so I stop. Doctor Ann watches me, waiting to see if I'll continue. I don't.

"Have you thought any more about starting that journal blog I suggested?"

"Oh yeah," I say. "I almost forgot." And I fill her in on

everything—from my first post to the anonymous "your a fag" commenter, to getting five hundred followers in a week.

"Wow," she says, and then actually laughs out loud.

"Are you laughing at me?"

Doctor Ann recovers, shakes her head. "No. Psychiatrists aren't permitted to laugh at our patients." She smiles. "I'm glad you started the blog. I think other teenagers will benefit from your insight."

I let out a breath I didn't realize I'd been holding; I guess I wanted her validation—not just for the blog, but for the way I've been thinking and feeling.

Doctor Ann glances at her watch, and I sit up straighter. We're just getting started; I'm not ready to go yet.

"We haven't talked about my dysphoria," I say.

"Would you like to talk about your dysphoria?"

"Not really."

"Okay," she says.

"Just okay?"

Doctor Ann frowns. "I get the impression you want something from me. Do you want to tell me what it is?"

I open my mouth, then close it. Then I say, "I don't know. I feel like you listen, but you don't do anything to fix what's wrong with me."

"Well, okay," she says, "but I don't think there's anything wrong with you."

"Then why am I here?"

"Why do you think you're here?"

"It's really fucking annoying when you do that," I snap.

Doctor Ann exhales heavily, then nods.

"I'm sorry," I say.

"Riley, I don't know what you want me to do for you."

I lean forward. "I want you to fix my anxiety. Make me feel like it's okay to be who I am. Help me figure out how to . . . how to tell my parents in a way that will make them okay with it."

Doctor Ann folds her arms. "That's a lot."

I throw up my hands.

"All right," she says. "Let's start with the anxiety."

"Okay."

"So, first, I want you to know that everybody experiences some level of anxiety. It's a normal human response to stress. It's like your body's smoke alarm. If there's a fire, you want to know so you can put it out or call 9-1-1, right?"

I shrug. "I guess. But it feels like my alarm is going off all the time."

Doctor Ann nods. "Some people's systems are more sensitive than others'. For you, maybe all it takes is burning a piece of toast, and your alarm thinks the house is on fire."

I nod.

"But there's no doubt you're experiencing a lot of stress. You just changed schools. Your dad is running for office. That's enough to give anybody a little anxiety. But when you add the bullying at school, and the gender dysphoria you're experiencing, it can be overwhelming. And if we take your sensitivity into consideration, it's not surprising that you're having more frequent, intense episodes."

I sit back. I hadn't thought of it like that. And she's right—it *is* overwhelming.

"So how do I cope with it?" I say.

"You are coping. You're taking meds. You're going out with friends. Standing up for yourself. Writing about it. Screaming at your parents."

"And that's normal?"

"For a teenager in your situation? I'd say so. It's better than"—she pauses, as if catching herself before saying the wrong thing—"doing something extreme."

I fold my arms. "You mean like washing down a dozen Xanax with a bottle of whiskey?"

Doctor Ann's mouth drops open slightly, but then she recovers. "Yes," she says. "It's much better than that." She looks like she's waiting for me to say something more about it. When I don't, she leans forward in her chair and speaks again, more softly this time. "As for wondering if it's okay to be who you are—that's not a symptom of mental illness. That's a symptom of being a person."

"What about my parents?"

"Are you ready to tell them?"

"No. But I'm kind of afraid I will. Like, in a moment of anger."

"Do you know what you want to say?"

"No. Hell no."

"All right. Well, let's make an agreement. You won't tell them until we have a chance to talk about it first. How about that?"

"Okay," I say. And instantly, I feel a weight lifted. I put my face in my hands, and my shoulders start to shake. I hear Doctor Ann pull a tissue out of the box on her side table, and I take it from her, blow my nose, and look up.

"I feel like you should give me some deep advice or something."

"About what?"

"Like, I don't know, about life. Or how I'm supposed to deal with all this."

Doctor Ann scrunches up her face in concentration. She's quiet for so long that I wonder if she's forgotten I'm there. Then, finally, she speaks.

"Find a cause."

"Find a cause? What does that mean?"

"Take a stand for someone other than yourself."

"You mean, like, demonstrate for animal rights or something?" I squirm on the leather chair.

Doctor Ann raises an eyebrow. "If that appeals to you."

"How will that help?"

"Maybe it will get you out of your head. Get you to stop thinking about *you* so much. Get you engaged with other people."

Stop thinking about *me* so much? What's that supposed to mean? I want to say it out loud, to snap at her; but instead, I just sort of deflate in the chair. She's probably right—she usually is—but the last thing I want to do right now is engage with other people.

"Find a cause. That's your deep advice?"

She shrugs. "Take it or leave it."

CHAPTER 14

NEW POST: REBEL REBEL (WITHOUT A CAUSE)
OCTOBER 7, 10:22 PM

Forgive me, Bloglr, for I have sinned. It has been two whole days since my last post.

Thank you for your kind messages and comments. Also, thank you to all my new followers. I know that most of you probably found me through QueerAlliance, so thanks to them for featuring me on their site. I honestly don't know what I did to deserve that, but I'll try to live up to the honor.

⊙ *NOW PLAYING: "Rebel Rebel" by David Bowie*

But now, dear readers, I need your help. The next phase of my therapy includes an assignment: I MUST FIND A CAUSE. Something that will get me out of my own head. Stop me from thinking about *me* so much. So here are my ideas, in no particular order:

Animal rights (vegan activism, protests, and stuff)

Community Service (the helping-old-people kind, not the picking-up-trash-in-an-orange-vest kind)

Antibullying club (if they have one at my school)

Aaaand that's all I have. Seriously, I need your help on this. Badly. Please send me ideas.

#genderfluid #animalrights #vegan #anxiety #recovery

I click Post, then start sorting through my inbox. Mostly, I've received nice messages from new followers, thanking me for sharing, or inviting me to check out their blogs. There are a few negative anons, but none of them are quite as rude as "your a fag," and I delete them quickly. The good messages outnumber the bad by at least five to one. After about half an hour, I come to a particularly interesting, but utterly inappropriate, question, and I decide to issue another smackdown à la my apostrophe post.

Anonymous: Okay, so sometimes u feel like a boy, and sometimes u feel like a girl. How do u have sex?

Alix: Well, I haven't actually had sex yet, so technically I'm not qualified to answer. And, while I understand you're curious, you need to know that "How do you have sex?" is a cataclysmically impolite question. Like, would you ask your cismale[1] friend how he has sex:

You: Yo, Bif, you have a penis. How do you have sex?

Bif: What, you want me to describe it?

You: Yes, please.

Bif: Why?

You: I have a nearly sociopathic disregard for both your privacy and your feelings.

Bif: Wow, that's . . . really honest. I am strangely compelled to grant your request.

You: Please provide graphic anatomical detail. Visual aids would help. Perhaps a series of animated gifs.

Bif: Sounds like a lot of work. How about I just use a vulgar euphemism instead?

You: Sold.

Bif: Okay. The airplane lands in the hangar, and then it takes off again. And then it lands again. And then it takes off again. . . .

You: This is a terrible metaphor. It sounds like you're describing feeding a baby.

Bif: I did say it would be a vulgar euphemism.

You: Wow. I am filled with regret for having pursued this uncouth line of inquiry.

Bif: I forgive you. Here, I have made for you an elaborate stop-motion film using Play-Doh and the camera on my phone. This should explain everything.

You: This is very informative. I hope you are nominated for an Oscar.

[1] Footnote: For those of you joining us from outside the LGBTQ bubble: "cis" (pronounced like the "sis" in "sister") is sort of like the opposite of "trans." More specifically, it means you identify as the gender you were assigned at birth. To put it crudely, cismale = you have

a penis and you feel like a boy. Cisfemale = you have a
vagina and you feel like a girl. Okay, that's a gross over-
simplification, but it's the best I can do on short notice.
Feel free to Google it. /Public Service Announcement

I sort through a few more messages, and then, just as I'm
clicking Post on my final answer of the night, the envelope
icon turns red again.

Anonymous: Hi Alix. I hope you answer this. I'm
writing from my phone at the train station right now. I
don't know where else to go. I don't even know how to
start so I'll just say it. I came out to my parents about 2
hours ago that I'm a trans girl. After I told them, my mom
sort of shrank back and put a hand over her mouth and
didn't say anything. My dad started yelling at me. He said
I'm not his son. I told him I wish I could be his daughter
instead. And then he hit me. And I left. And now I keep
staring at the train tracks and thinking I should just throw
myself down there. Please reply.

I let out a long, slow breath. This one is *not* a joke; it's
serious. And I don't feel qualified to respond to something this
intense—maybe even life-or-death—but at the same time . . .
she reached out to me, and she's desperate. I check the time
stamp. The message was sent less than three minutes ago; if I'm
going to reply, I should do it now. But what do I even say?
Hands shaking, I start typing.

Alix: First off, please don't kill yourself. I can't imagine how much pain you're in . . . but don't, please. Go here, if you want to: translifeline.org. They're way better at this than I am—I'm just a kid on the internet.

I consider just clicking Post; but it doesn't seem like enough. I take a deep breath. What would I want to hear? After staring at the screen for a minute, I put my fingers back on the keys and continue.

I am so sorry your parents reacted that way. And I know this might not make it hurt less, but I have to say thank you for being so brave. You have so much guts to be so honest like that. To say that to your dad. You're probably the bravest person I've ever heard of. If I were with you at the train station right now, I would hug you until you couldn't breathe, and then we would go to the little store and buy root beer and Red Vines, and bite off the ends and use them as straws to drink the root beer while we waited for the train. And then we'd get on and go somewhere very, very far away, like Pennsylvania or Prague. And we would find people like us and live in an apartment and make art and sell it and have a garden on the roof and just be happy.

But I know we can't do that. So I'll just keep writing until I come up with something real that might help.

You have to know that there is NOTHING wrong with you. Your parents' reactions have zero to do with you, and everything to do with them. For you, coming out is about finally understanding who you are, and then admitting it to the people who are most important to you. But for your parents, maybe they see it as this big, shocking change. And they aren't equipped to handle it. To them, it's like you suddenly made this huge choice they don't understand.

I know what you're thinking: it's not a choice! It's how you were born. It's who you are. You're not making some arbitrary decision to make your life and theirs more difficult—you're just finally accepting who you already are.

But the thing is, you did make a choice: you chose to COME OUT.

You know what's messed up? People tolerate secrecy. I see it in my life. It's like, it's okay to have gay feelings or trans feelings or gender fluid feelings—as long as you keep them inside. As long as you don't "act" on them. Whatever that means. People don't condemn you for being trans. They condemn you for embracing it.

So. See it from your parents' point of view for a second: They're sitting there on the couch, and you come downstairs, and in less than five minutes you turn their world completely upside down. And they didn't have a chance to prepare, so all their bad and ugly feelings rise to the surface. All the worst parts of them just flood out and fill the room and drown your heart.

And the thing is, they probably already wish they could take it all back.

So, anonymous, please don't throw yourself onto that track. Because this is the worst part, right here, right now.

If you can just get past this part, it gets better.

If you're reading this, and you still have battery and signal, go to QueerAlliance.org. I just checked, and they have contact info for shelters and safe houses in almost every major city. There's a hotline you can call. They can help.

We're with you.

I click Post and sit back in my chair. I'm worried that I've said the wrong things, or that I'm too late, and that the anonymous sender has already done something drastic. I wish I had said more. I wish I had been cleverer, more compassionate.

Suddenly tired and out of things to say, I reach for the keyboard to log off. Just then, the envelope icon blinks red again. I click it; there's only one message. It reads:

> Anonymous: go back where u came from dyke
> r school doesn't need another faggot

CHAPTER 15

I SIT COMPLETELY STILL AND stare at the screen.

It's like someone slapped me in the face. My pulse doubles. I read the message again.

I don't know what to do.

I look up stupidly at the closed door to my room, as though my father might walk in and *tell* me what to do.

Do I delete the message? Do I report it to someone?

I sit for a moment, waiting for the shock to turn into anger; but instead, a cold fear spreads through me, like ice water in my veins. I sit there, staring at the screen, and then I remember that low, mocking voice:

What she's trying to ask is, are you a dyke *or are you a* faggot?

Almost the exact words Jim Vickers used two days ago.

I stand and cross to my window to make sure it's locked; it is. I sit back down at the computer.

Could Vickers have found my blog? Has he somehow connected Alix from Bloglr with Solo's friend from school?

Does he know who I am?

My heart palpitates once, twice. If Vickers knew, he could tell everyone. He could post it online, send out a mass email. Everyone would know about me. I couldn't go back to school, not after that. And then—someone could connect the dots to my father. My *congressman* father. His campaign . . . it would be over. His career would be ruined.

Oh God.

I run back to my computer, my heart pounding in my throat. I click Settings and scroll down to "delete user account." I click the link. A box pops up:

Are you sure you want to delete your account?

My finger hovers over the trackpad. All I have to do is click OK, and Vickers won't be able to expose me. He can tell people about me, sure, but it will be his word against mine.

But if I do it, I'll be giving up the only thing that seems to relieve my anxiety. And on top of that, I'll lose my new friends, all 624 of them. I already hide from my parents, from my classmates—even from Bec and Solo. This blog is the truest part of me. If I delete it, if I erase any record of who I am, what will be left?

I close my eyes, take three slow breaths, and click Cancel. I go back to the inbox screen and open the message one more time.

go back where u came from dyke

r school doesn't need another faggot

Okay. So the sender used "dyke" and "faggot," the same words Vickers called me in the cafeteria. But how common are those words? They get thrown around every day, in and outside of high school, and certainly all over the internet. Hell, that first anonymous sender called me "fag." There's nothing here that points specifically to Vickers.

And the second line: "r school doesn't need another faggot." Not "Park Hills High," but "r school." Anyone could have sent this message; it's just an empty threat. Anonymous hate. My panic starts to subside.

I consider replying—and then, almost without deciding to, I delete the message.

I close my laptop and lie back on my bed, but my mind won't shut down. I think about what Solo said, about how I walk around assuming everyone is a bigoted asshole. I try to reconcile his live-and-let-live attitude with the message I just received. I can't.

And then I think about the girl at the train station. About how scary it must have been to tell her parents the truth right to their faces, and how crushed she must have felt when they rejected her. To be cast out by your own parents. And I think about her now, wondering if she read my reply. Wondering whether she's still sitting on that bench, or if she's already thrown herself onto the tracks.

I get very little sleep, and when I walk into school Monday morning, I'm completely exhausted. It's only my second week at Park Hills High, but it already feels like my second year.

I'm feeling super guyish, so I didn't really bother to put

myself together this morning. I'm wearing a baggy T-shirt and the same jeans I wore all weekend—but I did take the time to tease the top of my hair into a fauxhawk.

Solo comments on my scruffy appearance via text, and I reply with a stealthily taken phone pic of my middle finger. When Miss Crane isn't looking, Solo retaliates by bouncing a Starburst off the side of my head.

Bec is absent from Government—again.

The lunch bell rings, and I start across the quad toward the cafeteria. I'm still a little uncertain of where I stand with Solo; sure, he invited me to sit with him, but I think he knew I would refuse. Regardless, I've decided to let it be, for now. To "pick my battles," as Mom would say.

I descend the stairs and enter the Gauntlet without hesitation. As I approach the football table, I brace myself for an onslaught—but it never comes. Solo gives me a curt nod as I pass, but nobody says a word to me.

And then, just as I'm about to declare victory, Jim Vickers looks up and makes eye contact with me. He smiles, but it doesn't touch his eyes. All at once, the fear from last night—that somehow he knows about my blog, that he'll expose me—comes rushing back, and I look down and walk faster.

Moments later I'm through the Gauntlet and standing in the lunch line. I try to clear my mind, but that cold smile seems to be burned into the backs of my eyelids. Did I see a deeper meaning behind it? An echo of the anonymous hate message from last night? Or was it just my imagination?

I'm disappointed but unsurprised to find the ramp empty; Bec must be traveling with her dad again. I figure I could eat here alone, or see if Miss Crane is still in her room—but then I look down at my dry cafeteria burrito and decide that I'm just not that hungry. Solo is with his people, Bec is with her dad, and I'm alone on this stupid ramp. By myself. Thinking about being alone by myself.

And for the first time I can remember, I'm actually disgusted by my own self-pity. I hear Doctor Ann's voice in my head, telling me to stop thinking about *me* so much. To get engaged with other people. To find a cause. And she's right; I really should do *something*. Reluctantly, I stuff the burrito into my bag and head up toward the activities office.

I'm approaching the counter when the pretty blond girl behind it looks up and says, "*Bonjour,* Riley."

I stare at her for a minute, caught off guard by the greeting, until I recognize her: it's Casey Reese, the girl who sits in front of me in French. At my lack of response, her smile fades.

"Sorry," she replies. "Need to work on my accent."

"No," I say, too quickly. "No. It's really good."

Casey's smile returns at full wattage. "I love your hair," she says, absently reaching up to run her fingers through her own. "How do you make it do that?"

"Oh, I don't know. I just, like, brush it up, sort of, with my hand." I demonstrate.

She cocks her head. "You don't use hair spray or anything?"

I shrug. "My hair is naturally sticky-uppy. Plus, it's shorter than yours."

She nods. I think she'll say something else, drive the conversation deeper, but she just sort of spaces out. Finally, I clear my throat. "Um, do you have, like, a list of clubs on campus?"

"Oh. Sure!" She retrieves a green three-ring binder from her desk and sets it in front of me. "They're all in here. Let me know if you need anything else." She smiles again, then crosses back to her desk and starts sorting through a pile of paperwork.

I stand there at the counter, flipping through club flyers and sign-up sheets. There's a young investors society, an academic decathlon team, and a chapter of the Orange County Teen Republicans Network. I could join the Fellowship of Christian Athletes (if I were an athlete, and if they take deeply conflicted Catholics), but I'm really looking for something more service-oriented. Now I'm halfway through the binder, and what little hope I had is dwindling fast. There's no animal rights club, no vegan teens association, no antibullying coalition. I don't really expect to find a transgender group—and when I do finally come cross the Park Hills Gay-Straight Alliance, I'm unsurprised to see only two names on the sign-up sheet, both dated three years ago.

I'm about to slam the binder shut and walk out of the office when a pink flyer catches my eye.

JOIN "P.A.L.S!"
PEER ACADEMIC ASSISTANCE AT LUNCH!
MONDAYS IN THE LIBRARY

I read it twice, rolling my eyes at the cheesy name. Peer tutoring isn't exciting or political, but it does meet Doctor Ann's requirement of "getting engaged with other people." Reluctantly, I close the binder, say *au revoir* to Casey, and set off for the library.

∩

I spot Sierra Wells as soon as I walk through the front door. She's sitting at one of the long tables next to the entrance, talking to a younger girl who's stuffing her books into a red backpack. I'm about to turn around and walk out—but then the girl mumbles something, and Sierra replies in a surprisingly gentle tone, "I know, *receive* still trips me up, too. Just remember 'it's better to *give* than to *receive*.' Both words end in *I-V-E*." And then her face splits in a wide, genuine smile—this hardly looks or sounds like the same sneering girl who asked if I was a dude or a chick. I pause, half turned toward the door. The younger girl stands, says good-bye to Sierra, and walks past me out the door.

That's when Sierra looks up and sees me—and her smile dissolves.

"Oh," she says. The gentleness is gone from her tone. "Here." She reaches into her book bag and extracts a small package wrapped in purple tissue paper. She holds it out to me, and I stare at it. What could she possibly want to give me?

"Your mom ordered these," Sierra says, thrusting the package at me.

"Oh, right. The essential oils. Thanks," I say, taking it.

"Yeah," she replies, then closes her planner and starts packing her things. She's wearing a long-sleeved sweater, but as she reaches down to put her binder away, her sleeve slides up, exposing a scab-like patch of discolored skin on her forearm. I've seen marks like this before, on one of the other patients at Pineview. His were from obsessive scratching; it was the way he dealt with stress. I wonder what Sierra's are from.

I feel a sudden wave of sympathy for her—and I speak without really meaning to. "I'm sorry about the other day," I say. "At my house." Sierra looks up at me, surprised. I'm surprised, too, but I keep talking. "I hate it when my parents use me like a prop."

Sierra's face takes on a green tinge, and she looks away. "Yeah, well," she says, shouldering her bag, "whatever." She stands, pushes in her chair, and walks out.

I watch her leave, feeling stupid for even trying to talk to her. After the way she treated me, what made me think I could change her mind? And why would I bother? I guess it's like Dad says: You only get one chance at a first impression.

When I get home, I find a note from my mom explaining that she and Dad will be out late at some dinner event. I reheat the tofu rice dish she left me and eat it standing in the kitchen.

I consider checking my blog, but decide against it. I have a bad feeling about the trans girl from last night—the one who wrote to me from the train station. I'm afraid of what she might say if she replies. What if she calls me out? Like, what gives me the right to give *her* advice? What experience do I have that could possibly compare to what she's going through?

Or worse, what if something happened, and she hasn't replied at all?

On Tuesday, Mr. Hibbard informs the class that we have a Precalc test on Thursday. It's my least favorite subject, and I haven't done any of the homework. The news sort of derails my day, and I decide I'm definitely not up for lunch in the cafeteria from hell. I intercept Solo as he's walking out of Algebra and persuade him to sneak off campus with me.

Since Bec wasn't in Government, I hold out little hope that she'll turn up at the ramp, but I convince Solo to walk past it on the way to the parking lot anyway. She's not there.

On the way to Shock-o-Tacos, I pick Solo's brain for volunteering ideas.

"My church does a potluck soup kitchen on the first Sunday of every month," Solo says, shrugging. "Or maybe you could pass out juice at the High School Football Association blood drive." I could probably get my mom to make a dish for the potluck, but that doesn't qualify as *me* doing something. And the thought of waiting on a room full of Solo's bleeding teammates makes me queasy; I'll have to keep looking.

That night, I sit down at my desk, thinking I'll have the courage to check Bloglr—but when I get to the log-in screen, I stop. Between Mr. Hibbard's looming test and my failed attempts to "find a cause," the buzz of anxiety has been pretty much constant for the last few days—and the thought of getting another hate message like "go back where u came from dyke" amplifies it even more.

The trans girl from the train station crosses my mind, too— but I push the thought away. I'm already a month behind; I need to study. So I close my laptop and open my Precalc book.

On Wednesday, Bec is absent from Government again, and I'm beginning to think she's not coming back. I shoot her a text, but I get no reply. Still, I'm disappointed when I find the ramp empty. I sit down anyway, and I'm just starting to unwrap my burrito when I hear a familiar voice from behind.

"You're just racking up the tolls, aren't you?"

CHAPTER 16

I TURN TO FIND BEC standing over me. She's wearing a Cure T-shirt with the neck cut out, black leggings, and a plaid skirt that gives me Catholic school flashbacks. She's been gone for nearly three days, and she looks like she spent the whole time at Super-Hot Goth Girl Makeover Camp. Her expression is, as ever, unreadable behind her mirrored sunglasses.

"Hi," I say. Bec smirks.

"First," she says, counting off on her fingers, "there's the toll from last week, and then I actually *gave* you two juice boxes— plus one for today. And I figure you've come looking for me every day this week. So honestly, at this point we're way beyond Amazon gift cards and deep into narcotics territory."

I hold back a smile. "What makes you so sure I came looking for you?"

Bec drops her backpack and sits next to me on the ramp.

She pulls her shades down and looks at me with those blue eyes.

"Riley, if I were to disclose to you the full extent of my powers, the shadow government would be here within moments to whisk me away in an unmarked black helicopter. Have you ever *ridden* in a helicopter?"

"No," I admit.

"Well, let's just say that if I ever decide to tell you my secrets, I will need a triple dose of nondrowsy Dramamine in addition to the aforementioned narcotics."

"I see."

Bec reaches into her backpack and extracts a three-foot-long stick of beef jerky. I grimace. I take a bite of my bean-and-no-cheese burrito, and for a moment, we just eat in silence.

"So," I say. "Were you traveling with your dad?"

"No. I was . . . taking care of some family stuff."

"Oh." That's all I get? I want to ask where the hell she's been, and why she hasn't called me since our date—if that's even what it was. And then it occurs to me—maybe she expected *me* to call *her*. All these thoughts lock up in my head, and none of them make it to my mouth.

Bec extracts a juice box from her backpack. "I heard you had words with the football team."

I gape at her. "How did you know?"

"Everybody knows. You were, like, yelling in the middle of the cafeteria."

"I never yelled."

Bec shrugs. "Well, you made some waves." A wide grin

splits her face. "People are talking about you behind your back."

Great. Not only have I failed to blend in, but I'm *making waves*. I swallow hard. "What are they saying?"

Bec pulls off her sunglasses and considers me. "They're saying how the new kid totally owned the couple from hell in front of everyone at lunch."

I smile, though I suspect she's embellishing for my benefit. "'The new kid.' Is that all they're calling me?"

Bec shrugs. "One person may have referred to you as 'that androgynous chick-dude.' But I slapped his hat off."

My smile widens considerably.

"But listen," Bec says, narrowing her eyes. "You should be careful. Jim Vickers is not a guy you want to piss off."

I remember Vickers's look, and I suppress a shudder. "I'll be okay. I'm friends with someone else on the team."

Bec nods. "Jason Solomona. Aka Chewie. Used to be one of us until Coach Terrance turned him."

"Turned him?"

Bec sighs and stuffs the half-eaten Slim Jim back into her backpack. "You can't be on the football team and still hang with the freaks and geeks. Chewie learned that a long time ago."

"Well, he's friends with me," I say.

"Then why aren't you eating with him?"

I smile. "Maybe I prefer the company of cute girls with lip rings."

And then I realize that I actually said that out loud, with my actual voice, and my stomach sort of ceases to exist, leaving a large vacuum where my guts were just a moment before.

But Bec seems unperturbed by the comment. She puts her

shades back on and says, "What are you doing this weekend?"

My guts are back, but now they're doing somersaults.

"Nothing," I say. "I mean, I'm grounded."

"When does your sentence end?"

"Saturday."

"Perfect. You're coming with me to a club in LA."

Oh my God. She's asking me out. Again.

"I'm—I don't have ID."

Bec laughs. "It's all ages."

"I don't think my parents will let me."

Bec puts a hand on my shoulder and leans in. Her face is inches from mine. I catch that scent again. Smells like . . . vanilla, but with something spicy underneath. Warmth spreads through my middle.

Bec speaks, her voice soft, the beginnings of her words coming out in a purr. "If your parents knew the crushing weight of your debt to me, and if they understood that coming with me Saturday night was the only way to repay that debt, short of acquiring nearly a metric ton of schedule one controlled substances, they would say yes, Riley."

I swallow. Bec doesn't move, just keeps her face close to mine, waiting.

I open my mouth to reply—but someone interrupts from behind me, breaking the spell.

"Hey, Bec," a vaguely familiar voice says.

Bec leans back and lets her hand drop into her lap. I turn to see Erik standing on the other side of the railing.

"How can I help you, Erik?" Bec says, her voice dripping with irritation.

Erik hesitates, his eyes flicking in my direction as though he wishes I wasn't here to witness this conversation. He tugs at the hem of his sweaty shirt with a pudgy hand.

Bec clears her throat impatiently, and Erik finally speaks up. "Can I have five bucks?" he says.

Bec rolls her eyes. "Why should I lend you five bucks?"

He shoots me another uncomfortable glance, then looks back at his sister. "Lunch," he says quietly.

"Oh yeah," Bec says, and I could swear her face goes slightly pale. She plunges a hand into her backpack and extracts a crumpled bill. "Here's ten."

Erik looks down at it. "I really only need five."

"It's fine," she says, waving the ten at him.

"Thanks." He takes the bill, turns, and walks away with his head down.

I look back at Bec, but she's focused on rearranging the contents of her backpack. I want to ask what that was all about, why they both seemed so uncomfortable. But she seems pretty embarrassed by the whole thing, and besides, asking about family stuff would open the conversation to topics I'd rather avoid, too—at least, for now.

Bec zips her backpack and looks up at me. "So," she says, "Saturday."

"Yeah. Yes," I say, then bite my bottom lip to stop myself from endlessly rambling on in the affirmative.

Bec smiles, stands, and throws her backpack over one shoulder. "Pick me up at six."

"Where?"

"I have explained all of this in the note," Bec says.

"What note?"

Bec produces a folded piece of notebook paper and leans over to hand it to me. As she does, the cutout neck of her shirt falls forward, revealing the gentle line of her collarbone where it meets the slope of her neck. She clears her throat, and I look up at her face. She smirks as I take the note, and then she turns abruptly and walks away.

I sit down at my desk after school, intending to cram for my Precalc test, but I can't concentrate. I have a date on Saturday night. I mean, I think it's a date. My face heats up at the thought of standing next to Bec in some dimly lit club—and I get out of my chair and start pacing my room. Will I have to dance? What should I wear? I curse, wishing I had someone to call who could give me advice about these things.

And then I remember my blog followers. Statistically speaking, at least one of them has to have been in a situation like this before.

I drop into my desk chair, open my laptop, and start to log in to Bloglr—but my fingers pause above the keyboard, and I remember why I haven't logged in since Sunday: the trans girl at the train station. I have a sinking feeling that my advice didn't help—and that, if I log in, I'll find out she hasn't replied. And I'll know it's because she jumped onto the tracks after all.

And then I remember the anonymous hate message, and the cold smile from Vickers. Are they connected? Will another message—an even worse one—be waiting for me when I log in?

I stare at the Bloglr home screen, watching the little green frog logo catch animated flies with its long, pink tongue. Am I one of those flies? If I log back in, will I get caught and eaten?

I can't hide forever. Like Solo said, there will always be haters, but I can't let them stop me from doing what I want. And, if I'm too scared to look, I might as well delete my blog.

No longer feeling remotely like asking for dating advice, I log in and bring up my dash. My reply to the trans girl has gone viral. More than a thousand users have liked, commented on, or reblogged my reply to her call for help. I click on the post and scroll through the comments.

> DZboy:Stay strong girl! We're with you.
>
> Anonymous: Hang on, sweetie. It gets better :\
>
> shy-town-refugee: if ur in Chicago u can come crash w us. msg me!

They go on and on, an outpouring of love, support, and resources for the girl at the train station. My heart beats faster—I still haven't seen anything from the girl herself. Is she still alive? In the hopes that she's sent me another message, I click on my inbox and start reading.

> MustangGrl96: Please tell anon I went thru the same thing. She can msg me.
>
> Expecto_Patron: So brave. Please tell her we love her!

There are dozens like this, and as I scroll through them, my fear dissipates. The impact of one anonymous hate message seems insignificant compared with this demonstration of support.

Finally, I come to this message, sent in the early hours of Monday morning:

> wak1ng-up: Hi Alix. I'm the trans girl who wrote you from the train station. I just wanted to say thank you so much for your reply. You made me feel like I'm not so alone. When the flood of responses came in, I totally started crying. I called one of the hotlines and they told me about a safe house nearby, but I think I am just going to go home. I think if I don't, it will only make things worse with my parents. Anyway thanks again. You kind of saved me.

I put my hands over my face. My shoulders shake once, then once more. Two hard sobs, and I think there will be more, but they taper off. Relief surges through me. I wipe my eyes and read the message again, and then I reply.

> Alix: Thank you so much for writing back. I'm glad you decided to stay. Please message me if you want to talk more. Hang in there.

It doesn't feel like I'm saying enough, but I don't know what else to say. I click Send.

There's one more message in my inbox.

> MiMi_Q: Hi Alix. My name is Mike/Michelle Weston. I'm the curator of QueerAlliance.org, and I've messaged you once before. I don't know where in the world you

are, or whether you're interested, but we can always use contributors to QueerAlliance, or "the Q," as we call it around here. Send me a message if that interests you—or, if you're near Los Angeles, you could always visit the center. Check the website for address and hours.

By the way—in case you haven't realized it yet: I believe you've found your cause.

—Mike/Michelle

My shoulders shake one more time—in a sob or a laugh, I honestly can't tell. I sit back and stare at the screen.

I've found my cause.

CHAPTER 17

THE NEXT COUPLE OF SCHOOL days are the best so far: talking music with Solo before English, laughing with Bec on the ramp at lunch. I doubt I'll make the prom ballot, but I do feel like I'm finally settling in at Park Hills High; I practice speaking French with Casey Reese, and I even exchange civil nods with Erik. I have a couple more fluctuations at school—two on Thursday alone—but I'm less self-conscious about them, and I don't have any more panic attacks. I may not be "blending in"—but if I'm standing out, at least I feel like I've found a place to stand. Knowing that I have my blog community— even though it's anonymous and online—makes me feel like I belong, like I have a purpose, and that gives me confidence as I walk through the halls. I still endure occasional looks as I'm heading to my locker or standing in line for food, but for the most part, the people who don't like me just leave me alone.

At lunch on Friday I stop by the admin building to drop off the last of my transfer paperwork. When I walk in, I spot Jim Vickers seated outside the counselor's office. The sight of him elevates my heart rate instantaneously, and I almost turn and walk right back out—but then I notice that he's slumped in the chair, his shoulders hunched, his jaw propped in one hand. He looks defeated. He glances up as I approach the counter, and I can tell he recognizes me—but he just looks away.

The office door opens, and a tall man in a beige sports coat emerges. His resemblance to Jim is unmistakable—this has to be his dad. He shoots Jim a sharp look, and then heads for the exit. As he turns, I notice that he's wearing a white clerical collar, similar to the ones the priests at Immaculate Heart wore. Jim stands hastily and follows him out, looking like a dog who just had his nose rubbed in his own poop. I wonder what he did to earn that sharp look, let alone a trip the office; whatever it was, he probably deserved it. As I wait for the registrar to find my file, another thought occurs to me: I hope my own dad never has to make an appearance on campus. Having a preacher for a dad might suck, but it can't hold a candle to being a congressman's kid.

By Saturday afternoon, I still haven't worked up the courage to ask Bec if our date is actually a date—so I decide to treat it like one anyway. Just in case.

I lie on my bed and pull her note out of my messenger bag. I unfold it and read it for perhaps the tenth time since Wednesday.

Bullet Hole
12629 W. Imperial Hwy, Suite 7K
6PM. Come as you are.

I'm not sure what Bullet Hole is. I consider looking it up, but I'm kind of enjoying the mystery, and I have a feeling that's what Bec intended. The address is on the west side of town, in an industrial area maybe ten minutes past the railroad tracks. But the final line is the reason I've reread the note so many times:

6PM. Come as you are.

I run my thumb across the letters, which were written hard with a ballpoint pen. *Come as you are.* What could that mean? Maybe it's just her way of telling me that the club has no dress code. But something about it makes me think there's more to it. Does she know . . . about me? The idea that she might have figured it out on her own brings me a fantastic sense of relief; but just underneath that, there's the fear that, if she *hasn't* figured it out, she'll reject me when she finally does.

I reread Bec's note three more times, trying in vain to find some secret meaning in the handwritten lines, some hint at what she might know about me, or about what she has planned for tonight. I glance at the clock: It's only three. I have hours to kill before I leave to pick her up—and if I don't distract myself, I'll spend the whole time poring over her note like a psycho. I think about Doctor Ann telling me I'm not crazy, and I wonder what she'd think now as I press the letter to my face to see if it smells like Bec. Nope, no vanilla. Just notebook paper. Gah!

I've got to get out of my own head. Think about someone else. "Engage," as Doctor Ann would put it. Maybe she's right about this whole "having a cause" thing.

So I stuff the note back into my pocket, roll over, and log in to Bloglr. I hit the jackpot on the very first message.

> KimmieG1995: Hi Alix! I'm writing to you because I just found a box of girl clothes in my little brother's closet. He's sixteen. I've thought he was gay for a long time and I'm totally cool with it but I don't know how to talk to him about it. Anyway I saw your "Both and Neither" post and now I think my brother might be gender fluid too. What do I do?

Tentatively, I start typing a response, referring KimmieG to a transgender allies support group—but I stop. I sort of already know what they're going to tell her—and maybe my perspective could help this girl. So I delete my generic response and start to write what's in my heart. After a half hour of typing and deleting and rewriting, I come up with this:

> Alix: Hi Kimmie. Your brother is lucky to have such a caring sister. That said: if I were him, I would be completely weirded out if my big sis told me she had been going through my closet. So don't start there. You don't know how he feels about all this; he could still be trying to figure it out. He may not be ready to talk. Hell, for all we know, the clothes might belong to a secret girlfriend.
>
> The thing is, he probably just wants to be accepted.

Don't think of him as a kid with some kind of disease or disability. Just treat him like an equal. Don't walk on eggshells trying to figure out what's going on. There's no need to have "the big talk." Maybe you could find subtle ways of letting him know you're open-minded about gender identity stuff; mention a book, or a movie with a trans character in it. Make positive remarks. He'll get it.

But the most important thing is—just be the kind of person he will want to turn to when he—or, she—is ready.

#genderfluid #advice

I post it, and then I have a minor panic event in which I reread it three times and almost delete it. I sound . . . stupid. Not at all as witty and charming as I sound in my own head. But I think the advice is right—and it feels good, replying. Reaching out. So good that I move on to the next message.

Anonymous: Alix, thank you for writing that apostrophe thing the other day! I was having a horrible day and I really needed that laugh. I wish I could be witty like that in real life when I get made fun of. Anyway, sometimes I get really depressed and just want to die. Reading your post made me want to hang on a little longer.

I stare at that last line. It's hard to believe my joke made that big a difference. But there's something undeniably honest, even raw, about the message that resonates with me. I think about my own "down" moments, and how hard I try to appear happier or less broken than I feel. That's what this message feels like to me—the false cheeriness of a desperate person. Carefully, I type out a reply.

> Alix: Dear Anon, please don't think I'm witty IRL. I could never think of stuff like that in the moment, that's why I post it here! Seriously, I should rename this blog "Clever S#%! I Should Have Said."
>
> Thank you for being brave and sharing about being depressed. I wish I could say I didn't understand what you mean, but I do. Last week, I couldn't walk through the cafeteria without having an anxiety attack. Some days I don't even want to get out of bed; I just want to pull the blankets over my head and let the void suck me down into its depths.
>
> But then I started sharing. Writing this blog. And it kind of saved me. In a way, you saved me—by reading it, and writing back and sharing yourself. All of you did.
>
> So. There's something to remember: we're here for each other. We may be strangers on the internet, but we're real. And we're here.
>
> If only we could all get together and form an Academy for Lost Souls*.
>
> The art department would kick ass.
>
> *Academy for Lost Souls is the name of my new indie rock group.
>
> #genderfluid #depression #anxiety #suicide

I click Post, feeling gratified and, honestly, kind of fired up. Giving advice to strangers felt weird at first—but I'm starting to like it. It makes me feel like my own situation isn't so hopeless. It makes me feel brave.

And maybe it's because I can't stop thinking about going out with Bec tonight, but my internal compass needle is absolutely pegged on F. Like, just the thought of wearing pants makes my legs start to feel plasticky. But I still don't know how Bec perceives me; and while I really want to present as a girl tonight, I'm worried that if I'm *too* girly, I'll turn her off. So I have to go with neutral.

On the other hand, I don't want to pick her up while I'm in a dysphoria spiral, either, because panic attacks aren't exactly alluring. So, feeling a little brave, I decide to do a couple of clandestine girly things. First, I go into the bathroom and dig out the crate of unused styling products my mother has bought me over the last few years in an attempt to make me conform to her repressive twentieth-century hair values. By mixing a few of them a white waxy substance and a brownish paste—I'm able to tame the cowlick on the top of my head and shape my shaggy bangs into a more feminine sweep. It's not a Hello Kitty barrette, but it definitely makes me feel more girly. Then, I go back into my room and grab the unopened bottle of lavender oil my mother bought from Mrs. Wells—it's supposed to be some kind of homeopathic antianxiety thing—and dab some on my wrists and behind my ears. It's super subtle, not too perfumey, but I absolutely love it. I press my wrist to my nose and look at myself the mirror. My face breaks into a wide smile; I feel 100 percent better. My heart is beating fast—but in a good way.

I bring up Bikini Kill's "Rebel Girl" on my phone, plug in

my earbuds, and jump around my room like an absolute freak for the next two minutes and thirty-seven seconds.

At five thirty, I head downstairs to see my parents off; they're going to dinner with some big oil company rep. Mom is in the kitchen, packing homemade peanut-butter fudge into an enormous tin.

Dad is parked in front of the big TV, watching himself on some talking-head show. The interviewer says, "Your new education bill calls for massive budget increases. But just two years ago, you voted against a similar initiative. Can you explain that?"

On screen, Dad smiles. It's his congressman smile, but I'll be damned if I don't believe it. "Absolutely, Debbie," he says. "Since I cast that vote, I've visited over fifty schools in ten states. I've seen what's happening on the front lines, and we've got to make some big changes."

"So you changed your position?" the interviewer says.

He nods. "I know, I know. My advisers warned me against it. Said it was a bad move politically. But it was the right thing to do for our kids, and for our country."

Debbie steeples her fingers. "This isn't just another example of the famous Cavanaugh folksy underdog routine?"

Dad laughs. "'Folksy underdog routine.' That's good. I wish my team had come up with that." In fact, they *had* come up with it—I overheard that exact term being discussed during one of their late-night meetings—and now the press is using it. Watching my dad onscreen, I can see his charm working on the interviewer like it works on everybody he comes into contact with. On the one hand, it makes me wonder if he's ever used his powers on me; on the other, I envy his charisma. Why couldn't I have inherited that?

Dad flips off the TV and stands. "Sharon, if we don't leave now, the Ellises are going to beat us to Angelo's."

As she passes me on her way to the garage, Mom looks at me and cocks her head. "Did you do something different with your hair?"

I touch it self-consciously. "Um. Sort of."

"It looks . . . good." She smiles.

"Thanks," I say, wondering which word was on the tip of her tongue before she changed her mind and said "good" instead.

Once the Lincoln has pulled out of the driveway and turned the corner, I get in the minivan and type the address Bec gave me into my phone. I follow the directions to the industrial side of town. After ten minutes, I'm as far west in Park Hills as I've ever been. I'm surprised and a little uneasy when my phone tells me to turn right into an industrial park that looks almost abandoned.

According to the signs mounted above the rusting roll-up doors, the complex contains a trophy manufacturer, a furniture restoration workshop, a defunct T-shirt screen-printing place, and several other now-deserted office/warehouse suites. The last building is number seven, and I pull up behind it and stop the minivan.

There's a red logo on the door: a tattoo-style drawing of a human skull with a hole in its forehead, inscribed in a circle of text that reads "Bullet Hole Studios." I hear a cacophony of drums and electric guitar issuing from within. I'm about to turn off the engine when the door to suite 7K opens, and a tall, stubbly-faced guy in a red flannel shirt emerges and lights a cigarette. He spots me, then pulls open the studio door and yells something inside.

A moment later Bec comes out, toting a guitar case in one hand. She's wearing a black denim jacket over a white scoop-neck tank top, and my eyes linger a moment on the exposed skin. She sees me through the passenger window of the mini-van, and her mouth turns up in that familiar smirk, sending warmth radiating through my midsection. And then the tall guy reaches out, grabs her by the hand, and pulls her into him. She goes up on her tiptoes and throws an arm around his neck. He kisses her cheek.

The warmth in my stomach goes instantly cold. Bec has a boyfriend?

After a moment, she pulls away and punches the guy play-fully in the gut. He parks his cigarette back in his mouth and waves her away. She approaches the van, stows her guitar in the back, then comes around to the front and climbs in.

"Hi," she says.

"Hi," I say, trying to sound normal through the knot that has now formed in the back of my throat.

"Hey." Bec leans toward me, concern on her face. "You okay?"

"Yeah," I say, faking a smile. "Fine. Um, where are we headed?"

"Pull out the way you came in and head back to the fifty-seven," Bec says, buckling her seat belt.

It's not until we're back on Imperial that I realize I've been holding my breath, and I let it out slowly. There's a long silence.

That guy—he was so . . . *masculine*. If that's what she's into, I haven't got a snowball's chance in hell. Not on my most guy-ish guy day. But it doesn't matter, because I can't choose to fluctuate; it just happens. I can usually fake it when I need to—mostly around my parents, and for short periods of time—but, for some reason, when I'm with Bec, I can't. Something about her, something in her presence seems to short out my ability to pretend.

Maybe that's why I like being around her. ·

I should be making small talk, asking about her band or something, but all I can think about is my stupid sweepy hair, my lavender-scented wrists, and Bec, up on her tiptoes with her arm around that guy.

"Hey. Riley," Bec says, shocking me out of dark thoughts. I look at her, and she says, "I'm glad you came." There's an uncertainty in her voice I've never heard before. A vulnerability. And before I'm really aware of it, the words are coming out of my mouth.

"Was that your boyfriend?" I ask, heat rising in my cheeks.

Bec blinks, and her mouth twitches like she's suppressing either a laugh or a frown, I can't tell which. "Um. He's my drummer," she replies.

"But you guys are, like . . . together?"

Bec cocks her head. "People are not canned goods, Riley. We don't need labels."

I tighten my grip on the wheel. What kind of answer is that? I want to press her, but I don't want to seem desperate, or drive her away. So, instead, I change the subject.

"What's the name of your band?"

"Fluorescent Sunburn."

"Oh. What kind of stuff?"

"It's, like, late shoegaze, early grunge." Bec pulls out her phone and plugs it into the port on the center console.

"Is this you?" I ask, gesturing at her phone.

"God, no," she says. "I made you a playlist."

I shift in my seat. *She made me a playlist.*

Bec goes on. "It's mostly live Bad Religion, for educational purposes, but there's some bootlegged Pixies stuff, too, since I know you're a complete pop whore."

I gasp in indignation. "I am not a pop whore!" But I'm laughing as I say it.

"Please," Bec says, cranking up the volume and rolling down her window. "Ramones, Pixies, the Police. Your T-shirt collection is like a tour through the eighties." She glances over at me. "You look hot, by the way."

The skin on my face bursts into flame.

"My cousin has that," Bec says.

"What?" I reply.

"The blushing-for-no-reason thing." I glance over at her, and she twists her lips into that mischievous smirk that seems to set my guts on fire. All thoughts of tall stubbly dude evaporate. She made me a mix, and she thinks I look hot. My eyes linger on Bec, her hair blowing, her blue eyes bright in the glow of the streetlights, and I see that vulnerability I heard in her voice a moment ago. I'm stricken with a sudden compulsion to ask her about it. To break through this weird wall she seems to put up at random.

"Hey, eyes on the road," Bec says. I realize that I'm staring at her, and I turn my focus back to the road just in time to avoid drifting out of my lane. We pass under the freeway, and I turn and gun it up the on-ramp.

The conversation comes in fits and starts, with Bec interrupting frequently to turn up the volume and scream over the music that I *have* to listen to this song. She sings along with such a complete lack of self-consciousness that when we come to a song I actually know—"Where Is My Mind?" by the Pixies—I feel comfortable enough to join her. When we pull off the 101 freeway in Hollywood, we roll down the windows and scream the lyrics at the top of our lungs.

"Make a right," Bec says, breaking off from the song. "Turn here. Pull in the back."

We pull into the parking lot behind a three-story brick building. It looks like one of the older structures in LA; maybe a hundred years ago it was an office building or a textiles factory. I park the van and follow Bec to a heavy steel door, probably the deliveries entrance. I don't hear any music coming from inside, and when I look around, there are only half a dozen cars in the parking lot. There's no marquee, there's no velvet rope, there's no line around the block.

I turn to Bec. "What kind of club is this?"

She bites her lip, making the little silver ring twitch. "Don't be pissed, okay?"

I frown. "Why are we going in the back?"

"Have you not figured out by now that I like a little mystery? Come on." As she moves past me, she takes my hand as if it's the most casual thing in the world, and the goose bumps travel up my arm to the back of my neck, where all the hairs stand on end. Bec pulls open the door and we walk in.

It's an open space, like the basement of an old store, with a concrete floor and wooden columns supporting a ceiling of exposed beams. A dozen folding chairs are arranged in a circle at the center of the room.

The first person I notice is a large woman in an ill-fitting blue suit. Upon closer examination, I see stubble on her cheeks. She—or he—is holding hands with a slim Hispanic guy who looks like he could be an actor. Next to him sits a girl in combat boots, fidgeting with an unlit cigarette as she glances nervously around the room. Near the back wall, someone with short, vividly green hair is pouring water into a big electric coffeepot. From the back, I can't tell if the punk hairstyle belongs to a guy or a girl.

Then, as I'm turning to Bec to ask her what we've just walked into, the most striking woman I've ever seen waves and starts toward us. She's well over six feet tall, lean and graceful, and even in the dim incandescence, her dark skin glows. She walks straight up to Bec, wraps her long arms around her like an affectionate octopus, and lifts her off the ground.

"Baby, baby, baby," she says. "Where on earth have you been?"

Bec's face is red when her feet finally touch ground again. "Just . . . busy."

"Well, it's wonderful to have you back." The woman calls over her shoulder. "Mimi! Come look who's here!" She turns to me. "And who is our new friend?"

I wait for Bec to introduce me, but she doesn't. The tall

woman bends her knees so her eyes are on a level with mine, flashes a wide smile, and extends her hand.

"I'm Kanada," she says. "Like the country, but with a K. And I am very pleased to meet you." She squeezes my hand with surprising strength; and that's when I notice that, from this angle, I can see that she has a very pronounced Adam's apple. I look over at Bec, who smiles at the dawning recognition on my face.

Kanada turns to Bec and makes a *tsk* noise. "Is this a surprise party?"

Bec shrugs.

"Mimi!" Kanada yells again, glancing toward the back of the room. A tall, professional-looking woman in a cranberry dress approaches.

"I'm right here," she says, laying an affectionate hand on Kanada's shoulder. Something about this woman is vaguely familiar. Like maybe I've seen her on TV. When she recognizes Bec, she smiles broadly and embraces her. "We've missed your sense of humor around here," she says.

And then she turns to me and offers her hand.

"Welcome to the Q," she says. "I'm Mike/Michelle."

CHAPTER 18

TIME SEEMS TO FREEZE, AND I stand there with my mouth slightly agape. After a moment, I sputter, "Mike/Michelle Weston?"

She raises her eyebrows. "Have we met?"

We have, in a way. She's sent me messages online—well, technically, she sent them to Alix—but of course, she wouldn't recognize me. How could she?

"I've been to your website," I say.

Kanada laughs and throws an arm around her. "Girlfriend is *famous!*" She turns to me. "What's your name, baby?"

"I'm Riley," I say.

"It's very nice to meet you, Riley," Mike/Michelle says. "We're just about to get started."

We make our way to the center of the room. I pick a seat with empty chairs on either side, and Bec sits down between me and the woman in the blue suit. Feeling a bit bigoted myself,

I glance from Kanada's prominent Adam's apple to the hint of stubble on the big woman's face. This "club" is obviously some kind of LGBTQ support group—which means Bec brought me here for a reason: She knows.

When the realization hits me, I expect my heart to start pounding, or my fingers to start tingling—but instead, I let out an involuntary laugh of relief. If Bec *does* know, the fact that we're here together proves she's already accepted me. My laugh morphs almost instantaneously into tears, and I hastily wipe my eyes. I shoot a glance at Bec to see if she's noticed, but she's deep in conversation with the handsome Latino guy and appears to have missed my mini meltdown.

Mike/Michelle calls the meeting to order, and the rest of the group take their seats.

"Hello, everyone," she says. A handful of people say hello, and a few clap. "Welcome to Queer Alliance, which we affectionately call 'the Q.' We're a gender and sexuality support group, and you don't have to fit into any specific category to be here. Some of us are gay, some of us are trans, and some of us are genderqueer. Some of us are out, and some of us aren't. This is a safe place where we share what we're going through. And tonight, we have some new faces, and some old friends, too." She nods toward Bec and me, and most of the heads turn in our direction. Bec smiles warmly. I give an awkward wave. Mike/Michelle continues, "Let's start with our dedication." Everyone clasps hands; I take Bec's in my right, and Kanada reaches out to take my left. Most people bow their heads, and some just close their eyes. Mike/Michelle looks up as if talking to the sky. "Tonight we come together as a community—not to focus on our flaws, but to celebrate our uniqueness. To share our pain, our joy, and our love, and to create a better tomorrow."

Bec lets go of my hand as people start to applaud. Apparently, clapping is big with this crowd. When the applause dies down, Mike/Michelle continues.

"We'll start by going around the circle. But there's no pressure." Mike/Michelle talks as though she's addressing the whole room, but I can tell she's speaking to me. "Feel free to introduce yourself, share something about your week, or just pass the conch to the next person. I'll start. I'm Mike/Michelle, the mediator of this group and the administrator of Queer-Alliance.org. Even though my transition is complete, I go by Mike/Michelle—because when I meet someone new, my name becomes an opening for dialogue, and that's what I'm all about." Her face splits in a smile that includes the whole room. "Okay," she says. "Who's next?"

"I'll go." It's the girl in the combat boots. She's sitting to Mike/Michelle's left, and speaks in a low monotone. "I'm Chris. I do IT at a big financial group." She makes eye contact with me, but only briefly. "For the new people, I know I look like a girl, but that's not how I identify. I started transitioning about ninety days ago. I have to live with being addressed as a girl all day, so I'd appreciate . . ." Her—*his* voice breaks, and he stops.

I catch myself staring at him, and then I look down at my lap instead. This is the second time in as many weeks that I've misjudged someone else's gender identity. I feel a pang of shame; like everyone else, my instinct is to put people in a category.

Chris continues. "Yesterday, I was informed that my insurance will no longer cover my hormone therapy."

The woman in the blue suit grunts in disgust. "You should sue," she says. "I'll take the case myself."

Chris shakes his head. "Companies don't have to fund birth control if it goes against their 'moral values.' They argue the same for transition treatment. I just . . ." Chris buries his face in the crook of one arm. "I can't go back there. The way they look at me . . ." His speech dissolves into sobs.

I sit back in my chair and stare at my hands. My problems suddenly seem small, even ridiculous, compared to this man's. I glance around the group. Everyone, Bec included, is watching Chris with expressions of empathy and concern—and I start to feel like I'm intruding. Like I shouldn't be witnessing this stranger's vulnerable moment.

Once Chris has composed himself, he goes on. "I'm going to start looking for another job. And I'm *not* stopping therapy; I'll just have to figure out how to pay for it out of pocket." The group applauds him, and he accepts their acknowledgment with a teary smile.

The big woman in the blue suit volunteers to share next. She introduces herself as Bennie, and says that she identifies as a trans woman. After twenty years of hiding, Bennie explains, she finally came out to her wife—who promptly filed for divorce. Now she's going through hormone therapy and struggling with the accompanying weight gain. Herman, the tall Latino man, is Bennie's straight, cismale boyfriend. When they met at a law conference last year, Bennie was still presenting as a man— but Herman somehow saw past that, and they fell in love. It's

155

a beautiful story, and they laugh as they take turns retelling it.

A few times, I find myself glancing at the person with the short green hair. She—or he—looks to be around twenty-five, has very fine features, and doesn't appear to be wearing any makeup. A puffy green flight jacket obscures the more telling parts of his or her anatomy. At one point our eyes meet, and I look away, embarrassed.

Bec goes next. She says hi and that it's good to see everyone— and that's when I wonder: How did she even know about this place? She seems to know everybody by name, as though she's been here dozens of times before. What am I missing?

And then it's my turn to talk. Mike/Michelle said I shouldn't feel pressure to say anything, but I do; after hearing everyone else share their most personal thoughts, I feel like I owe them something. As the eyes turn toward me, my heart starts to beat faster, and the saliva seems to evaporate from my mouth. After a long, uncomfortable silence, Kanada takes mercy on me by launching into a story about her daughter. I'm not really listening—I'm too busy trying to control my breathing—but I'm grateful for the rescue.

Eventually, the formal, go-around-the-circle format dissolves into a more open discussion. As everyone shares what's happening in their lives, I start to feel more *normal*. I feel lucky to have figured myself out at sixteen instead of waiting until I was married with kids. Some of these people grew up without the internet; they had no way of reaching out, no way to find out *why* they felt the way they felt, or even to discover that it had a name.

At one point, Mike/Michelle invites the member with the

green hair—who apparently goes by Morgan—to share, but Morgan graciously declines in a soft, alto voice. By the time Mike/Michelle calls the meeting to a close, reminding the regulars that next week's session has been rescheduled for Friday, I already know I want to come back.

It's 10:15 when we pull out of the parking lot and then make a right on Sunset. Traffic crawls along the Boulevard; even the sidewalks are full of life, but I don't really see any of it. Every part of my brain not required to operate the minivan is trying to make sense of the last three hours.

What kind of second date was this? Or, was it a date at all? Furthermore, how did Bec know about the Q, and why does she seem to know all of its members? I want to ask her a hundred questions.

"Hey," Bec says. "You okay?"

"Yeah. Just thinking."

Bec adjusts her seat belt and turns to face me. "You were pretty quiet at the meeting."

I shrug. "I wasn't really prepared for that kind of thing."

"I know," Bec says. "I'm sorry. I shouldn't have surprised you like that." She glances out the windshield, gently punching her thigh with a fist. "I have an overdeveloped sense of drama."

"You say that like a person with an overdeveloped sense of drama."

She laughs.

"It's okay," I say. "Really. I just didn't know what I was walking into."

"See? Mystery. Not a bad thing." She smiles, and I smile back.

"So, how did you know about that place?" I ask. Bec turns away, maybe to look out the window, or maybe to avoid my gaze. "Bec?"

After a long silence, she turns to face me again, and that crooked smile is back on her face. "That's not really second-date material," she says.

Second date? Fireworks go off in my midsection. Questions rush to the top of my mind—but before I can ask any of them, Bec says, "Wait. Where are we? Did you already pass San Vicente?"

I shrug. "I have no idea."

"Oh, great. Hang on." She pulls out her phone and checks the map. "Okay. Turn right up here. On Larrabee."

Just as I pull into the intersection, Bec shrieks and starts pointing frantically out the driver's side window. I almost drive off the road.

"Look! Look! It's—ohmygod ohmygod! It's— Look, it's him!"

But I can't look, because I'm trying to pull the van back into my lane while simultaneously recovering from a minor cardiac event.

"Jesus, what? Who?"

"Him, with the . . . from the . . . band!"

"Who?"

"The . . . guy, with the— Dave! Standing right outside the Viper Room. Dave Grohl!"

"Foo Fighters' Dave Grohl?"

"Yes! Yes! Right there!" She's unbuckled her seat belt and is now hanging out the window.

"Do you want me to stop?"

She drops back into her seat and gapes at me. "Stop? Oh God, no. What would I say? Just keep driving."

I glance into the rearview mirror just in time to see the faint green glow of the neon sign, and then it passes out of view. Bec sinks into the passenger seat, taking deep breaths.

"So, Dave Grohl, huh?" I think of that flannel-wearing drummer kissing her cheek. "Really? That's your type?"

Bec refastens her seat belt and rolls up her window. "Don't be ridiculous. I don't have a 'type.' And even if I did, Dave Grohl transcends all sexual boundaries."

"I guess," I say, feeling a twinge of jealousy. "You looked like you were having a fit back there."

"Ugh! I know. I can never spit out words when it's important," Bec says. "Like, I was at the zoo once with my sister when I was a kid, and we were standing outside the monkey enclosure. And she was just staring through the bars at these two adult spider monkeys, who were, like, picking fleas off each other and eating them or whatever—but she didn't see the baby monkey hanging right above her, with a handful of poo, about to fling it. And you'd think I would be able to yell, 'Sister, beware! Monkey poo from above!' Or, 'Incoming!' at least."

"So you didn't warn her?"

"No! All I could muster was 'Monkey! Monkey! Monkey!' But it was too late. Splat."

"No."

"Yup. She took a load of monkey dung right in the skull.

Ugh. We couldn't shampoo all of it out. We had to cut off so much of her hair!"

I laugh, and Bec does, too. But the laughter fades quickly, and the silence rushes in to fill its space. Bec looks out the window again.

After a moment I sort of blurt, "How did she die?"

Bec doesn't reply right away, and I'm afraid I've gone too far. "I'm sorry," I say. "You don't have to answer that."

"It's okay," Bec says, and I believe her. "She had a bad reaction to some medication, and they couldn't resuscitate her."

"Oh. God, Bec. I'm so sorry." It's not enough, but I don't know what else to say.

Bec nods and then falls quiet, and I pull onto the freeway. The traffic is horrible, and we inch our way through downtown at about fifteen miles per hour. Bec reaches over and turns on the stereo. Bad Religion breaks the silence, and for a while, we just listen. Finally, I reach over and turn down the volume.

"So, how come you don't sit with the Hardcores anymore?"

Bec turns to me. "The who?"

"Oh yeah, sorry. I sort of nicknamed your table 'the Hardcores.'"

"The Hardcores. That's funny." Her smile fades a little. "But it wasn't my table."

"You said sometimes you need a day off. But that was, like, a week ago."

Bec turns to look out the window. "People are okay one on one. But get them in groups, and they start adopting this hive mind. Like we all have to like the same band and buy the same brand of hair dye."

She hasn't answered my question, any of my questions, really, but I decide not to push it. I'm enjoying her company, and I don't want to spoil that. The conversation ebbs and flows. We talk about music—we like a lot of the same bands—but mostly, we avoid talking about the big issues. Sex, family, stuff like that. It's a pretty superficial conversation, to be honest, but I sort of don't care. With her, even the surface stuff feels . . . I don't know. Deep. Alive.

The traffic breaks up just south of Hollywood. Downtown recedes behind us, and before I know it, we're back in Park Hills, pulling off the 57.

"Should I take you home?" I say.

"Nah, just back to Bullet Hole."

I pull up at the studio and kill the engine. We sit there for a while, neither of us moving or talking. Just sitting and breathing. I sense more than see her hand resting on the center console. It seems to have its own magnetic pull, drawing my hand toward it. I release my death grip on the steering wheel and let my right hand fall gently into my lap. Then, slowly, I inch my arm toward the console.

"I'm glad you came," Bec says.

"Me too." I take a slow breath, and then reach for Bec's hand—but, at the same moment, she turns and grabs the door handle.

I waited too long. I put my hand back on the wheel and look away.

"So," Bec says. "You want to do this again next week?"

My breath quickens, and I turn to look at her. I want to scream YES! YES! YES! But instead, I say, "Yeah, that would be good."

And then the van door opens and Bec hops out, grabs her guitar from the back, and slams the sliding door shut. She waves, crosses the parking lot, and disappears into the studio in a swell of crashing cymbals.

I get home thirty minutes before curfew. As I pull into the driveway, the light goes out in my dad's den; he waited up for me. I kill the engine and head inside.

Lying on my bed, my laptop whirring to life next to me, I stare up at the ceiling and just breathe. I feel like a completely different person from when I left the house just a few hours ago. The kind of person who drives to LA with a hot girl on a Saturday night. The kind of person who lies to their parents and goes to support groups and tries to make a move on said hot girl in a parking lot with live punk rock thundering through the walls.

A few butterflies still twitch in my stomach, and I savor the delicious discomfort. I wonder how things might have gone if I had reached for Bec's hand just a moment sooner. Would we have kissed? What would her lips feel like? At this thought, the butterflies flap up a hurricane. But kiss or no kiss, she still asked me out on a third date. A slow, triumphant smile spreads across my face.

My laptop emits its welcoming chime, informing me that my immersive online experience is only moments away. I roll over onto my stomach and log in.

When my dash pops up, my jaw drops.

FOLLOWERS: 10,161

I stare at the number for a solid minute, not moving a finger.

From five hundred–something to over *ten thousand*? How the hell could that even happen? It has to be a glitch. I click Refresh. The page goes white and then comes back to life—but the numbers remain the same. I expect a swell of excitement to rise within me; instead, I feel a wave of cold dread that drowns whatever butterflies remain.

I click on the envelope icon: I have hundreds of messages. I start scrolling through.

> yell0wbedwetter: OMG have you seen the article?
> QueerBoi1996: Guess ur gonna be bloglr famous now! ;-)
> Anonymous: Alix, I can't believe you responded to that kid. WAY above your pay grade. You're responsible for what happened and I hope they prosecute you.

My panic rises as I skim message after message that makes reference to some news story. I have to scroll through a dozen before I find one that includes a link to the article. I click it and begin to read.

Transgender Teen Survives Alleged Assault by Father
Nicholas Price, special contributor to The Advocate
NORMAN, Okla.—An Oklahoma teen sustained a severe

beating by her father after coming out as a transgender girl to her parents on Sunday, police said.

She was treated for a fractured jaw, two broken ribs, and multiple cuts on her face and arms at Oklahoma University Medical Center and was released early Monday.

Her father, Douglas Gingham, 42, was arrested on suspicion of assault and is being held at the Cleveland County Jail, Norman Police Department Sergeant John Harmonson said.

The alleged attack reflects a growing trend of violence inflicted on US teens who reveal their nonconforming gender identities to family or classmates. While it is The Advocate's *policy to conceal the identity of minor victims, Andrew "Andie" Gingham requested that her name be used—with the permission of her mother—and that her story be told to put a human face on the issue.*

"When I told them, my dad hit me in the face," said Gingham, 17. "So I just left."

That was when Gingham said she reached out online. She sought the advice of a gender fluid blogger named Alix, whose diary-cum-advice column, Hiding and Other Social Skills (bloglr.com/alix), has been gaining popularity in the LGBTQ community.

"That blog saved my life," Gingham said. "When I left my parents' house, I was lost. Ready to end it. But then Alix responded. And just knowing that one other person out there knew what I was going through—and cared enough to write back—made me stop." (Click **here** *to read the original blog post.)*

Gingham said she didn't sustain her severest injuries until she returned home in a second attempt to reconcile with her parents.

That was when the beating ensued, police said.

"Dad had been drinking," Gingham said. "He just lost control."

Gingham's mother was eventually able to calm her husband and call an ambulance, Harmonson said.

Neither of Gingham's parents was available for comment.

Despite the severity of her situation, Gingham remained hopeful about the future.

"If I can live through this, I can live through anything," Gingham said. "It's time for all of us to come out. Trans girls and trans boys and everybody. The longer we hide, the more of us will get hurt every day. I don't want to be a part of that anymore."

Gingham spent the night at Oklahoma University Medical Center before being transferred to a Child Protective Services facility in Oklahoma City, but said she expects to be returned to her mother after a closed hearing later this week.

I read the story twice, and by the time I'm finished, my face is tingling.

She listened to me—and she got beaten for it.

In the next moment, I'm overcome by an ironclad conviction that the link is a fake, that this is some kind of elaborate prank. Hastily, I Google the headline—but sure enough, the *Advocate* story comes up as the first search result. I go to Queer-Alliance. The article is the top story, along with a special profile on my blog, including my now-notorious David Bowie avatar. Finally, I open a new browser window and go directly to *The Advocate*'s website. Andie Gingham's story isn't on the home page, but I find it after only a few clicks. I stare at her photo, and it feels as though a hand is squeezing my heart. My eyes blur, and then the tears spill out, running down my face.

Her father *beat* her. She went back, and he beat her.

I stand up, start to close my laptop, then sit back down again. I clap a hand to my chest as if I can somehow slow my heartbeat from the outside. I take a deep breath.

I'm not responsible for her injuries—of course I'm not— but I'm not innocent, either. I got involved. It may not have been my fists that beat her—but my words left their own marks. Very real, very tangible marks. But Andie didn't blame me—she *thanked* me.

This can't be my life; it feels like I'm watching it happen to someone else. And yet, I know it's real. I know it's true. And what started out as a half-assed attempt to appease my doctor has now affected someone's real life—and potentially the lives of ten thousand other people who read what I wrote.

It's too much. It's too big. I can't wrap my mind around it.

I click over to my inbox and start skimming through again. Many of the messages are from transgender people— adults and teenagers—expressing their sympathy for Andie and praising her courage. The others are directed toward me, and they're split more or less evenly between support and criticism. DocMama82 tells me in raging capital letters that I'm unqual- ified to give advice to anyone, while Outguy-in-Denver says I should pursue therapy as a career. One anonymous sender claims Andie wouldn't have been beaten if it weren't for me— but another insists I prevented her suicide.

But it's the message from DanielD87 that gets to me.

DanielD87: Wow. I almost came out to my dad because of what you wrote to that girl—but I changed my mind at the last second, and now I'm glad I did. I'm not ashamed of what I am, but I'm sorry, if coming out is gonna get me beat or kicked out of my own house then it's not worth it. I'd rather stay in the closet.

Tears blur my vision a second time. I'm enraged at Andie's father for hurting her, and I'm angry at DanielD87 for letting his fear keep him in the closet—but mostly, I'm ashamed. Ashamed that, just like Daniel, I'm too afraid to come out myself. Ashamed that I've been hiding behind this fake name, pretending to be some kind of counselor, some kind of activist—when the truth is that I can't even face my own problems. I'm only a scared kid, just like Andie was.

I read the rest of the messages—all of them. I take particular satisfaction in the hateful ones; reading them hurts, and the hurt feels like punishment. Punishment that maybe I deserve.

Finally, I come to the last message in my inbox. I click it, and I freeze.

Anonymous: c u at lunch. fuckin tranny

CHAPTER 19

THE NEXT FEW DAYS go by in a dark haze; my sense of belonging seems to evaporate, along with my confidence. Sierra Wells glares at me when I walk into AP English, and Cole, Vickers's stringy-haired teammate, grabs his crotch at me as I pass him on the way to my locker before Precalc. I try not to let it get to me, but it does. In fourth period, Casey Reese tries to cheer me up, but I brush her off; I just want to be left alone.

I have vague, humorless conversations with Solo, and when he asks me what's wrong, I just shake my head. Bec shoots me concerned looks, but she doesn't say anything. Maybe she's trying to give me space. It's hard to tell, because I feel so detached, like everything is unreal, and I can't seem to relieve the pressure that's settled on my chest.

c u at lunch. fuckin tranny

The message plays over and over in my mind—and instead

of paying attention in class, I'm compulsively trying to puzzle out who sent it, and why. I figure it comes down to two scenarios.

Number One: The message is an empty threat by a stranger. It contains no names, no places, no specifics—just a vague "c u at lunch." But *everyone* eats lunch—so while it's reasonable that I immediately think of Vickers and his gang because they've been harassing me in the cafeteria, there's no actual evidence to suggest that they're involved. Anyone could have sent that message—in fact, it's probably the same anon who wrote "your a fag" and "r school doesn't need another faggot." In other words, it's just some random troll trying to scare me. This is the most likely conclusion. But the one I find myself turning over and over in my mind is Number Two: It *is* someone from school—most likely Jim Vickers. If it's him, it means he's somehow managed to connect me with my blog—which means he could do much worse than harass me: He could *expose* me. The thought turns my stomach to ice water.

But if he wanted to out me, why wouldn't he just post a link online, or email it to all his friends? That clearly hasn't happened, because the looks and comments I receive would be getting worse instead of slowly tapering off, as they seem to be doing now.

Still, even though there is absolutely no evidence to support it—I can't shake the feeling that it *is* someone at school. That someone knows. And, if not Jim Vickers, then who?

I can think of only two other possibilities: Bec and Solo. And the thought that either of them would out me, even by accident, let alone *threaten* me, is so devastating and far-fetched that I don't even want to think about it.

But I do.

I know Bec knows something. She seems to understand something about me that I've never been able to say out loud; it's almost as if she's read my diary. She invited me to the Q, after all. But she's been nothing but supportive; she'd have to be hiding some serious issues to be capable of sending a message like that, and I just don't think that's the case. Could she have let my identity slip out while she was talking to one of her Hardcore friends? It's possible—but she hasn't been at school much, and when she is, she seems to be spending her time with me. I just can't believe it's her.

Which leaves Solo. Just thinking about it makes my heart sink and my throat constrict. He was the first friend I made at Park Hills, and even when we had our big disagreement, he was always straight with me. I can't imagine him typing out a message like that. But, if he's figured out I'm gender fluid, could he have told someone about me? Let it slip to one of the football guys who he thinks might keep his confidence? It's possible— but it doesn't ring true. It doesn't seem like him.

Still, I find myself playing back all these possibilities.

To make matters worse, by Monday afternoon, the Andie Gingham story has been covered by every major gay and trans rights blog in the country. The *Huffington Post* does an editorial on Tuesday, and my blog's readership expands to fifteen thousand followers. On Wednesday, CNN.com picks up the story, and I hit thirty thousand.

The focus of the story in the LGBTQ community is

Andie's call for transgender people to come out, while the mainstream media are selling the drama of a family hate crime. But regardless of the angle, most of the stories mention Alix—especially the online ones. Some paint me as a dangerously irresponsible child who put Andie at risk; others cast me in a much more positive light, as some kind of anonymous, gender fluid celebrity.

Meanwhile, I haven't posted at all on Bloglr—each time I log in, I'm intimidated by the massive increase in followers, and I log out without even checking my inbox. I feel guilty for abandoning my followers, and for not reaching out to Andie when she probably needs it most—but I'm terrified of the messages that must be waiting for me. Not just responses to the story, but more threats from the anonymous sender I've come to think of as my stalker. Twice, I've sat down at my laptop with the intent of deleting the whole blog, only to chicken out at the last minute. The anxiety I've worked so hard to eradicate over the past two weeks has crept back in, and now I walk around with it constantly buzzing in the background, a vague tingling in my cheeks, an unrelenting pressure behind my eyes. I get very little sleep. My mom asks me several times if I'm feeling well, and I have to lie and smile. I'm doing my best to fake it at school, but I know I can't fight the pressure much longer. Something has to give.

On Thursday, Bec and I eat lunch on the ramp as usual. I won't go near the cafeteria, so I'm eating the peanut butter and banana sandwich I packed, while Bec subsists on her traditional fare of beef jerky and juice boxes. Between bites, she's her typical, witty self, but today I can't seem to keep up. I try to nod and laugh in all the right places, but I'm too distracted; I keep thinking about the message. I keep thinking maybe I should tell someone.

I set down my sandwich, wipe my hands on a napkin, and look up at her.

"I want to—" I start to say, just as Bec says:

"So what's going—"

And then we both stop. Neither of us laughs.

"You first," she says.

I shift on the uncomfortable concrete ramp. "I want to . . . tell you something."

Bec nods as if she expects this. "Okay."

I take a deep breath, open my mouth, shut it. Bec waits patiently. I want to continue, but it feels like all the saliva in my mouth has suddenly turned to glue, and I have to swallow before I can speak again. "I have this . . . I mean, I've been writing. Online. And . . ."

I stop, because Bec's eyes have wandered over my shoulder and out of focus; she's no longer listening. I clear my throat. "Bec, I'm trying to tell you something important."

"I know," she says, still looking past me and frowning slightly. "But maybe you should wait."

Something inside me recoils, and suddenly I'm certain Bec thinks I'm about to confess my feelings for her. I'm convinced that she's interpreted my strange behavior this week as a sign that I have a massive crush on her, and she doesn't want to hear me say it. Even through my fog of confusion and paranoia, the rejection stings like a slap.

And then I hear movement behind me, heavy footsteps on

the rough concrete, and I turn around.

Solo is tramping toward us, pizza box in hand, a determined expression on his face. He walks to the foot of the ramp and stands there looking down on us.

"Erik said I might find you here," he says.

Bec looks up at him. "Chewie," she says.

Solo frowns.

"What a surprise," Bec continues. "The League of Douchebags must keep you very busy playing with balls, because I haven't seen you around our table much for, oh, the last year and half."

Solo glances at me, then back at Bec. "Haven't seen you there much, either, Francesca."

Bec stiffens. Her pale face flushes red, and the ring in her lip twitches. "Don't call me that," she says. It's almost a hiss.

"Don't call me Chewie," Solo says, "and you've got yourself a deal." They stare at each other.

Finally, Bec says, "Fine."

Solo turns to me. "Mind if I join you?"

"Not at all." I scoot back to make room for him.

He sits, and the three of us form a lopsided triangle on the ramp. Solo folds his pizza into a grotesque, wedge-shaped, quadruple-decker cheese and pepperoni sandwich, then takes an enormous bite.

Bec grimaces. "Disgusting."

"Delicious," Solo says around his mouthful of pizza.

I take a bite of my sandwich, Bec tears off a piece of jerky, and for a minute, everything feels normal. Just three friends eating lunch on the ramp behind the auditorium. In that moment,

I feel ridiculous for having thought either of them might be my anonymous hater. Solo swallows a huge bite of pizza, then fixes his eyes on me, and I feel a question coming.

"So," he says. "You've been off in another galaxy this week. What's up with you?"

I set down my sandwich and wipe my hands on a napkin, stalling for time. Next to me, Bec shifts on the ramp.

"Sorry," I say. "There's been a lot going on."

"I gathered," Solo says. "Thing is"—he gestures at Bec with his pizza sandwich, and a pepperoni slips out and drops into the box; he ignores it—"you're supposed to talk to us. We're your friends."

Bec folds her arms. "Don't lump yourself in with me. You haven't spoken to me outside class for almost two years."

Solo smiles, retrieves the fallen pepperoni, and stuffs it into his mouth. "I've actually missed arguing with you, Bec. Did you know that?"

Bec rolls her eyes. "Of course you've missed it. You spend your time in a locker room, slapping asses with a herd of witless sweat rags. You must be dying for intellectual stimulation."

Solo shakes his head, but he's smiling. "You're incredible." He turns back to me. "Seriously. You've been distracted. You're not laughing at my hilarious jokes." He pauses as if waiting for a smile or a laugh, which I don't give. "You're acting strange. Even for you."

I glance at Bec, hoping she'll defend me, but she only shrugs and says, "He has a point."

"So," Solo continues, "what's going on?"

And then both of them are staring at me, waiting for me to

talk. I look down at my lap and wait for the tingling to come.

As if he senses my turmoil, Solo relents. "Hey, I didn't mean to add pressure. Talk when you're ready. Just know we're here for you."

Bec cocks her head at him like a curious predator.

Solo blinks. "Okay, *I'm* here for you. I can't speak for Bec."

Bec leans back and grips the railing casually. I brace myself for another argument.

"I'm here in ways you wouldn't understand," Bec says.

The ferocity in her voice sends a warm sensation through me; but now, it's Solo's turn to stiffen.

"Why are you so pissed off at me?" he says. "Because I decided to play football?"

"Because you abandoned your friends to join a bunch of assholes who shit on the people you used to hang out with."

"I don't shit on people," Solo says, defiant.

"But you don't defend them from your 'friends,' either," Bec says, making air quotes. "Or are you telling me that you and your gang of apes are actually grooming Erik for a spot on the team?"

Solo folds his arms. "No one groomed me. If Erik wants it, he has to fight his way in just like I did."

Bec throws up her hands. "See? This is what I'm talking about. 'Fight his way in'? That's not how friends treat each other. Who would want to fight their way into *that*?" She shakes her head. "You don't even see it. It's like you're a different person."

Solo regards her with the coldest look I've ever seen on him. "That's really how it seems?"

"That's how it *is*," Bec says.

Solo looks away, nods. "Then I get why you're pissed." He gestures toward me, then locks eyes with Bec. "But don't you think it's telling that the first two people Riley meets, less than a week after coming to a new school, are you and me?"

Bec releases her grip on the railing. She glances at me, then back to Solo, then shrugs.

"I have a proposal," Solo says, wiping his hands on his jeans. "The two of you come to my game on Saturday."

Bec and I look at each other. I picture the two of us, climbing the bleachers side by side to shouts of "*Fag!*" or "*Dyke!*" Bec blinks, looks at Solo, and lets out a grunt of contempt.

"Hear me out," Solo says, raising his hands defensively. "You can sit by the exit. You can leave at halftime if you want. But come to the game." He lets his hands drop to his lap. "I know you think football is stupid. But I really love it. I don't love all the people involved—but then, I don't love all *Star Wars* fans or all Whovians, either." Bec and I glance at each other again. Solo continues, "I think if you watch me play, maybe you'll understand. And if you don't think differently about me after that, you don't have to speak to me ever again."

"I don't have to speak to you ever again *now*," Bec says.

Solo opens his mouth, shuts it. "Fair point. So. What do you want in return?"

Bec regards Solo coldly, as though sizing him up. After a moment, she leans forward. "We'll go to the game," she says, "but first, you have to come to a club with us. Tomorrow night."

My head snaps toward Bec. What is she doing? Agreeing to go to the game is bad enough, but inviting Solo to the Q? I open my eyes wide in protest, but Bec's are locked on Solo.

He gestures at his chest. "You want to unleash all *this* at a club? Do you have any idea what kind of devastation that could cause?"

I consider speaking up to tell Solo it's not that kind of club—but Bec replies before I have the chance.

"Those are my terms," she says.

Solo glances at me, then turns back to Bec. "Done." He holds out one fist. It's like the head of a plump, brown mallet. Bec stares at it for a moment, then slowly extends her own. Suddenly, their arms whir into action, fists and elbows flying in a complex and ridiculous dance. They finish by touching index fingers and uttering, in unison, "Ouch." Solo smiles. Bec tries not to, but I see the telltale twist at the corner of her mouth.

Solo crams the remains of his lunch into his mouth, brushes off his hands, and gets to his feet.

"Tomorrow," he says, the word almost indistinguishable around his final mouthful of pizza sandwich, and then he walks off.

CHAPTER 20

ON THE RIDE TO SCHOOL Friday, I notice that my mother is biting her cuticles again. Dad left for Washington this morning, last-minute—something about his education bill—and Mom always worries when he flies. I start to reach out, like I'm going to pull her hand away from her mouth, but I think better of it, and let my arm drop into my lap.

"When does he get back?" I say.

Mom, suddenly aware that she's gnawing on her own flesh, puts her hand back on the steering wheel and glances over at me, embarrassed. I stare out the windshield and pretend I don't notice.

"Monday night at the latest, depending on how his meetings go. He's so tense about this bill." She starts chewing her thumb again. The affect makes her look younger, somehow, an odd contrast with the worry lines forming on her forehead. I wonder if she secretly loathes this whole election business as much as I do.

There's another fund-raiser on Tuesday, a big one, and my attendance is mandatory. Thinking about being in a huge hotel ballroom with two hundred people, smiling my campaign smile and wearing what I have to wear, is usually enough to send me into a spiral of anxiety—but right now, I've got other problems to distract me.

I don't know why it bothers me so much that Bec invited Solo to the Q. He already knows I'm different, so I'm not too worried about him rejecting me. It's just . . . I thought of the Q as *our* place. Bec's and mine. And there's also the fact that it was supposed to be our third date. At least, I thought it was.

But it's more than that. When I'm with Solo, I tend to behave more like a guy, because I think that's how he sees me. But around Bec, I'm inclined to be more . . . I don't know. *Feminine* is the word that comes to mind, but it's too simple a word for what I feel. There *aren't* words for what I feel, because all the words were made up by people who never felt like this.

As if that dilemma weren't enough, I'll be in a room full of people who expect me to be open about my gender identity. Regardless of which direction my compass is pointing tonight—how am I going to satisfy all those different expectations without acting like a crazy person?

Behind all this, buzzing in the background like an unseen wasp's nest, is the threat of my anonymous stalker. I start to turn over the possibilities for the thousandth time—but my thoughts are interrupted when Mom pulls into the circular driveway and stops at the curb.

"How about you?" she says, squinting at me. "You're dreading the fund-raiser, aren't you?"

I open my mouth, then close it again without saying anything. It's not at all what I was thinking—but she's right. I am.

"I don't blame you," she says. "All you can eat at those things is bread and ketchup."

I actually laugh out loud.

"We'll get On the Vedge before, so you're not starving. Okay?"

"Okay," I say. And then she reaches toward me, and I'm not sure if she intends to ruffle my hair or pat my cheek. She ends up sort of gripping my shoulder and giving me a weird concerned-mom smile.

As she pulls away, I wave good-bye, and she starts chewing on her thumb again.

I expect Miss Crane's classroom to be empty, as it usually is when I get to school early—so I'm surprised when I open the door to find Sierra Wells standing at the far end, facing one of the windows. Her head is down and her phone is pressed to her ear.

"No," she says. "Mom. Dad's . . . Okay, I'm not saying he *is*. I'm just . . . you're—okay. Fine."

She ends the call abruptly, drops her phone on the nearest desk, and buries her face in her hands. I didn't hear enough to understand what she was talking about, but it's clear from the way her shoulders are shaking that she's upset. For a moment,

I consider walking right back out the door—but then Sierra turns around. Her eyes are red and puffy. When she sees me, she stiffens at once and her expression hardens into a glare. This is the second time I've witnessed her in an embarrassing moment—the third, if you count the time I cut her down in the cafeteria—and I regret it immediately.

"Sorry," I say, taking a step back. She sniffs, looks away. "Are you . . . okay?" For a second, I think she might actually answer me, but then she snatches her phone, drops it into her purse, and heads for the door.

"Mind your own business," she says. Then, under her breath, "Fucking freak."

As she storms out, I notice she's scratching vigorously at her wrist.

I drop into my usual seat, and not long after that, the classroom begins to fill up. Solo comes in and starts trying to tease information out of me about "the club" we'll be hitting tonight. I deflect his questions with humor, but I'm distracted; I'm still thinking about walking in on Sierra's phone call, and her obsessive scratching. I almost tell Solo about it—I want to—but something stops me. Maybe I'm just being polite, or maybe I'm scared of what Sierra will do if she finds out, but I think it's something else. I think I just sort of understand what it's like to have a fucked-up secret, and I don't want to be the one who tells someone else's. Not even hers.

When I get home from school, there are still a few hours left before I have to get ready for tonight, so I head straight upstairs and fire up my laptop.

I haven't posted since I received the "c u at lunch" message; I haven't had the courage. But over the past week, the story of what happened to Andie Gingham has become a national news item. And with all the attention driving my follower count into the stratosphere, I feel pressure to respond. To get back on Bloglr and address my part in what happened.

It's still hard for me to believe that something I wrote created so many ripples—ripples that became waves—but whether I believe it or not, I have to deal with the consequences. At least, that's what I think Doctor Ann would say.

My computer emits its welcoming chime, and I go to Bloglr and type in my username and password below the smiling frog logo. My finger pauses above the keyboard, and I feel my heart skip. I take one deep breath, and then hit Enter.

MESSAGES: 500
FOLLOWERS: 35,144

This time, I'm prepared for the ridiculously high numbers. I manage, as Bec would put it, to contain my overdeveloped sense of drama, so there is no gasping or jaw dropping or anything like that.

My finger moves to click on my inbox, but I stop. Whatever is inside—hate or threats or gratitude—it has no bearing on what I want to say.

I click on New Post instead.

NEW POST: COMING TO TERMS
OCTOBER 19, 4:46 PM

Hi.

First, I want you to know I haven't opened a single message since the night I read Andie's story in *The Advocate*. I haven't even logged in until now. I apologize for my silence. I just got overwhelmed—by the massive response, sure, but also by little things in my own life.

It's easy to sound wise on a blog, easy to engage in clever banter and dispense advice to anonymous strangers. It costs me nothing.

Andie's stand cost her plenty. It almost cost her everything.

⏵ NOW PLAYING: *"Low Point"* by *Trespassers William*

Andie, I'm so sorry you were hurt. And I'm sorry if anything I said put you at risk. I only wanted to help. And I'm so grateful that you're going to be okay.

I don't know how else to respond or what else to say. I'm humbled by your gratitude, but I don't know what to do with it. I'm inspired by your bravery, but I'm not ready to match it. I feel like a coward, hiding on the internet behind a fake username. But I'm not just hiding on this blog—I'm hiding in real life, too. I don't have the guts to come out like you did. I'm afraid.

So, right now, nobody knows who I am. Nobody but strangers.

But when my time comes, I'll try to summon the kind of courage you showed us.

I click Post and slam the laptop shut. I think about how brave Andie was to come out to the world, and what she got as a reward for that act of courage: a nation of supporters. An extended family of people who believe in her, even admire her. I have that, too, from my blog followers—but in an artificial, anonymous way, as Alix. If I want the real thing—the support, the admiration—I'll have to do what Andie did. And I don't know if I can.

A cold feeling settles in the center of my chest. The only person in my life who knows who I really am is Doctor Ann, and my parents pay her to care.

For the first time, I consider the consequences of coming out. School would be unbearable, obviously. The taunting I get just for *looking* different is a drop in the ocean compared with the torrent of discrimination I would suffer for being openly gender fluid. Bec would stay friends with me—I'm almost sure she would. But Solo? I don't know. He tolerates my weirdness, but if I were to come out, would he be willing to endure the harassment from his team?

My mom would accept me, I think. It might take her a while to wrap her old-fashioned mind around it, but she would come around. My father, on the other hand—what would it do to him? He's worked so hard to carve out his spot in this ultraconservative county; a breaking story about his secretly gender fluid kid might be enough to cost him reelection.

Then I think about my stalker, and a shiver goes through me. The thought of being exposed, of being outed before I'm ready, terrifies me. It makes me want to shut down my blog and just go back to trying to blend in.

But there's another voice in my head—maybe it's Andie

Gingham's voice, or Doctor Ann's. Or maybe it's my own. The voice is telling me that all those things aren't reasons, just excuses.

And maybe this isn't only about me anymore.

CHAPTER 21

DESPITE MY PROTESTS ABOUT GETTING carsick, I end up in the backseat of Solo's hatchback on the way to LA—windows down, music up, and heater cranked to full blast. For the first ten minutes, Solo and Bec fight for control of the stereo; Solo wants to play XTC, but Bec has just acquired an Against Me! bootleg that she insists is "the proper soundtrack for tonight's festivities." Which prompts Solo to assert that he doesn't actually know what "tonight's festivities" are, which leads to an argument over whether Solo ought to know where he's driving us. I had almost forgotten he doesn't know what the Q is.

That's when the vague nausea of carsickness gives way to stomach-dropping dread. Even if I don't say a word tonight—even if I sit quietly and just listen to everybody else in the group—Solo will know. Maybe not the specifics, but he'll know something. Of course, he must suspect something already; our talk at the Reagan Years proves that. But when he sees the whole picture—when he finds out what I am—what if he's repulsed? My guts churn again.

Solo turns down the music and glances at me in the rearview. "You okay?"

"Yeah," I say. "Just tired."

"We're almost to the exit. You need me to pull over? You want a 7UP or something?"

I shake my head.

"All right." Solo turns the music back up, but not as loud this time. A moment later, I feel a hand touch my shoulder.

It's Bec's.

I sit up when we pull into the parking lot. My temples and upper lip are slick with sweat—whether from nerves or from Solo's heater, I'm not sure—but the cool air feels good when I step out of the car, and my stomach settles a little.

"Where the hell are we?" Solo says, glancing around at the empty buildings.

"West Hollywood," Bec says. "Almost Beverly Hills."

"Are you sure?" He glances down the alley, then frowns at Bec. "It doesn't look very safe."

Bec looks him up and down. "I'll protect you."

Solo laughs. Bec smiles.

We start across the parking lot, Bec to my left, taking her short, quick strides, and Solo ambling along on my right. Suddenly, I don't know how to walk. Almost sixteen years of doing it without thinking seem to vanish in an instant, and now I'm just putting one foot in front of the other in a series of awkward, robotic lunges. Part of me wants to lean toward Bec and take her hand, and the other part wants to jam my hands in my pockets and match long strides with Solo. Instead, my arms just swing dead at my sides, making me feel like some sort of ballerina ape. I'm so distracted and self-conscious that I catch the toe of my Chucks on a pothole and barely stop myself from eating asphalt.

"You all right?" Solo asks.

"I'm cool," I reply. My voice comes out oddly low, as though I'm imitating some rapper. Bec shoots me a bemused glance. I blush and look away.

This is what I was afraid of: being caught in some kind of relational limbo between masculine and feminine. I close my eyes for a second and try to sense which direction my internal compass is pointing—but it's as if there's too much interference, and I can't get a clear reading. So instead, I concentrate on walking and try to pretend nothing is happening.

Kanada greets us at the door. She performs an elaborate European cheek-kissing ritual on Bec, then collects me in a tight hug as though she's known me for years, her strong, lean arms almost squeezing the breath out of me. At first, it's overwhelming, and I feel a claustrophobic instinct to withdraw; but after a moment, I find myself hugging her back. I can't actually remember the last time someone hugged me like this, and I don't want to let go. I feel a pang of disappointment when she releases me and turns to Solo, her smile widening even further.

"Well, look at this hunk of pure love," she says, extending her hand. "I'm Kanada."

"Solo," he says. And then, instead of shaking her hand, he

bends deftly at the waist and plants a kiss on it. "Enchanted."

Kanada squeals with delight and throws an arm around Solo's neck. "Ladies best back off. Her Majesty claims this one for her own."

Solo smiles, and I think I see a tinge of red on his brown cheeks.

Kanada leads us in, and we gravitate toward the table in the back as the rest of the group begins to show up. Bec goes from member to member, exchanging hugs and making small talk—she's almost a different person here, so much more social and outgoing than she is at school. Solo and I hang out by the refreshments table, him gnawing on a stale grocery-store cookie, me sipping at a Styrofoam cup of coffee. When the room starts to fill up, Bec comes back and ushers us to the ring of chairs in the center, and we sit.

Mike/Michelle is dressed as a man tonight, in gray slacks and a white dress shirt, her hair parted on the side and combed back. "Welcome, everyone," she says. "In case you've never seen me present as a man before, this is what *Mike* used to wear to work." She strikes an elegant pose, to which the group responds with scattered laughter and applause. Mike/Michelle smiles. "We have some new faces tonight, but don't worry, I'm not going to single anyone out. So if you want to introduce yourself, just raise your hand and say hello."

I glance at Solo, wondering how he feels at this point. He sits quietly, observing the group's members and clearly doing his best not to stare. He probably looks exactly how I looked last week.

The cast is pretty much the same: Kanada sits next to

Mike/Michelle, and then there's Chris, the trans man with the combat boots. Next to him is Herman, the good-looking guy who was holding hands with Bennie last week—but there's no sign of Bennie herself. Morgan—the group member with the awesome green hair—takes the chair to my left. I recognize the fine-featured face and baggy flight jacket from last week, but this time, only a few strands of that shocking green hair are visible, peeking out the back of a baseball cap with a "T" embroidered above the bill. I'm trying not to stare like I did at my first meeting, but I think I detect a hint of lip gloss.

Mike/Michelle rubs her hands together. "Okay then. Let's have our opening words." She reaches out to Kanada, and then everybody clasps hands. It's kind of cheesy, and I glance around to make a face at Solo, but he's solemn as a choirboy. So is Bec, for that matter. I wipe the smirk off my face and turn to look at Mike/Michelle. She closes her eyes and tilts her face toward the ceiling.

"Tonight we come together as a community—not to focus on our flaws, but to celebrate our uniqueness. To share our pain, our joy, and our love, and to create a better tomorrow."

For a moment it's quiet, and I have to stifle the urge to say, "Amen." Then Mike/Michelle looks up and there's a subdued round of applause.

"First, a few announcements. Herman tells me that Bennie couldn't be here tonight because she's meeting with her soon-to-be ex-wife and divorce attorney. So let's all take a moment to send her loving thoughts."

We clasp hands again, and everyone is quiet for a moment.

"We also want to congratulate Kanada, whose daughter

was accepted into the very prestigious All Southern Youth Orchestra!" More applause. Kanada wipes tears from her eyes and waves at the group to stop. Mike/Michelle continues. "There's another person I'd like all of us to acknowledge, but she's not officially a member of our group. I'm sure you all must have heard about Andie Gingham by now? The trans girl in Oklahoma?"

A chill runs down my spine. Everyone nods.

"Good. Because I want to acknowledge Andie. She didn't back down or hide, even in the face of rejection by her own family. Even in the face of violence. She could have let it stop her, and no one in this room would have blamed her."

"No way," Kanada says. There are murmurs of assent.

"But she didn't," Mike/Michelle continues. "She took the beating and then came out *again*—to the world. She took a stand not just for herself, but for every one of us. And I want to thank her for that."

Even though there are fewer than a dozen people in this little room, the sound of applause bouncing off the concrete walls is almost deafening.

"And finally," Mike/Michelle says as the applause dies, "I want to thank you for agreeing to switch nights this week. As you know, Trans Health Con is coming up in a few weeks. Remind me, who's coming? Raise your hand if you're planning to attend."

Mike/Michelle, Kanada, Herman, and Chris raise their hands.

"Bennie's going, too," Herman says.

"Oh, good," Mike/Michelle says. "For those of you who

haven't registered yet, there are still spots open. I know you would find it inspiring. In any case, the reason I had to switch nights is that there's a planning session tomorrow. They're holding a panel about online community building at the conference, and the chairperson asked *me* to be the mediator!"

This time there are cheers mixed in with the applause.

Mike/Michelle smiles broadly and raises a hand to quiet the group. "Okay, okay, thank you! Wow." She laughs. "Now, if nobody objects, I'll start the sharing."

"Share away, my love," Kanada says.

"As you can see, I didn't have time to change before tonight's meeting. I went to my son's debate competition, and I have an agreement with him to present as a man when we're together in public."

Everyone in the room nods. Even Solo. I wonder what he's thinking right now.

"Well, I just—I just wanted to share that I'm bothered by it. Right now." She puts a fist to her mouth as if to cough. Kanada takes her other hand, and then Mike/Michelle continues. "I've been out for years, but it's still a struggle. And I was really looking forward to wearing this periwinkle top Kanada bought me."

"And you should've seen her in it," says Kanada. "I mean, *damn.*"

We laugh.

Mike/Michelle smiles. "My son placed third, by the way. Okay. Who's next?"

For a moment, everyone just looks around at everyone else—and then Morgan breaks the silence.

"I know I don't talk much," Morgan says, and I hear the hint of a drawl in that alto voice. "But I guess I'll go."

"That's great," Mike/Michelle says. "What's on your mind?"

"Well," Morgan says, glancing around the group, "y'all know I came out here from Texas to get away from my family."

Most of the group nods their heads.

"When I left, my dad pretty much disowned me. I didn't actually come out, not in so many words, but to my family, moving to Cali and being genderqueer are pretty much the same thing."

A few people laugh, but not me; I'm transfixed. *Genderqueer.* I realize this may be the first person like me—or *close* to being like me—that I've ever met. I look at the trace of lip gloss, the green hair protruding from the back of the baseball hat—and all at once, I understand what it must be like for someone else to see *me* for the first time. When I saw Morgan, my first instinct was to wonder: Boy or girl? And if I saw *me*, with my untamed midlength hair and my ambiguous wardrobe, I'd probably wonder the same thing. I think of all my mother's scrutinizing looks, all the lectures about appearance I've endured from my dad. Were they really judging—or just trying to figure me out? The idea reverberates in my head like a low gong, drowning out all other thoughts.

"Anyway," Morgan continues, "I've been here about three months. Haven't heard nothing from my family till last week." Morgan pauses. When he—or she—speaks again, I expect that calm, alto voice to break, but it doesn't. "I got a letter from Momma. She told me I ought to get my scrawny ass to church and pray to Jesus I don't get corrupted by y'all."

This time I do laugh, along with everybody else.

"It wasn't the best thing, but . . . well, she wrote. So that's good. Right?"

"Yes it is, precious," Kanada says.

Morgan glances around the room. "Anyway. I just wanted to say I'm glad y'all are here."

Herman shares next, something about Bennie and the turmoil around her divorce, but I'm not really listening—I'm watching Morgan listen. Even after hearing him—or her—speak, I have no idea which pronoun to use, which gender label to apply. And I realize that, while I tend to think of myself as drifting between the two poles of male and female, that's my individual perception—and, in some ways, it's too binary for a person like Morgan, who seems to hover somewhere in the middle, or maybe doesn't envision gender as a spectrum at all. It's weird to think that now *I'm* the one clinging to old ideas. Just then, Morgan catches me staring and flashes me a brief, tight-lipped smile. I smile back.

As the applause dies following Herman's sharing, I notice Mike/Michelle looking in my direction.

"Riley," she says. "Welcome back. How are you tonight?"

My heart gives a throb of protest. Mike/Michelle must sense my distress, because her face falls, and I get the feeling she's searching for a way to shift the focus to someone else. In my peripheral vision, I see Solo turn his head toward me.

"I'm okay," I say.

More heads turn, and now all the eyes are on me. But it's not like the Gauntlet, not like walking through the halls at school;

those eyes are invasive and penetrating. These are curious and patient. These people genuinely want to hear what I have to say.

Mike/Michelle leans back in her chair as if to give me more room to breathe. "Would you like to share?"

I nod. "Hey, everybody, I'm Riley."

The room responds with nods and hellos. My heart is now a lump in my throat, and my breath is shallow. I talk anyway. "I'm sort of . . . fighting off a mini anxiety attack right now," I say.

"Do you want some time?" Mike/Michelle asks. "Kanada can take you out for a little fresh air if that would help."

"No." I'm surprised at the strength of my voice. "I think I just need to sort of push through, if that's okay."

"You bet it's okay," Kanada says. "We're here for you."

The group murmurs their agreement. I close my eyes and take three long breaths. I look up and glance at Bec. She nods encouragement.

"I was inspired by what Mike/Michelle said, about having to dress a certain way around her family. Such a normal thing, for us, feeling out of place. I feel that way all the time. Like I'm from some other planet, you know? Like my soul was stuffed into the wrong body and then dropped off here by mistake."

The group responds with murmurs of assent, and Morgan nods. But Mike/Michelle narrows her eyes just a little. Her gaze is curious, but intense. I swallow. Why is she looking at me like that? I look away and try to pick up the thread of what I was saying.

"I think everybody has moments like that. It's not just us.

Everyone feels lost. Everyone is just . . . looking. Looking for somewhere to stand. For someone to stand next to." I look at Bec. "And even though we're on the outside of everything, maybe we're the lucky ones. Because we already have that."

Bec nods slowly, but doesn't smile. I look around the circle. Kanada is nodding, too, her mouth tight. Chris wipes at the corners of his eyes with his sleeve.

Then I glance at Solo. His head is inclined, his brow furrowed. I realize I'm holding my breath.

"I'm gender fluid."

I hear the words echo off the concrete before I realize I've spoken them. The whole room seems to freeze in place.

For a long moment, Solo is still as a statue. Finally, he glances around the room and then leans closer, as if it's just the two of us having a conversation.

"I figured it was something like that," he says. "I've sort of been doing homework on gender stuff." He shakes his head. "God, I hope my mom never looks at my browser history."

I laugh, and that seems to give everyone else permission to laugh, and they do. Bec does smile now, then turns and punches Solo's arm. A few people applaud, and Herman blows me a kiss. Kanada stands up and gives me a long-armed hug. I hug her back as hard as I can, and tears creep into the corners of my eyes. I've never been so accepted by a group of strangers—or friends, for that matter. I've never felt so . . . normal. And, other than some raw nerves—understandable after sharing something so personal—my body feels amazing. Whole. Almost like I belong in it. It's the first time I can remember not feeling a single trace of dysphoria; but, rather than exhilarating me, the realization kind of depresses me, because I think about how much time I've spent feeling *wrong*.

When the meeting is over, a few people come up to me and congratulate me on coming out. I smile and try to be polite, but I'm sort of emotionally exhausted, and I'm sure I seem distant. Kanada stands near the refreshments table with Herman and Solo, having an animated conversation I can't hear. I look around for Morgan, but he or she must have slipped out as soon as the meeting ended. I wish I could do the same. Bec seems to sense my fatigue, because she leans in and whispers, "I'll get Solo," then crosses the room to retrieve him.

"Hi, Riley."

The voice comes from behind, and I turn to find Mike/Michelle walking toward me.

"Hi," I say.

"Can we talk for a minute?"

"Sure."

She leads me away from the ring of chairs. "I want to ask you something. But if you don't want to answer, it's okay. And I won't share this information with anyone unless you specifically ask me to. Okay?"

I don't know what she wants—but the way she's asking is making me nervous. I glance around the room to make sure no one can overhear. "Okay."

"What you said tonight, about feeling like your soul had been stuffed into the wrong body. That was . . . very moving. It reminded me of something Alix wrote on *Hiding and Other Social Skills*. Do you know that blog?"

My breath catches in my throat. So *that's* why she cocked her head at me when I said that. She recognized it from my blog. She knows.

After a moment, she continues. "I think you're Alix. I think you're the one who responded to Andie Gingham. And I would really like to know if I'm right."

I don't say anything, but the heat rushing up my neck tells me that my skin and my blood vessels have already spoken on my behalf.

Mike/Michelle nods. "Okay," she says. "You don't have to say anything. This is between you and me. I am not in the business of telling other people's secrets. But I have an invitation for you. Or, maybe it's a request. You don't have to decide tonight, but I'll need your answer soon, because it's in two weeks."

I swallow hard. "What's in two weeks?"

Mike/Michelle clasps her hands, almost like she's praying. "I'd like you to be on my panel at Trans Health Con."

At first, I mistake the sensation that rushes through me for anxiety—but there's a hopeful edge to the feeling, a lightness instead of the usual darkness. I realize it's not panic I'm feeling; it's excitement.

"Riley, you have a gift for words. The way you write, and the way you speak—you have the ability to move people. You saw it tonight, the way the group responded to you. The way I responded. The way Andie Gingham responded." She puts a hand on her chest. "I know you haven't come out to your parents yet, and you would probably want to do that before you spoke at the Con. I know you're only sixteen, and I know it seems like I'm asking an awful lot. But, Riley—there are so many more Andie Ginghams out there. And they need to hear someone like you."

I blink at her. The blood rushing past my ears sounds like an army marching on dry leaves. My mouth is dry.

Come out to my parents. Speak in public. In two weeks.

"Please consider it."

I feel my head nod as though someone is pulling an unseen string. "I will."

CHAPTER 22

ON SATURDAY MORNING I WAKE up to the sound of knocking on my bedroom door. I grab my phone and check the time: it's almost nine thirty.

"Riley, are you awake?" It's my dad's voice.

"I am now," I say, sitting up and rubbing the sleep out of my eyes. "Come on in."

He opens the door and takes a step in. Standing there in his blue pajamas and bathrobe, he looks like a dad from some old TV show. He sips from his University of Notre Dame coffee mug and surveys my bedroom over the rim of his reading glasses as if he's never been in here before.

"I didn't know you were home," I say.

"Got in late last night, decided to sleep in." He walks over to my record collection and starts flipping through albums.

"How did your meetings go?" I ask.

A giant grin spreads across his face. "Better than I'd hoped. The teachers' unions are on board, and that makes a big difference. There's still a long way to go, but we might just pull this thing off."

"And that's good for the campaign?"

"It's good either way."

"That's awesome." I smile at him, and he smiles back. He pulls out *London Calling* by the Clash, flips it over, and starts reading the back cover.

It's been a long time since my dad came into my room while I was still in bed—and longer since I felt so . . . I don't know, *normal* about it. I'm usually pretty self-conscious in the morning, at least until I've had a chance to read my internal compass and figure out how I want to present myself. But right now, it's not so bad. I'm already feeling extremely guyish—like the needle is all the way on M—and I tend to feel less vulnerable on guy days.

"So," Dad says, putting the record back, "your mother and Shelly are off to some sort of baking expo and then to the spa." He puts one finger on the turntable and gives it a spin. "And I'm going to get my lazy butt dressed and head into the office. I have a thousand emails to catch up on, then meetings this afternoon." He glances up at me. "Want to come with me? We could get bagels."

I can tell he really wants me to go—but I haven't spent much time alone with my father. I don't know what we'd say to each other.

"No pressure," he says, taking an intentionally nonchalant sip of coffee. "I was just thinking you could keep me company.

Bring your laptop. Do some homework. When you get bored, Elias can take you home." I consider. The game isn't until five thirty, and I was planning to do some reading anyway. Dad stares down into his now-empty coffee cup. "I want to pick new walk-in music for Tuesday. Something . . . different. I could use your expertise."

As usual, he's reserved a carrot to dangle in front of me—I've been bugging him to let me pick his walk-in music since he announced his candidacy last year.

"Can we get On the Vedge instead of bagels?"

He looks up at me, and I can tell he's pleased. "You've got yourself a deal."

An hour later, Dad's bald and burly head of security, Elias, picks us up in his black SUV. When I get in the car, he hands me a paper bag emblazoned with the On the Vedge logo. It smells amazing.

"You rule," I say.

"Good to see you too, Riley. How's school?"

"It needs drastic reforms, Elias."

He laughs. "To the office, Congressman?"

Dad nods. "To the office."

Dad spends the morning behind his giant mahogany desk, catching up on emails. I sit at the small conference table by the window, trying to get through Act 2 of *The Crucible*. But, after rereading the same page three times, I give up and start clicking around the internet.

Shortly before noon, Dad stands, takes off his reading glasses, and rubs his eyes. "If I read one more email, my eyeballs are going to pop out of my head." He walks over to where I'm sitting, plops down in the chair next to me, and puts his feet up on the conference table.

"You're in a weird mood," I say.

"I'm in a *good* mood. You're just not used to it." He smiles. "So, what do you think for walk-in music?"

I bring up my list. "I figured you'd want something education-themed."

"Good thinking."

"How about 'Another Brick in the Wall'?"

Dad frowns. "Isn't that the 'we don't need your education' one?"

I smirk.

"Very funny."

"Not safe enough? Okay. How about . . . 'ABC' by the Jackson Five."

He wrinkles his nose. "No, come on. That's too . . . I'm, I don't know, I'm edgier than that," he says.

"*Edgier?*" I say, unable to keep the sarcasm out of my voice.

"Yeah. Edgier." Dad gives me his best TV face, cocks his head at an angle, and says, "It's time for an *edgier* Orange County. I'm Sean Cavanaugh, and I approved this message."

I roll my eyes. And then my dad emits this weird bark of laughter.

"Sean Cavanaugh," he says in a caricature of his congressman voice, "your *edgy*-cation candidate."

And he starts to laugh, a deep, booming chuckle, until his eyes get moist. At first, I just shake my head, but I feel a smile forming. This seems to egg my father on, because now he's leaning forward, slapping the conference table with one hand, laughing so hard he's gasping.

"Call Shelly!" He motions helplessly at the phone. "We're changing the posters!"

Now I'm laughing, too—not a full-on belly laugh, but the closest thing I've had in a long time. It feels good—like something that's been building up inside me finally finds a vent, and the pressure lessens.

Finally, Dad manages to get control. "Okay," he says, wiping away tears and putting his glasses back on. "Seriously. Next suggestion?"

"How about 'School's Out' by Alice Cooper? That's your generation."

"Wrong message," he says. Then, he sits up straighter. "Wait . . . the Ramones!"

I frown. "Which song?"

"You know . . ." And then he sings in a horrible imitation of Joey Ramone. "Rock, rock, rock, rock, rockin' the high school!"

"Oh my God, Dad. Please don't ever do that again."

He feigns a hurt look.

"Now I know where my lack of musical talent comes from."

"All right, all right. But seriously, that's an upbeat song. It's sort of silly, but it's catchy, and it's education-related."

"Um, have you ever listened to the words?" I bring up the lyrics in a new browser tab and angle the laptop toward him so he can read. He scans them, frowns.

"Wow," he says, sitting back in his chair. "I almost pulled a Reagan."

Oddly, I immediately picture Solo inhaling his chocolate malted. "As in President Reagan?"

Dad nods. "He used 'Born in the USA' during his campaign. Springsteen was huge, and he thought it sounded patriotic, but it's actually a protest song. Made himself look like an idiot in front of the whole country." Dad sits back and gazes out the window, tapping absently on the tabletop with his index finger. "I guess I'm pretty out of touch." His voice sounds soft and uncertain, not like him at all—at least, not like any part of him I'm allowed to see. He turns his head away from the window and looks at me, and it's as if he's seeing me for the first time since I was a little kid. We sit there for a while, looking at each other. Then his eyes drop to his lap and he clears his throat—but before he can say anything, the phone rings. He reaches for the extension on the conference table.

"Cavanaugh." He looks at me, mouths the word *edgy*, and gives me a thumbs up. I shake my head at him. "Yeah, okay," he says, glancing down at his watch. "I'll still be here. Okay." He hangs up. "Superintendent Clemente will be here in five. You want to stay, or . . ."

"No, that's okay. I need to head home. I'm going to the football game tonight."

Dad raises his eyebrows. "Really?"

"Yes, Dad, really."

"With whom?"

"My friend Bec. We're going to go watch Solo play."

Dad frowns, folds his arms. "Bec is a boy?"

I turn the laptop back toward me. "Bec is a girl, Dad."

"Oh, right. So, are you two . . ."

"I don't know yet," I say, feeling my cheeks get hot. Dad cocks his head, and I can almost see the wheels turning.

My breath quickens. Is this my opening? My moment to tell him? I don't feel ready—and yet, I've known the truth for a long time now. I've been in therapy for months. I've come out to two friends, half a dozen strangers, and the entire internet. For Christ's sake, I've been invited to speak about it publicly in two weeks. If I'm not ready now—will I ever be?

I open my mouth to speak—and then all at once, I change the subject. "You want to finish picking a song?"

"Yes. Absolutely," Dad says. He sounds as relieved as I feel. "What else have you got?"

"Well," I say, turning back to the screen and swallowing the lump in my throat, "this one isn't about education, not at all, really, and it's kind of weird. But it might work."

"What is it?"

I bring up the lyrics and turn the laptop back toward him. "'Changes.' David Bowie."

He pulls the computer closer and scrolls down, reading. A faint smile turns up the corners of his mouth—it's the same smile I have—and he nods.

"It's perfect."

The phone bleeps, and Elias's voice comes through the speakerphone. "Congressman, Superintendent Clemente is here."

"I'll be right out," he says, and punches the hang-up button. He turns back to me, folding his hands. "Okay, well. Thanks for the song."

"Don't thank me. Thank Mr. Bowie."

We stand, and he waits till I've packed up my laptop and tossed my copy of *The Crucible* into my bag. Then I follow him through the door into the outer office.

"Felicia," he says, striding across the small lobby and extending his hand. I walk behind him.

"Good to see you back on the home front, Congressman," she says. She's tall, and the heels she's wearing make her even taller than my father; I can only see her shiny black hair over the top of his head. I step out from behind my dad, and the superintendent looks from him to me with a bright smile. "And this must be your . . ." She pauses for a split second—but in that time, I see her smile falter just slightly.

Dad, being the consummate politician, jumps in a millisecond later, defusing the awkward moment with his usual charm. "Riley," he says, "this is Superintendent Clemente. She's here to hold me accountable for all my campaign promises."

She recovers her smile immediately, but I know my dad noticed.

"Nice to meet you, Superintendent Clemente," I say. We shake hands. Her grip is weak.

Dad turns to me. He smiles, but it's that no-teeth smile, and his eyes have gone distant. It's as though I've already left the room, or as though he wishes I had. The warmth of the last few minutes evaporates.

"Have a good time at the game, Riley. Be safe. Text before you head home."

"Okay," I say, and then Elias ushers me out of the office, and the door closes behind us.

CHAPTER 23

THAT AFTERNOON, I TRY TO forget the uncomfortable exchange with Superintendent Clemente so I can study, but I can't. God, why couldn't we have run into one of his junior aides, or the janitor in his building? Why did it have to be the effing superintendent?

I play back the moment right before Elias took me home, remembering the cold tone of Dad's voice; it was like he was trying to distance himself from me. As though, instead of being his kid, I'm some politically dangerous *thing* that he needs to disassociate from.

I slam my book shut, slide off my bed, and get ready for the game.

To my relief, there's no sign of the scruffy drummer when I pick up Bec at Bullet Hole. We drive to school—which feels strange on a Saturday. The lot is almost full when we arrive, and

I have to park the minivan at the far end by the tennis courts. I shut off the engine, and we just sit there for a moment, neither of us eager to get out and face the chaos of the game.

"Do we have to go?" I say.

Bec glances out the window, then back at me. "If we leave now, we could be in Mexico before the game ends. No one would know we were gone."

"We could take on fake names."

"We could wear sombreros."

"And six-guns." I smile. Bec smiles back. Then she reaches for the door handle.

We get out of the car and walk toward the field slowly, delaying the moment when we have to join the noisy throng on the other side of the bleachers. We're passing an old green pickup truck when Bec stops.

"I just . . . ," she begins, then pauses. "I just wanted to tell you that I'm totally cool with it. With you being gender fluid, I mean."

Air rushes out of my lungs in a sort of dry, silent sob—and it's like I've been holding my breath for as long as I can remember, and now I can finally breathe.

Bec continues, "I mean, it probably goes without saying. But I wanted to—"

"No, I'm glad you said it. I'm . . . glad." I laugh. "Gladdy-glad-glad-glad. I think I caught your speech disease."

"Monkey, monkey, monkey?" Bec says.

"Yeah, that one."

She shakes her head. "On the contrary. What you said last night, about having somewhere to stand and someone to stand with . . . you have a thing with words."

I blush so deeply that it shows in my reflection in the truck's window. "*I* have a thing?"

"You have a thing."

"That is a supreme compliment coming from the girl who coined the phrase 'slapping asses with a herd of witless sweat rags.'"

Bec smirks. "I have my moments."

Just then, a voice comes over the PA, announcing, "Kickoff in five minutes!"

But I don't really want to move; I like standing here in the parking lot, talking to this strange, attractive girl. I try to think of something to say to postpone the inevitable end of this moment we're having, whatever it is.

"I told my dad about you today," I say.

"Oh yeah?"

I nod. "He wanted to know if you were a boy or a girl."

She cocks her head at me.

"I think he was trying to figure out if it was a date." I feel my cheeks go hot again.

Bec reaches out, takes my hand, and interlaces her fingers with mine. "Come on."

We're still holding hands when we queue up to buy tickets, and a few people shoot glances in our direction. I feel a strange pang of pride and grip Bec's hand tighter; her touch is at once reassuring and exhilarating. We get our tickets and then stop at the snack counter, where Bec purchases a soda roughly the size of a bathtub. I smile when she grabs two straws.

The first few rows of bleachers are completely packed, so

we mount the steps and head for the top. The crowd is loud and the PA is blaring; I'm not surprised when I feel a buzz starting up in the back of my head.

We make it halfway to the top before the harassment starts.

"Which one's the dude?"

I turn my head, and my stomach goes cold. Jim Vickers sits five feet away from me, one arm still bound in a yellow cast, the other draped around Sierra's shoulders. She says nothing, but doesn't take her eyes off me.

Seated between us and Vickers are the bespectacled red-headed kid and Cole, the broad-shouldered football player with long stringy hair. He should be on the field; I wonder what he did to get suspended.

Vickers points at me. "That one's got to be the dude. No tits."

Cole laughs. "The other one doesn't have any tits either." The redheaded kid pushes up his glasses and looks away.

Bec squeezes my hand tighter, and we start to move past.

"That's right. Keep walking, queers," Vickers says.

Bec stops, turns, and looks at him.

Vickers says, "What are you looking at?"

Bec smirks and says, "A very wet boy."

Vickers's smile wilts. Bec squeezes her soda cup until the lid pops off—and then she takes a step forward and upends it over Jim Vickers, sending sixty-four ounces of ice-cold purple drink cascading into his lap.

He leaps to his feet, gasping. "What the hell?"

"Oops," Bec says, and drops the cup.

Sierra stands up. There's a purple stain splashed across the thighs of her jeans, and her face is red with fury. "You little bitch," she says, taking a step toward Bec, but Vickers grabs her arm and pulls her back down to the bench.

"What's going on here?" says a low voice from behind, and Bec and I turn simultaneously. Mr. Brennan stands a few steps below, dressed in a Park Hills High sweatshirt and jeans, a frown of disapproval peeking out from under his moustache. "Mr. Vickers," he says, "is there a problem?"

Vickers glances at Bec, then back at Brennan. "Nah. We're cool."

"All right, then." Mr. Brennan turns back to us. "I suggest you two go find your seats."

"We will," Bec says. Brennan shoots a warning look at Vickers, and then starts back down the stairs.

A few rows up, a group of girls stands and starts applauding. One of them calls down toward Vickers, "How do you like that, douchebag?"

Sierra glares at me.

Bec takes my arm, pulling me away, and we move past them, climbing until we reach the very top of the bleachers. I sit, taking deep breaths, trying to abate the tingling that is rapidly spreading out from my cheeks to the rest of my face. Bec squeezes my hand.

"You're shaking," she says. "Are you okay?"

"Yeah," I reply.

A squeal of feedback issues from the speaker overhead, and a voice begins introducing the players. The list is long and mostly unfamiliar until the announcer says, "Jason Solomona!" At first I don't react, but when Bec stands and starts cheering, I join her. The announcer says something else after his name, but it's a string of words and phrases so foreign to me they might as well be in another language.

"What was all that about?" I ask.

"One of the defensive linemen was injured, so Solo's filling in."

I start to ask what the hell that means, but then the announcer introduces the star quarterback, and the crowd explodes to its feet. The noise is tremendous—and that's when my vision starts to tunnel. I sit down quickly and draw my thighs up to my chest. Bec reaches behind me and rubs my back.

"I know it's loud," she says, "but we're okay up here."

I nod.

"And we can leave if it gets bad."

I close my eyes and try to paint the whiteboard black. I make it about three quarters of the way before the black paint starts to drip away—but combined with Bec's touch, it's enough to calm me. The numbness recedes, leaving only that frenetic buzzing in the back of my head. I start to watch the game.

To me, football is like a poorly organized war in which two groups of guys face off at an arbitrarily drawn line. Someone yells "hike," and then they all try to kill one another while four or five others chase a ball like cats after a laser pointer.

Solo isn't even one of the cats—he appears to spend most of his time wrestling with the only guy on the other team who comes close to matching his size. At halftime, the scoreboard reads:

LIONS: 0
VISITORS: 14

The other team is from Anaheim Lutheran, and I understand enough about football to appreciate that today, it's the Christians who are eating the Lions.

When the fourth quarter begins, the other team is already in what Bec refers to as "the red zone." They line up only a few yards from the big Lions logo spray-painted in the grass. The crowd is hushed, the mood tense. I'm watching Solo. When the other team's quarterback yells "hike," Solo darts forward with unexpected speed, knocking his sumo partner onto his back. Two other guys in white Lutherans jerseys rush in to block him, but they're smaller, and he shunts them aside like bowling pins. Now, the Lutherans' quarterback—who, for some reason, is not throwing the ball—starts to dodge around, trying to avoid Solo, but Solo pursues him relentlessly. Finally, the guy turns and tries to run up the field in the opposite direction, but it's too late. Solo jumps on him, squashing him flat against a big number thirty painted white on the grass.

And then, all the other players run up and pile on top of them. Even the other Lutherans. It's as if Solo and the opposing quarterback have committed some sort of crime, and their punishment is being crushed to death.

All of a sudden, a guy in a green jersey emerges from the tangle of legs and helmets; he's holding the ball. He looks down at it in disbelief, and then starts to run.

Somebody in the crowd yells, "Fumble!" And then everyone is on their feet, Bec included, yelling, "Go! Go! Go!" Even

I stand up and raise my fists.

That seems to turn the tide of the game, and when it's over, the scoreboard reads:

LIONS: 17
VISITORS: 14

Bec stands up, ready to leave, but I pull her back down by the hem of her jacket.

"Let's wait until the crowd clears a little," I say.

"Okay."

"Besides, I need you to explain what happened so I can compliment Solo without sounding like an idiot."

Bec laughs. "What happened is that, the very first time Solo ever played defense, he sacked the opposing quarterback and caused a fumble that led to a momentum-shifting touch-down. Which is epic. They would have lost without him."

"Why do you know so much about football?"

She shrugs. "I am mysterious and unpredictable."

We watch the bleachers clear out. When Vickers and his gang are gone and the seats are mostly empty, Bec says, "Good to go?"

I nod, and we stand and start down the stairs. The buzzing is still there in the back of my head, as though the anxiety is just taking a nap, and too much noise or excitement will wake it up again. I take a few deep Doctor Ann breaths. They help, but it doesn't quite go away.

It's getting dark when we finally exit the field. Parents are pulling out of the lot in their SUVs, the opposing team's players are filing onto their bus, and groups of students stand around, discussing the game or deciding where to go next. We're stepping off the curb and into the lot when I spot Jim Vickers and his crew huddled next to an old green pickup truck. It's the one Bec was leaning against before the game. Vickers looks at me, glances at Bec, and says something to his friends. They all look over at us. Instantly, the buzzing in my head grows louder. I want to reach for Bec's hand, but I'm frozen.

"Hey," Vickers says, walking toward us. I want to walk away—to *run* away—but Bec stands fast. Two of Vickers's friends trail behind him. Sierra leans against the bed of the truck, arms folded, watching with a smug look on her face.

The buzzing in my head spreads until my whole body is thrumming.

Vickers stops maybe three feet away and points at Bec. "If you were a dude, I would beat your ass."

Bec cocks her head. "That's a bit sexist, don't you think?"

Vickers shrugs. "I don't hit girls. Even titless wonders like you."

I feel my jaw tighten.

"But it's okay to comment on our bodies?" Bec says.

"I just call them like I see them," Vickers says. Cole laughs.

"Huh," Bec says. "Let me give that a try." She gestures at the purple stain on his crotch. "Based on the lack of bulge, even if we allow for shrinkage because of the cold, I'd say you've got your own anatomical shortcoming."

Vickers frowns.

"I mean you have a small dick," Bec says.

Vickers's face darkens, and he clenches his good hand into a fist. He steps forward and puts his face right in Bec's.

My chest is tight, my heart pounding. My head throbs with adrenaline.

"You better walk away before I decide you *are* a dude. Dyke."

Bec's nostrils flare, but she says nothing, and she doesn't move.

I'm surprised when I hear my own voice cut through the silence. "Back off."

Vickers glances at Bec, then back at me. "Fuck you, queer. This is none—"

But I don't hear anything after the word "queer." That word isn't his to use.

I fly at him. My vision goes blurry. My head feels full of burning cotton. Vickers tries to shove me, but I knock his good arm aside and lunge forward. Instinctively, I grab his cast in both hands and pull hard. Something pops. He grunts in pain and staggers back—and then there are hands on me. Bec's hands, pulling me away. Vickers drops to the ground, clutching his arm and groaning. Sierra yells a curse and rushes toward him.

I stand there, looking down at Vickers sprawled on the asphalt, not quite believing what's happening.

His friends kneel to help him. One of them, the redhead, looks up at Bec.

"You'd better get out of here," he says.

She takes my arm, and we do.

CHAPTER 24

I'M STILL BREATHING HARD WHEN Bec guides me into the passenger seat. She gets in on the driver's side, slams the door, and starts the engine.

"You okay?" she asks.

My heart pounds—but in my chest, not in my throat. The roar of the crowd still rings in my ears, and the glare of the stadium lights is a hovering red blur when I close my eyes. But this isn't anxiety; it's adrenaline.

"Yeah," I say. "I think I am. I'm just really . . . amped."

"Well, buckle your seat belt, Bruce Lee. Let's get the hell out of here."

A squeaky, slightly hysterical laugh escapes my throat as she backs out of the parking space and heads for the exit.

"Wait," I say. "Can you drive?"

"More or less," Bec replies.

As we're pulling out of the lot, I shoot a glance back toward the green pickup truck. Vickers is on his feet now. Sierra tries to put an arm around him, but he pushes her away. For an instant, I think I see Bec's brother, Erik, standing by the truck's front bumper. And then we turn the corner and pass out of sight.

"Did your brother come to the game tonight?" I ask.

Bec looks over at me. "I doubt it."

"Is he still trying to get in good with the team?"

She shrugs. "Honestly I haven't been paying much attention to him. There's been a lot of other stuff. . . ." Bec pauses, shakes her head. "Anyway."

"What other stuff?"

"A lot of family bullshit I don't really feel like going into," she snaps. I shrink back in my seat a little. Bec glances at me. "I'm sorry. Let's change the subject."

"Okay," I say, still a little hurt.

"I'll start," Bec says, affecting a cheery voice. "You want to go to the movies with me?"

I smile. "Yes, I do."

Bec drives like she's trying to outrun the cops: she zigs and zags through traffic, exceeding the speed limit by at least fifteen miles per hour. At first, I just grip the door handle and stare—but then Bec rolls down the windows and turns up the music, and something inside me seems to break loose. She starts singing along to "Anesthesia," and I join in with my own atonal shouting.

We careen down East Imperial Highway and shoot right past the Cineplex.

"Where are we going?" I yell over the music.

"You'll see."

We turn south on Richfield Avenue and keep driving until we cross the Park Hills border into Fullerton. Bec clicks off the stereo and lets out a long, slow sigh.

"What's wrong?" I ask.

"I guess I'm still pretty shaky. I thought my heart was going to beat right out of my chest back there."

"Welcome to my world," I say.

I turn and stare out the window. We pass a hardware store my dad used to frequent and an old appliance showroom with a banner that reads: EVERYTHING MUST GO! On the plywood planks covering the broken windows, someone has spray-painted EVERYTHING IS GONE.

"I'm sorry I freaked out back there," I say, my face still turned away from Bec. "I don't know what happened."

"Hey," she says, and I turn to look at her. "It's okay. You're human. You have a breaking point. Vickers found it."

I nod. "I think I might have rebroken his arm."

Bec considers. "Well, he and his friends haven't exactly made life easy for you. And tonight, he said some really nasty shit. And then he got right up in my face."

"Yeah," I say.

"Yeah," Bec repeats, with emphasis.

She turns left, pulls up to a 7-Eleven, and sets the parking brake. "You stay in the car," she says, then gets out, leaving the keys in the ignition and the engine running. "I'll get snacks."

I watch her through the window as she browses the snack aisle. She has this confidence in her walk—as though nothing bad is ever going to happen—and I try to memorize how she looks in the store, lit from above by the harsh fluorescents and filtered through two layers of glass. I feel something inside me twist and untwist, like a wet rag being wrung out. It's a good feeling.

When she gets back in the car, she hands me a plastic bag containing a Slim Jim, a bottle of grape soda, and a bag of mini Oreos.

"They're accidentally vegan," she says, and the pleasant twisting sensation intensifies.

We head east for three more blocks and pull up behind a crumbling, windowless three-story brick office building. Despite the packed parking lot, there's not a soul in sight—and, somewhere on the other side of the building, a strange electric glow lights up the sky, growing and fading at random, like the lightning from a miniature thunderstorm.

"This is it," Bec says.

"This is what?" I ask.

Bec just smiles and gets out of the van. I follow as she slaloms through the parked cars, working her way toward the back of the building. She stops under an ancient, rusting fire escape and looks up at it.

"You're not going up that thing," I say.

"We both are," she replies, her eyes locked on the wrought-iron ladder protruding from the bottom of the fire escape.

"That's crazy."

Bec looks at me, and my stomach twists again. "So are we," she says, holding out the 7-Eleven bag. I take it.

And then, without warning, she bends her knees and leaps into the air, grabbing onto the lowest rung. The catch gives under her weight, and the ladder comes down with a tremendous *clang*. Bec brushes flakes of rust off her hands and gestures at the ladder, which now hangs a foot above our heads.

"You first," she says. I stare up at the ladder dubiously. Bec takes a step back. "I'll give you a boost."

I step forward, and Bec puts her hands on either side of my waist. Even with layers of shirt and jacket between us, my skin heats up where she touches me, and then it spreads through my whole body. I'm grateful there's only one flickering sodium lamp overhead—because I'm certain I've just gone completely red. I jump and Bec lifts, and I grab ahold of the ladder and start to climb.

By the time I make it to the top, I'm flushed and out of breath, but the exertion seems to have expelled the last of the buzzing from my head. With the 7-Eleven bag clenched between her teeth, Bec ascends the ladder like a fireman, vaults onto the roof, and motions me forward. "Come on."

I follow her across the rooftop, careful not to trip on the warped, peeling surface, which is littered with cigarette butts, candy wrappers, and empty beer cans. When I catch up to Bec, she's standing at the edge of the building, looking down on the courtyard of an abandoned shopping center. There are people down there—two dozen or more—sitting on planters and blankets and lawn chairs. Someone has rigged up a projector, and they're showing an old movie on the side of the four-story building facing us.

"What is this?" I ask.

"Movie night," she says. "One of the churches around here organizes it, I think." She gestures at the old adobe-style bell tower on the other side of the courtyard. When she speaks again, her voice is so quiet I have to move closer to hear her. "I used to come here a lot, until the football guys found it and ruined it. Probably Chewie's fault. But since there was a game tonight, they're otherwise occupied."

And then she's silent for a long time—thinking, I guess, or maybe remembering something. Either way, I don't want to disturb the quiet, so I just watch her face, lit intermittently by the flickering projection on the far wall. Finally, she leads me to another part of the roof, where she reaches behind an exposed ventilation duct and pulls out two corroding lawn chairs. She sets them near the edge, then gestures for us to sit. The old movie dialogue echoes faintly off the bricks, blending in with the sound of crickets and the distant whoosh of traffic on the freeway. For a moment, it feels like we're alone in the world.

"I used to come here with my sister before she died," Bec says. Her voice is suddenly small, almost like a little kid's. "Today would have been her fifteenth birthday."

"Oh, God, Bec. I'm so sorry."

Bec nods. "I thought I could handle coming back here, if you came with me, but I . . ." She stops, swallows, and then starts to speak again. "She was transgender, Riley. That's how I knew about the Q. How I know Mike/Michelle and everybody. Because of my sister."

I stare at Bec for a second, then nod absently and look away. If I'm really honest with myself, I'm not surprised. How else could Bec be so attuned to what I'm going through? I feel a deep swell of sorrow for her, and for her sister.

And then the sorrow is overpowered by a pang of something

else, a knot of doubt that leaves a bitter taste in the back of my throat: What if Bec was never attracted to me in the first place? What if she only followed me to the ramp that day because I reminded her of her dead sister? It would make sense; I mean, we spent what I thought was our first date in the bedroom they shared. And then she took me to the Q, a place they went together. And now, we're at another one of their spots. On her dead sister's birthday.

I turn and look at Bec, worried that she's somehow been reading my thoughts—but the distance in her eyes tells me she's a million miles away, remembering something impossibly painful. I'm surprised when she speaks up again.

"I guess I knew from the time she was about six. We were coloring, and she traded me dinosaurs for princesses. She always wanted the princesses. We used to play dress-up, and she would beg to wear my patent leather Mary Janes, even though they were too big for her." She laughs, but it fades quickly. She picks at a flake of oxidizing metal. "When she finally told me how she felt, I tried to help. I researched on the internet with her. We found the Q. But after she came out to the family . . . things got worse. My parents started fighting. Erik withdrew. When she died . . ." Bec looks away. "It wasn't an accident." She falls silent.

"What happened?"

"Mom and Dad were asleep. I was still awake, reading, and I heard her get up, go to the bathroom, flush the toilet, and go back to bed. I've replayed those sounds a thousand times, and I . . ." She shakes her head defensively, as if some unheard voice is cross-examining her. When she speaks again, the words come out tight and flat. "It was my fault. I was the one who encouraged her to come out. But the way the family reacted . . . She thought we would be better off without her. She even wrote it in her note." Bec looks up at me. "She didn't wake up. I found four empty pill bottles, all tightly closed and neatly replaced in the medicine cabinet. She was thirteen."

Bec turns her unfocused eyes back to the movie. I reach out and take her hand. It's freezing. I want to say something, to say I'm sorry, to say it's horrible, but the words seem stupid and empty. So I just hold her hand until she's ready to talk again.

"It broke my mom. She just fucking gave up. And then Dad left. I don't blame him, I'd have left too, if I could've. The rest of us were hurting, too, you know? What right did she have to just *stop*?" She draws in a deep breath. "Anyway. That's where I am when I'm not at school. At home, taking care of my"— she seems to swallow an unkind word—"mom. She can't hold down a job. Dad sends money, but I basically have to be a parent from the time I get home from school to the time I leave the next day. And on tough days, I have to . . ." Bec trails off. "And, since this is Gabi's birthday month, they're pretty much all tough days. So." Bec looks at me uncertainly.

"Gabi," I say. "That was her name?"

Bec nods.

"It's beautiful. Named after the angel, right?"

She nods. "My mom's choice. They named her Gabriel, and she shortened it to Gabi." Bec withdraws her hand from mine and crosses her arms. She glances at the movie projected on the bricks, then turns back to me. "You must hate me."

"Hate you? For what?"

"For using you. For treating you like some kind of emotional crutch instead of just being there for you."

I shake my head. "No."

Bec sniffs once, wipes her eyes on her jacket, and looks me in the eye. "Be straight with me."

I pick at a thread on the knee of my jeans. "Okay," I say. "I did hate you, a little, but only for, like, a second."

"That's fair."

And we just sit there for a minute, not talking, but not really watching the movie, either. For the first time, I notice it's in black-and-white.

"What movie is this?" I ask.

"*Casablanca*, I think," Bec replies.

We're quiet for another few moments, and then I ask, "Do you want to go home?"

Bec shakes her head. "No. Let's just . . . let's just watch the movie. Okay?"

I nod.

"I'm sorry," she says.

"For what?"

She takes my hand. "For ruining our date."

CHAPTER 25

I DON'T EVEN TRY to sleep.

The last five hours feel longer than the whole last year of my life. The images and sensations—good and bad—flash through my head like a slide show: Sierra Wells's face, red with rage. The pop of Vickers's arm as I pulled it, and the thump of blood rushing past my ears. Bec's crooked smile. The feel of her fingers between mine.

And all at once the buzz is back in my chest; I wish my dad wasn't guarding my meds. I haven't felt the need to sneak an extra one since my little freak-out, but I could use one now. But if I can't have my pills, I need distraction. I pull my laptop toward me and turn it on.

I've only posted once since Andie Gingham's story went public, and I still haven't gone through the hundreds of messages clogging my inbox. If this is my new cause—helping other people deal with their gender identity issues—then I'm doing a horrible job of it. I feel guilty for neglecting my blog, for not writing back to my followers—but it took me a week to get over one anonymous hate message, and I've been too afraid that if I log in, I'll only find more abuse.

But now, alone in my bedroom, my need for distraction outweighs my fear. No, not distraction—connection. I need *someone*—someone anonymous. Someone who can't judge me. Or see me.

Or know me.

My follower count has risen to just over forty-eight thousand, but my messages have maxed out at five hundred. I take a deep breath, then scan through a few of them. There are some random compliments, and considerably more criticisms, but most of the messages are requests for advice. At the moment, I don't feel qualified to help anyone. So I start clicking Delete.

The first few times, I see the message counter on my dash going down: 499, 498, 497, and so on. But after I've deleted maybe a dozen messages, the number starts creeping back up. Could new messages really be coming in that fast?

I scroll down to the very bottom of my inbox and see six—no, seven new messages all time-stamped within the last minute. I click on the first one.

Anonymous: i guess 50,000 fans can't be wrong

I sit back against my headboard and stare at the screen. What does that mean? A vague sense of dread settles in, tightening my chest. I open the next:

Anonymous: but i think u just want attention

My nose begins to tingle, then my cheeks. I should just log out, but something about this message compels me to read the next.

Anonymous: get it while u can. cuz no one is going to love u once they find out
Anonymous: u. r. a. freak.

I want to be angry. I want to be furious, but instead, heat builds up behind my eyes, and I feel tears coming.

Unable to stop myself, I click the next message. And the next.

Anonymous: who wants to love a dickless sewn up faggot dyke tranny
Anonymous: why dont u just go to the bathroom right now
Anonymous: and take all ur pills and kill urself

I think of Gabi's bottles lined up neatly in the medicine cabinet. The first tears stream down my face.

Anonymous: u know u want to
Anonymous: so easy. easier than facing what u r

My chest heaves in a sob.

Enough. I click Delete. I erase the hateful messages one

by one, as quickly as I can. But new ones pop up, one after the other, piling up faster than I can click.

> Anonymous: ur school will be happy
> Anonymous: ur fake friends will be happy
> Anonymous: ur dad will be happy

Sobs shake my body. I pound at the keyboard, trying to stop the cascade of opening messages, but they just keep coming.

> Anonymous: no one will cry for
> Anonymous: poor.
> Anonymous: little.
> Anonymous: RILEY

The messages stop. I stare at the screen. At my name spelled out in all-capital letters.

My real name.

RILEY.

Unaware of what I'm doing, my whole face thrumming, tingling, numb, I dash to the bathroom. Hot bile rises in my throat. I open the tap, lean over the counter, and dry-heave into the basin as cold water runs down the back of my neck. All at once, the tingling in my face spreads like wildfire in a hot wind, head to chest to arms to toes. I try to take a deep breath, but my chest is too tight. My lungs won't expand. I can't breathe.

My heart pounds in my chest, stutters, pounds again. My vision goes dark at the corners.

poor.

little.

RILEY

A low moan rumbles up from inside me, and when it gets to my throat, it becomes a scream. Time and vision seem to fade and I feel myself thrashing, flailing, screaming in a void.

There's a distant crash, like a window breaking. A jolt of pain shoots through my hand and up my arm, and I hear my father's voice from the doorway.

"Riley, what's going on?"

I flinch back into reality as Dad crosses to the sink and grabs my arm. Without knowing it, I've put my fist through the bathroom mirror.

Red droplets fall from my knuckles to spatter the white marble basin and swirl pink down the drain. I look up at the mirror. From the place I struck it, a spider web of cracks spreads out like ripples on a frozen lake. A dozen dark reflections stare back at me.

And then my mother is in the room, enfolding me in her arms.

"What's the matter, Riley? What's wrong?"

I try to answer her, but I can't get the words out through my heaving, irregular breath.

Someone knows who I am.

CHAPTER 26

WHEN WE PULL UP AT Doctor Ann's office, I start to get out of the car, but Mom lays a hand on my arm. "Wait," she says. I glance back at her, and she looks . . . old. The lines around her eyes seemed to have deepened, and I spot a few gray hairs among the auburn ones. I wonder if it's stress from the election that's causing it, or if it's me. I close the door and settle back into my seat.

"Riley, I'm . . ." She pauses, reaching up as if she's about to chew on her cuticle—then realizes what she's doing and lets her hand drop into her lap. "Your father and I discussed it. You don't have to go to the fund-raiser Tuesday if you don't want to."

I whirl on her. "You think I punched a mirror to get out of going to the fund-raiser?"

"I don't know," she says. But she doesn't sound angry; she

sounds worried. I start to reply, but I can't think of what to say. Mom stares out the windshield. "When I married your father, I knew what I was getting into. The crazy schedule, the media." She lets out an ironic laugh. "I thought it would be romantic. It hasn't been all roses and bunny rabbits, but I love him. So I get through it." She glances at me, smiles sadly. "But you can't stand it, can you? All the events, and the attention, and the dressing up. You hate it."

I consider for a moment before replying. "I hate feeling like a liability."

My mother shakes her head. "That's . . ." She stops and folds her hands in her lap again. "You've never been a liability. You're more important to us than this election. Than anything."

I turn my head to glance out the window, and then she makes a weird sound—somewhere between a laugh and a sob—and I look back at her.

"Your father is better at this sort of thing," she says. "He's the one who has the way with words. I never know what to say to people. To you." She tucks her hair behind one ear. "I just feel everything, and then try to hold it in. Good manners, but not much courage." She looks at me. "I guess you're somewhere in the no-man's-land between."

My heart contracts as though it's being squeezed. I've always thought my mom was clueless about me—but what she just said is so . . . true. I wonder if she knows more than I think she does. Before I can say anything, she goes on.

"Riley, this . . . thing that you're going through. You can tell me about it. All right? You can just tell me. Sometime." She looks at me. Her mouth is a thin line. Her eyes are moist.

She's never been this open with me—it's moving, and a little frightening, too.

"I will," I say. "I will when I know what to say."

When Doctor Ann finally calls me into her office, she's seated in her usual chair, her legs crossed at the knee. I flop into one of the cow chairs.

"Sorry for making you work on a Sunday," I say.

"No one is *making* me work, Riley."

"Yeah, but when a congressman calls, you sort of have to come. Right?"

Doctor Ann's smile fades slightly. "Is this a test?"

"What do you mean?"

"Well," Doctor Ann says, dislodging a stray hair caught in her lipstick, "sometimes we test people. We want to make sure they care, and that we're safe with them. We want to find out what their motivations are so we can predict their behavior."

"So you think I don't trust you because you came in on a Sunday?"

"I think you want me to say I'm here for some other reason than it's my job."

I stare at her. "Are you this honest with your other patients?"

She blinks. "I'm this honest before my second cup of coffee." I let out a small laugh. She says, "You want to tell me what happened last night?"

I shift in my seat, and then suddenly the words just sort of blurt themselves out. "I got in a fight at the football game and then I went on a date with a girl."

Doctor Ann raises her eyebrows. "You went to a football game?"

I manage to smile—and then I tell her about last night. I start with Bec holding my hand as we walked into the stadium. I recount the fight with Vickers. I even talk about Bec's sister committing suicide—but I end the story there. When I'm finished, Doctor Ann remains quiet for a long time, just looking at me. I catch myself picking at the bandage on my hand, and I fold my arms.

Finally, she says, "Are you going to tell me the rest?"

"That wasn't enough?"

Doctor Ann takes off her glasses and begins cleaning them. "For some people, there's a delay between experiencing a stress trigger and having an anxiety reaction. They get in a car accident, and they're fine afterward. But then, three days later, safe and secure in their cubicle at work, they have a massive panic attack." She puts her glasses back on and regards me. "That's not you. Your episodes usually have an immediate trigger."

I take a long breath and let it out through my nose. Where do I even start?

"Did you hear about the trans girl in Oklahoma?" I ask. "The one whose father beat her up when she came out?"

Doctor Ann nods. "Andie Gingham."

"Yeah. Well, I'm . . ." I wrap my uninjured hand into a tight fist, willing the fingers not to go numb. "I'm Alix."

She frowns. "I'm sorry?"

"The journal blog you had me start? I go by Alix. I'm the one Andie reached out to online. The one who told her to have empathy for her abusive parents. The one she thanked in all those interviews."

Realization dawns slowly on Doctor Ann's face: first confusion, then understanding, and then I think I catch a hint of fear before she puts on her clinical face again. "I see."

And then I tell her everything.

I start with my first post and the overwhelming response it received, about Mike/Michelle featuring my blog on QueerAlliance.org. I describe that first hate-mail message—"your a fag"—and my seething reply. My advice to Andie, the subsequent news coverage, and the explosion of followers that resulted. In as much detail as I can remember, I tell her about the anonymous threats—and finally, about the stalker who identified me by name.

When I'm done, Doctor Ann walks over to her coffee-maker, pours herself a second cup, and then leans against the edge of her desk. "So. What are you thinking of doing?"

I blink. "What?"

"What are you thinking of doing?"

"About what?"

"About all of it."

I cock my head in disbelief. "That's what you're asking me? I tell you that someone knows all my secrets—that I have a real-life stalker—and you ask me in that casual fucking tone, 'What are you thinking of doing?'"

Doctor Ann's face remains impassive. She sips at her coffee. I want to yell at her. Slap her coffee cup out of her hand. Anything to get a reaction. But she just sits there, waiting me out. When the silence grows too uncomfortable, I clear my throat and speak.

"I don't know," I say. My voice cracks. "What do you think I should do?"

Doctor Ann looks down at her feet—something I've never seen her do before. I think she'll look up after a few seconds, but she doesn't. She just stares at her tan flats, gripping her coffee cup in one white-knuckled fist. After an uncomfortably long interval, just when I'm convinced she's going to stand up and dismiss me as a patient, she says quietly, "Have you ever shaken up a two-liter soda bottle?"

I open my mouth, close it again, then reply, "Yeah."

She looks up at me. "That's you. Right now. You're the bottle. And the world just keeps shaking you up. Move to a new school: shake, shake, shake. Kids harass you at lunch: shake, shake, shake. Get a threatening email: shake, shake, shake. All that pressure building up. You feel like you've got to let some of it out, or you'll explode. So, every now and then, you unscrew the cap, just a little. Just enough to let out some of that pressure. You ditch school. You yell at your parents. You punch a mirror." She shrugs. "But no matter how many times you vent, life keeps shaking you up. And eventually, if you don't take the cap all the way off and deal with the mess, that bottle is going to explode."

"What does that mean?" I ask.

"What do you think it means?"

"I hate it when you do this," I say, standing to pace behind my chair. "I mean, what are we even talking about? Are we talking about coming out?"

"You tell me."

A spike of fear drives its way into my chest, and I shake my head. "I'm not ready."

Doctor Ann considers me over the rims of her glasses. "You know how you're always telling me to stop asking you 'therapist questions' and give you actual advice?"

I stop pacing and grip the back of the chair. "Yeah."

"Talk to your parents about what you're going through."

"You mean come out to them?"

"I mean talk to them about what you're going through. Tell them how it is at school. What it's like for you to get dressed in the morning."

I shake my head. "No way. Not two weeks before the election. He'd have a stroke."

"You don't know that's true."

"Trust me."

"Okay. But what if this anonymous person outs you before you have the chance? Wouldn't that be worse?"

"I'll delete my blog. I'll just shut it down."

"You could," she says. "But after all that publicity from the Andie Gingham article, I don't know if that will make a difference. Besides," she says, uncrossing her legs and leaning toward me. "I don't think you want to delete your blog. I think you're proud of it. Proud of yourself for writing it." I blush furiously. Is she mocking me? But then Doctor Ann leans back in her chair and says, "I know *I'm* proud of you."

I turn even more red—but this time, it's from embarrassment instead of anger.

I swallow, then drop back into the chair. "So. What do I do?"

Doctor Ann lets out another sigh. "Every therapist dreads this question."

"What? Why?"

"Because if it goes horribly wrong, we feel responsible."

"You're not making me feel better right now."

"Okay, okay. Three things," she says, ticking them off on her fingers. "One. You prepare what you want to say. Write it down, get it clear. That part should be easy for you." I smile. "Two. Find the right time—not just before some big event, and not right after an argument. Pick a calm moment. Three, do it on neutral ground."

"What's neutral ground?"

"Not in public. Someplace you feel safe. We could even do it here, if you want."

I nod, then let out a long exhale. The feeling starts to come back to my fingers. "How will I know when I'm ready?"

Doctor Ann folds her hands, smiles. "You'll know."

CHAPTER 27

TUESDAY ARRIVES WITH THE KIND of merciless velocity usually reserved for the last week of summer. The election is only two weeks away, and tonight's dinner event is the most important of my dad's campaign, if not his career. All day long, there's a faint buzz of anxiety in the back of my head, but thanks to a slight alteration in my meds—not to mention the support of Solo and Bec, who stay in touch with me throughout the day by text—I'm holding it together. I even manage to pay attention in Precalc.

It helps that I haven't heard anything more from my anonymous stalker. Whoever it is, they're probably just trying to scare me. Maybe they hacked my account and discovered my real name—but that doesn't mean they know who I am. I did a little Googling and found literally dozens of Riley Cavanaughs in the US and Canada; the knowledge helps to calm my nerves.

Still, I'm not eager for more drama—so I avoid the cafeteria, taking refuge in Miss Crane's room instead. Solo and Bec join me, and the three of us chat with Miss Crane about books and anime while we eat.

On the way back to class, I'm walking past my locker when a glint of something silver on the door catches my eye. I stop to look, and a cold knot forms in my chest: someone has covered the lock with duct tape. I take a step closer. The combination dial has been removed entirely.

Someone broke into my locker.

I look around, suddenly convinced that I'm being watched—but the hall is empty. Everyone is still at lunch or in class. I turn back to my locker, peel off the tape, and open it.

A tangy, pungent odor wafts out as the door swings back on its hinges. Vinegar? I wonder if the kid with the locker next to mine has left his lunch bag in there too long. At first, nothing appears to be missing. I can see my textbooks in their usual haphazard pile. I reach in to grab my copy of *The Crucible* off the top, but withdraw my hand immediately when it touches something sticky. I wipe my hand on my hoodie, pull out my phone, and use it to illuminate the inside of the locker.

My books—all of them—are spattered with coagulated blood. I stagger back and cover my mouth with my hand—but when I look closer, the vinegar smell hits me again, and I realize it's not blood, but ketchup. There's a drizzle of something faintly golden, too—it looks like honey. The sides of my locker are dripping with it. I reach in and gingerly lift the cover of my French textbook: the pages are soaked, sticking together in clumps.

I stare at the stack of ruined books for a long moment, feeling my heart creep up into my throat, and the heat and pressure build behind my eyes. I won't let tears come. I won't. I start to close my locker, but stop when I notice that something is pasted on the inside of the door.

It's a sequence of cutout magazine letters spelling the words

POOR LITTLE RILEY

My pulse pounds in my throat. I want to throw up. I want to scream, but nothing comes out. I look around to see if anyone is watching, and then—I'm not sure why I do it—I cross the hall and drag a trash can toward my locker. Pulling down the sleeve of my hoodie to cover my hand like a mitten, I reach in and slide the stack of books into the trash can. They hit the bottom with a thump, stirring up a cloud of tiny insects. Then I turn to the inside of the locker door and scratch at the edges of the pasted-on letters until they peel away. I drop the shreds of paper into the trash, then pull off my hoodie and drop it on top, concealing everything.

I stare blankly into the trash can as the buzzing in my head swells, drowning out all other sounds. I had thought—no, *hoped*—that my stalker might just be some random stranger on the internet, trying to scare me. But this proves that's not true. The stalker is here, at my school. And they know exactly who I am.

The bell rings, and I flinch so hard that I let out a grunt of surprise. Students start to flood the hallway. Hastily, I slam my locker shut and drag the trash can back into place, leaving it next to the restroom door.

Then I go inside, lock myself in a stall, and vomit.

It's an hour before we're supposed to leave for the fund-raiser. I'm standing in front of my closet, fighting the heaviest bout of dysphoria I've ever experienced. My whole body feels fake. My stomach roils with nausea. My palms sweat.

I can still smell the tang of vinegar, still see the cut-out letters. I shake my head hard, but it has no effect. I slap my face, like you do when you're falling asleep behind the wheel. It hurts, but it helps.

I stare at the outfit my mother chose as it hangs there in the closet. Finally, I work up the courage to put it on. I do it as quickly as I can, just trying to get it over with. Once I'm dressed, I stand in front of the brand-new bathroom mirror and force myself to look into it. I open the mirrored medicine cabinet just so, spilling an infinite trail of my own reflections deep into the glass. I stare at them, hoping that, like a word repeated over and over, my image will lose its meaning if I look long enough.

"Riley?"

I flinch and turn. It's my father.

"Sorry," he says, laughing a little. "I didn't mean to startle you." He holds out his hand: he's got three oblong tablets cupped in his palm. "Doctor Ann said you could have three tonight. If you want them." He bounces the pills in his hand like they're peanuts and we're at a ball game. I look at his face, and I see genuine discomfort in his eyes. "Listen," he says, looking away, "Mom told me what you said, and I . . . well, I wanted to thank you."

I cock my head. "Thank me for what?"

"I know that you . . . dislike these events. I know they're hard for you, with the anxiety, and . . . everything." He clears his throat. "And I appreciate you going. Not just for appearances, you know, but because it's nice to have you there. Supporting your dad." He shrugs. "That's all."

His lip trembles slightly. I've never heard him fumble for words like this—and for the first time, I'm ready to tell him. Right now. Ready to tell him how I feel in these clothes. How I long to be "one of the guys" with Solo, and how I want Bec to want me. I'm ready to tell him about Sierra calling me "it," and Vickers asking, "Is that the new tranny?" About the blood—no, it was *ketchup*—all over my books. The message in my locker. The stalker who knows my name.

I've been carrying around this pressure inside me for so long—not just since I started at Park Hills, or even since I got out of Pineview—but maybe since I was six years old. And after everything that's happened in the past few weeks, it's become too much. I want to let it go. I need to let it go. I need my parents to know who I am.

I'm ready to come out.

But then I look at my dad, and I see how the lines on his forehead have deepened, and the gray in his hair is no longer confined to his temples. Under his eyes, I see the dark semicircles he tries so hard to hide from the cameras.

In an hour, he'll be walking into a ballroom full of those cameras, and I'll be right behind him. So no, maybe now isn't the time. I'll tell him after the event. Tonight, when we get home.

I'll tell them both.

I hold out my hand. He tips the tablets into my palm, and I swallow them.

I'm silent in the limousine, just staring out the window and taking deep Doctor Ann breaths. My dad keeps shooting me worried looks. He thinks I don't notice, but I do. My mother, on the other hand, makes no attempt to hide her concern. Every few minutes, she glances over her shoulder to check on me. At one point, she says, "How are you feeling, honey?"

I force a brief smile. "I'll be fine once we're seated."

The Grand Entrance is always the worst for me. These fund-raisers are basically extravagant dinner parties that the candidate throws for himself, pretending the whole time that it was his supporters' idea, as though he and his staff haven't spent the last month deciding on the menu and tweaking the seating arrangements. For the sake of theatrical tension, the candidate and his family have to arrive fashionably late—which means we're always paraded through a crowded hotel ballroom amid camera flashes and deafening applause. In short, even without the dysphoria, it is a perfect storm of anxiety triggers. Which is why Doctor Ann upped my dosage for the evening. Xanax doesn't really make me feel less anxious, per se. It just makes me care less about feeling anxious. Like I'm distant from it. Like I'm watching some other Riley *down there* fend off an impending attack.

The limo pulls up in back of the hotel and a valet opens

the door for me. I step out and follow my parents up a short flight of steps, through a steel door, and into a service corridor. Dad's staff surrounds us now, Shelly's heels clicking on the white tile, Elias reaching up to adjust the radio mic clipped to his lapel. He flashes a big smile and says something to me, but I don't hear. I just nod.

They lead us through the kitchen, weaving among rows of tall stainless steel shelves and huge gas stovetops. Vaguely, I think how this is the part of politics they glamorize on TV. In real life, it just smells like frying grease and restaurant trash.

We're at the ballroom door, and Mom turns to face me for what she calls "last looks." She fixes an errant strand of my hair, then tries in vain to smooth a wrinkle in my clothes. "Are you ready?" she says.

I look at her. Somewhere in the distance, I can feel my heart beating against my breastbone. With a stifled laugh, I imagine it shattering my sternum and skittering across the rubber kitchen mat to freedom. I say a silent thank-you to the one and a half milligrams of Xanax roaring through my bloodstream.

"I'm ready," I say.

The PA system in the ballroom squeals to life and a muffled voice announces us. Then the doors open, and I'm ushered into the chaos of flashing lights and loud cheers. Elias is behind me, making sure I won't fall as we mount the steps to the stage so Dad can introduce his family and say a few words before dinner is served.

As I cross the stage behind my father, I feel 350 heads turn in our direction, and I'm suddenly aware that I don't know how to walk. My legs wobble, my knees twinge. I look down at my feet, stumble, and fall forward.

Elias catches me, but not before an audible gasp rises from the crowd. My father turns to look, his face a mixture of concern and embarrassment, as Elias pulls me to my feet. My mother takes a step toward me. I raise my hands to show I'm fine.

I turn to the audience and murmur, "So much for that gymnastics scholarship." One of the microphones on the podium picks up my voice, amplifying it, bouncing it off the silk-papered walls and into the ears of the constituents packed into the room. At first, there's a lull, and then an old woman in the back lets out a high-pitched cackle. A moment later, the room erupts in laughter and applause, and I take an ironic bow.

By dessert, the Xanax is starting to wear off, but it's okay. The hard part is over, and now all I have to do is nod and smile and pretend to eat the brick-sized wedge of gelatinous dairy products they've placed before me. My mom sees me pushing the cheesecake around with my fork and produces a square of dark chocolate from her purse. I take it gratefully, and she smiles.

After a while, someone announces my father, and he excuses himself to go up to the podium for his speech. I hear myself wish him good luck.

When he's finished, the audience bursts into applause and cheers. The noise is pretty bad, and I wish I could cover my ears, but I know if I just smile and clap along I'll be safe in the car in a few minutes.

My mom mouths, "Are you okay?"

I nod and smile.

And then it's over, and Elias and Shelly are leading us out the way we came in, through the ballroom and into the kitchen. It's less crowded here; my heartbeat slows. We weave through the stainless steel maze and into the service corridor. Just a few more steps, and we'll be at the car. My breathing becomes steadier, and I let out a relieved laugh; I'm going to make it. The hard part is over. We turn right down the hall, and then we're at the exit. Elias reaches for the door.

It opens to a burst of light as bright as a nuclear explosion. I throw up my hands to shield my face. The snap of camera shutters and the click of shoes on concrete crescendos into a wall of sound, mixing with the shouting voices of the crowd of reporters before us, making their words indistinguishable.

I'm used to being intercepted by media after an event, but the energy here is too frenetic, too high-pitched, like a pack of coyotes descending on their prey.

Something is wrong.

Elias steps in front of me, spreading his arms like a fence.

My father raises his hands. "Okay, everybody, please step back and give my family some room."

A tall blond woman elbows her way to the front and thrusts a microphone in my father's face.

"Congressman Cavanaugh! How will this revelation affect your campaign for reelection?"

But before my father can answer, a man in a gray suit calls out, "How will your conservative constituents respond?"

And then they're all pushing forward, calling our names and shouting questions, an undulating swarm of faces and microphones.

"Congressman Cavanaugh!"

"How long have you known about Riley?"

"Do you support your child's lifestyle choices?"

I glance at my father. His mouth hangs open slightly, his face a mask of confusion. Elias grabs me and shoves me between my parents, then moves in front to clear a path toward the car. We take a few steps, but the crowd of reporters only presses in closer.

And then a small woman in a pink suit breaks through the line and points her microphone at me.

"Riley," she says, "how did your parents react when you told them about your gender identity?"

CHAPTER 28

ONCE WE'RE OUT of the hotel parking lot, I expect my father to begin the interrogation; but he just looks at me and says, "We'll talk about this when we get home."

By the time we turn onto our street, it's clogged with reporters and news vans. Elias clears a path through, inching along in his SUV, and we follow behind in the limousine until we reach our driveway. And then we're out of the car and fighting through another mob of media people. Finally, Elias shoves us through the front door and slams it behind us. The doorbell rings twice, and someone pounds on the door—and then I hear Elias's raised voice, and the pounding stops.

We stand in the dark foyer, frozen, waiting for the tumult outside to subside. I stare at the floor, avoiding eye contact with my parents as Elias clears the media people off the front steps and urges them to leave the property. We listen as the voices recede. Two news vans start up and drive away.

Finally, Elias pokes his head through the door. "They're clearing out."

"Thank you, Elias," my father says.

"You should probably stay inside tonight. Call if you need anything."

My father nods, and Elias closes the door.

And then it's just the three of us, standing in the unlit house. I still can't bring myself to look at either of my parents, so I just stare at the tile and try to breathe. I'm grateful when my mother puts a hand on my shoulder and then turns on the hallway light.

"Let's sit down," she says. She turns and moves back toward the family room, and we follow.

I sit down on the long, brown couch. My mom sits next to me, leaving a small but noticeable gap between us. My father drops into the big chair opposite.

Dad exhales, loosens his tie, and yanks it off. "Riley," he says, "what were they talking about out there?"

I don't reply.

He folds his tie in half, then in quarters. "You've got to talk to us."

This is not how the conversation is supposed to go. This is not happening on neutral ground, I do not feel safe or calm, and this is not the plan I made with Doctor Ann. It's not fair. I feel tears welling up, but I force them back. I want another Xanax. I want this to be over. I wish I could just push the forward button and skip past this part like a bad commercial.

But I can't. It has to be now.

My mouth is dry, and when I speak, my voice sounds like someone else's. "I'm . . ." The words feel foreign and unwieldy. I force them out anyway. "I'm gender fluid."

There is no response. Not a gasp or a clearing of the throat. Only silence.

Not knowing what else to do, I say it again. "I'm gender fluid."

My mother shifts in her seat. "Does that mean . . ." Her voice breaks, and when she speaks again, her voice is gentler. "You're gay?"

I shake my head, searching for a better way to tell her. "No. It means that I . . . It's like—most people wake up, and they know who they are. Like you know you're a woman. You feel that way, you *feel* like one. It makes sense to you."

She blinks at me as though I'm speaking a foreign language.

"I'm sorry," I say. Tears of frustration blur my vision, and I wipe them away. "I had this all worked out, how to say this, but it just sort of . . ." I open my hands. They're on fire with pins and needles. I suck in a breath. "Gender fluid means that sometimes I feel like I'm a girl. And sometimes I feel like I'm a boy. So the . . ." I trail off.

It's quiet for a long time. Finally, I glance up at my mom. She's looking past me at some unseen spot on the wall. "Oh," she says. Her tone is polite, distant. "So it's . . . you're transsexual."

I hear a thin vein of contempt in that last word, and it sends a jolt through my heart. Mom reads my reaction and shakes her head. She opens her mouth to say something, but nothing comes out.

"No," I say. "It's like that, but it's more complicated."

Slowly, terrified of what I might see on his face, but knowing I have to look, I turn to my father.

His jaw is set, his cheeks white. "How long have you known?"

"I figured it out last year," I say, the words flowing more easily now. As though they need to come out. "Right before that big dinner, do you remember? I locked myself in my room?"

Recognition dawns on his face. My heart leaps; he understands.

"But I guess I always knew something was different. I just didn't have a word for it."

Dad nods.

"But I don't understand," my mother says, glancing at my father and turning back to me. "How did the media find out before we did?"

I try to swallow, but my throat is too tight. I glance back at my father, hoping he'll intervene on my behalf, but he only looks at me expectantly. I moisten my lips.

"I started a—a blog. It was anonymous, and then . . ."

I fall silent as my father stands abruptly. His face is crimson, the vein in his temple pulsing. He opens and closes his mouth like a fish out of water, but he can't seem to speak.

My mother cuts in, her voice shaking. "You put this on the internet?"

"I didn't—I used a fake name, but somebody figured out—"

"Well of course they figured it out!" My dad's voice, almost a bellow. "I'm a United States congressman running for reelection, Riley. For Christ's sake, you don't think there are people trying to dig up dirt on my family?" His eyes are wild, the cords in his neck tight with anger.

Trying to dig up *dirt*?

I swallow. "Dad, I'm so sorry. I never meant for this to—"

"One month out of Pineview, Riley. We're not even through dealing with *that* mess, now you want to broadcast your bisexual phase on the goddamn internet?"

The moment the words are out, his face goes pale. He looks at Mom, then back at me. He swallows. When he speaks again, his voice is low and tremulous. "Riley," he says. "I didn't mean—"

But I don't care. I stand up, shaking with rage. "You think I don't feel the pressure of your campaign every minute of every day? You think I don't know I'm just a PR problem to you? I changed schools for you. I wear *this* for you. I hide who I am for you. I go to the doctor and take the right pills and I did not broadcast this! I shared myself anonymously, and somebody fucking outed me!"

I stand there, trembling, out of my body. My heart is in my throat. It's going to explode. My father glares at me, his mouth tight, his eyes wide and red. I turn my glare on my mother so suddenly that she flinches.

I drag my arm across my eyes, sniff, and turn back to my father. "And this is not a *phase*, Congressman. This is who I am."

I turn and run for the front door, grabbing Mom's keys

from the bowl on the hall table as I pass. I hear voices behind me, calling me back, commanding me not to leave the house, but I don't care. I tear open the front door, climb into the mini-van, and peel out into the darkness.

CHAPTER 29

I JUST DRIVE.

My body is on fire with tingling. My chest is tight, my vision so severely tunneled it's like looking through the wrong end of a telescope. I can't tell if I'm going five miles per hour or fifty.

They know. *Everyone* knows. My father . . . I still hear the rage in his voice; I feel it in my body like a physical blow. A punch to the gut, knocking the wind out of me.

So I just drive.

I drive without thinking, tearing west down Imperial Highway. Over the train tracks. Toward Bec? I don't know. I reach into the cup holder where I stash my phone, thinking I'll call her, call someone—but my phone isn't there. I've left it at home. I don't even have my ID.

The lights are out at Bullet Hole, and it's quiet in the parking lot. I rattle the door; it's locked. I look around for something to break the glass, and then I realize how stupid that is—there's no one inside anyway. I run back to the minivan.

The clock on the dash reads ten minutes to midnight. It's Tuesday. Of course Bec isn't here; she's at home. And she's probably asleep—but I have nowhere else to go. I pull back onto Imperial and speed toward her house.

The streetlights on her block are still out, and her house is dark when I pull up. There's an old green pickup in the driveway. Erik's? I don't know. I reach for the keys to turn off the van, thinking I'll get out and go knock on Bec's window—and that's when the truck in the driveway roars to life. I flinch at the growl of the engine. A single headlight illuminates the garage door in a splash of orange.

"Hey!" a voice shouts from inside the truck.

Panic surges through me.

I peel out from the curb, make a sharp right, and step on the accelerator. I'm barreling the other way down Imperial now, pedal to the floor, not knowing where I'm going, not caring. The streets are almost empty; I pass no one. I check the rearview, looking for the truck—but I only spot one headlight, maybe a motorcycle, far behind me.

The buzzing in my head grows louder. My ears fill with the sound of static, like rushing water; the panic rises. And rising with it, a cold feeling in the pit of my stomach—a low, hopeless knowing: whatever I was hiding, whatever I was protecting, it doesn't matter now.

The tires thump as the minivan crosses the train tracks again. I think of Andie Gingham—

And suddenly, it's so clear to me why she wanted to jump.

The water seems to envelop me, rising to my mouth. I'm breathing in shallow, ragged gasps. Frantically, I roll down the window to try to get some air. The buzz of the engine echoes against the concrete freeway underpass. My body thrums with electric tingles. My vision blurs. I have to do something. I have to go somewhere.

At some point, I turn. I pass the old hardware store. I pass the closed furniture showroom with the painted message: EVERYTHING IS GONE.

I'm not even sure what I'm doing when I pull up behind the crumbling, windowless three-story building—the movie-night spot where Bec used to come with Gabi before the foot-ball crowd took it over—I just shut off the van and get out. A stiff autumn wind picks up, scattering the dead leaves piled against the Dumpster, then swelling to a gust that rattles the rickety fire escape.

The parking lot is deserted. There's no flickering glow from the courtyard. There's no Bec; there's no one at all. I'm alone.

I think of my dad's hands, folding his tie in on itself. The gap my mother left between us on the couch. I hear blood pumping past my ears. A fresh wave of cold tingles washes over me. I shake my head. I can't think about this. I have to do something.

Anything.

I glance up. Overhead, the sodium street lamp blinks intermittently, and I see the glint of new metal against the rusting frame of the fire escape. The ladder has been retracted, and someone has wrapped a brand-new steel chain around it, locking it in place, far out of reach.

And suddenly, I want to get on that roof. I *need* to get on that roof. I walk over to the Dumpster and start to drag it toward the ladder—but it stops short, jarring my arms almost out of their sockets; it's chained up, too. I look around for something else to stand on—a milk crate, a pallet, anything— but there's nothing.

Panic rises in me like cold bile, threatening to drown me.

I run back to the van, climb in, and start the engine. I inch toward the building until bumper touches brick, then shut off the motor and get out.

Heart pounding, I climb up the van's shallow hood and reach for the ladder. It's still three feet above my head. I take a deep breath, bend my knees, and jump.

My fingers barely brush the cracked and rusty surface of the lower rung, and then I fall. My foot comes down at an angle and I slip, falling sideways, my hip slamming into the hood just before my head knocks against the windshield.

My vision goes black.

When I come to, I hear laughter. The sound of an old engine idling. Doors opening and closing. Heavy doors. The truck from Bec's driveway—it must have followed me here. I open my eyes, and I'm blinded by a flood of orange light.

A voice says, "Look who it is."

I squint. My vision is blurry, but I see two, maybe three silhouettes moving toward me, casting long, low shadows in the throw of a single headlight.

"Looking for your girlfriend, you queer fuck?"

My stomach clenches; I recognize that voice. I raise a hand to shield my eyes from the light. There are three of them. A broad-shouldered guy with stringy hair stands closest to me. Next to him is a smaller kid. The glare of the headlight casts an auburn halo around his head and whites out the lenses of his wire-rim glasses. Behind them, lingering close to the truck, is the tallest of the three. I see him in silhouette, his arm posed at an awkwardly formal angle.

"I asked you a question," he says. He steps into the spill of the headlight, and I see that his arm is in a cast. Panic grips me.

It's Jim Vickers.

I try to swallow, but my throat is dry. Maybe they just came here to drink. Maybe they'll only harass me, and then let me leave.

"I'll . . . I'll just go." I turn, intending to roll off the hood and put the van between them and me.

"Wait up," Vickers says, his voice eerily gentle—and then a hand grabs my ankle. My heart spasms in my chest. I roll onto my stomach, trying to pull myself away, but he yanks on my foot, pulling me back toward him. My fingers grip the gap between the hood and the side of the car. I can't let him trap me. I have to get free.

Vickers grunts, yanks harder on my leg. One hand slips, but I regain my grip. "Cole," Vickers says. "Help me out."

I feel a hand grab my other ankle. I struggle to kick, but the hands are too strong.

"Oh, come on," Vickers says, almost laughing. They pull hard, and my palms make a squeaking noise as I'm dragged backward across the hood. My toes touch asphalt, and then someone slams my face down on the warm metal, bending me over the hood.

"You have the right to remain silent," the long-haired one says. There's laughter. I struggle to stand, but the hands push me back down.

"Hurry up, you guys," a third voice says. "I don't want to get caught."

"Shut up, Grady," Vickers says. "Anybody want to take bets on what we got here? I got ten bucks on chick."

"That thing is too ugly to have a pussy."

Another laugh. Then Vickers says, "One way to find out."

I feel a hand grip my upper thigh, and I scream. Another hand covers my mouth. I thrash on the hood, kicking wildly.

"Grady, get over here."

The third boy moves forward.

"Pin the arms."

My arms are pulled apart and pinned so that I'm spread-eagled on the hood. Someone takes a fistful of my hair.

And then his face is against my neck. His dry lips on my skin. His breath reeking of beer.

He whispers, "Not so tough now, are you? Fucking freak." My head is slammed against the hood again. Stars pop in my vision. I feel my body slacken.

He presses against me harder. Stubble abrading my cheek, foul breath in my face. His hand grips my thigh, then moves up to reach between my legs.

"What do you got down here, huh? What do you got for me?"

I find just one word. "Please," I say. My voice sounds weak, thin. "Please."

He turns his head. "Kill the lights."

Someone lets go of my arm, but I don't thrash. I don't cry out. I just hold still. The headlight goes out.

His thumb hooks the waistband of my underwear.

I feel the cool night air against my skin. I focus on the smooth, warm metal beneath my cheek. I stare at the windshield, watching the reflection of the flickering sodium lamp appear and disappear.

And then, all at once, everything lights up. *Camera flashes*, I think, vaguely. *They've come to take pictures.*

But the light doesn't fade.

And then he's off me. The hands release me, and I hear footsteps moving away. Doors slamming, the truck reversing, then peeling out on the crumbling asphalt. I want to move, but my whole body is numb. I just stay there for a moment, spread across the hood, and then I feel my shoulders start to shake. But it's not me crying. It's some other Riley. I roll onto my side and slide down the side of the van to the pavement.

And then a huge hand touches my shoulder. And I scream.

"Riley, it's okay. It's okay." It's Solo's voice.

I look up. Solo and Bec are standing over me.

"You're going to be okay."

CHAPTER 30

I SIT IN THE PASSENGER seat of Solo's car with my arms wrapped around my knees. Bec tries to hold my hand from the backseat, but I don't want to stop hugging my legs. Solo tells me they're taking me to Park Hills Community Hospital.

I thought there was a special place at hospitals for things like this. There isn't; I sit in the waiting room at the ER. Solo talks to the woman behind the counter, and Bec holds my hand. There's an old man with an oxygen tank sitting across from me. Against the far wall, a baby is screaming. A woman in a brown sweater tries to make it stop. I let go of Bec's hand to cover my ears, and I close my eyes.

I'm in a big room with ten other beds. I'm concealed from the other patients by a thin blue curtain—but the random shadows moving beyond it only make me feel more exposed. Finally, the curtain is pulled aside and a tall woman enters. She has a long, dark ponytail and a red blouse under her white coat. She tells me her name, Dr. Amala, and asks permission to examine me. I feel myself nod. She pulls on a pair of blue silicone gloves.

She frowns as she works, as though she's cleaning up an unpleasant mess.

My mother arrives before the police. I don't want to see her.

Officer Dinning is polite and gentle, but it doesn't matter. I hardly feel anything. I feel like a mannequin, like the parts being poked and prodded and inspected don't even belong to me.

I have to lie down for the swabs. My stomach cramps.

I'm okay until the police officer starts taking photographs. When the first flash goes off, I flinch hard, knocking the exam kit off the metal cart and scattering its contents on the floor.

Doctor Amala recites some soothing phrases. A nurse heaves an exasperated sigh as she collects the spilled contents and hurries off to get a fresh exam kit.

Officer Dinning waits while I regain my composure. "You okay?"

I nod, but I keep my eyes closed for the rest of the photos.

I think I talk to my mother. I don't remember what we say.

Finally, they offer me something to make me sleep. I take it.

I hear my father's voice, and I open my eyes. He's leaning over me, his face puffy. When our eyes meet, he lets out a breath as if he's been holding it for a long time. He squeezes my hand, but says nothing. I drift back to sleep.

When I wake again, I'm in a different part of the hospital. The lights are off and the room is empty. There's a window, but the blinds are drawn. I can hear the hum of machines and the sound of arguing voices in the hallway. I try to sit up, but a sharp pain in my abdomen stops me—so I lie back and fish around for the bed's controls. I find the remote and raise the bed until I'm in a sitting position. My head aches, and I reach up to inspect my face. There's a big square bandage on my left temple and another on my cheek. My lips are chapped, my tongue thick. I turn my head to look for water and realize my whole *head* is thick. Whatever they gave me to put me to sleep has left me extremely groggy.

There's a plastic cup on the table next to the bed. I reach for it and miss, knocking it to the floor with a clatter. The door opens and my father and a nurse rush into the room. I squint as the lights come on.

My dad leans over me and takes my hand while the nurse pours me another cup of water, which I sip through a straw.

"Hey, Riley," Dad says.

I can't look at him.

"I'll be right outside if you need anything," the nurse says, then leaves, closing the door behind her.

"How are you feeling?" my father asks.

I start to answer, but I can't find words. I shrug. He nods.

"Your mother is here," he says. "She's sedated. When we heard, she—well, we both . . ." His face goes hard. "Jason Solomona spoke with the police. They told us what happened. I mean, everything they could." Dad frowns, shakes his head. "Riley, I'm so sorry."

I want to nod. To say, "It's okay." I *expect* myself to. But something stops me, and I just look at him and take another sip of water. His eyes sadden, then go dull.

"What can I do for you?" he asks. It comes out a whisper, almost a prayer. I've never heard my dad's voice sound like that—weak, almost helpless. Anger courses through me, heating my face and making my whole head throb. What right does he have to be weak? To not know what to do?

But I can't say any of this. Not out loud. So I just shake my head and close my eyes. After a while, a nurse comes in to give me another sedative.

When I wake the next day, the grogginess is gone, but I'm sore all over. My head throbs, my legs ache, and there's a deep heat in my abdomen, as though I've swallowed a burning coal.

I open my eyes, blink, and then my mother is at my side, straightening my blankets and brushing hair from my forehead and fluffing my pillow and a hundred other things at once, the rustle of her clothing like the flapping of moths' wings. It doesn't feel like care, it feels like correcting, as though I should have straightened the blankets myself before she came, and fixed my own hair, made myself presentable so she wouldn't have to see me like this. As she pulls away to look at me, she fixes me with a soft expression of compassion and remorse, and I suppress a sudden urge to reach up and slap her.

She leans forward and presses her lips to my forehead. It's

how she used to tell whether I had a fever when I was little.
Now her lips feel cold and foreign on my skin, and I just hold
still until she's done. When she sits back, her expression hasn't
changed, but something underneath is gone. The look is somehow emptier.

"How are you feeling, honey?" she asks.

"Okay," I say, fishing for the remote. Mom finds it first and
offers it to me. I snatch it away with more force than I intend.

She flinches. "I'm so sorry I wasn't here when you woke
up."

I shrug. "I don't remember it, anyway. I was too doped up."

She smiles. I bite back the urge to tell her it's a lie. "Do you
have my phone?"

She shakes her head. "I'm sorry, in the rush to get here, we
just . . ." Then, off my look of disappointment, "I'll have your
father bring it."

I nod. "Are Bec and Solo still here?"

"Solo stayed until three, but we finally persuaded him to
go home and get some sleep. He promised he'd come back
today."

I nod. "What about Bec?"

She shakes her head. "I'm sorry, honey. I haven't seen her.
But they weren't letting any visitors in, just family. I'm sure
she'll be here later."

I nod, but I'm not sure at all. Something about the way
Bec acted when we got to the hospital, the way she avoided my
eyes, makes me think she won't come.

"Can I have some more water?" I say. Mom smiles and
refills my cup, and then we talk. Not about me, or about what

happened, or about anything important. We talk about hospital food, and how it rained last night for the first time since June, and she promises to bring my laptop and some Blu-rays since I'll probably be here for one more night. It's all so fake I can hardly stand it, like taking a bite of rice and finding that your mouth is full of hot plastic. I just want to spit it all out, to throw it up and scream at her.

And then she looks at me, and her face sort of contorts, as if someone is stabbing her. And I don't know if it's for me, or for her, or just because she can't hold in everything she's feeling for another moment. But for that split second, she's my mom again. Like before the election. Before Pineview. Before everything. And I stop talking. And she smiles at me. And I start to sob.

She comes to me, and I drop my water cup on the bed and just let the tears come. She wraps her arms around me, and I feel the tepid water spreading out on the blanket, wetting my leg and soaking through her sweater. I feel her powdered cheek against mine, her earring pressing into my face. The sobbing goes up and up until it becomes a frantic shuddering, and before I know it, a nurse is pulling us apart and injecting something into my IV, and the world goes fuzzy, then white.

I wake up again in the late afternoon. Mom is scrunched up in a plastic chair, fast asleep with her head cocked uncomfortably to one side. When my dad sees that my eyes are open, he nudges her and they pull their chairs up next to the bed.

"You slept for a long time," Mom says.

"Must be good stuff they're piping in," Dad says. He leans in as if to disconnect my IV. "Can I have a hit?"

I don't feel like smiling, but I try. The effect on my parents is palpable. My mom lets out a little laugh-sob and covers her mouth. My dad's shoulders relax.

"How are you feeling?" he says.

"I feel like if someone asks me that one more time, I'm going to start throwing things."

My parents look at each other. My mother licks her lips, and my dad clears his throat. "Riley, we want you to know that—"

I cut them off. "Can we not . . . not right now? Not in here?"

My mom's face falls. My dad looks relieved.

"Okay," Dad says. "Yeah, of course." He glances at the door. "Riley," he says. "The police want to take a statement."

"No," I say.

"Riley, sweetheart, the longer you wait, the more chance they'll—"

"No!" It's almost a shout.

Mom puts a hand on Dad's knee. "Okay, honey," she says. "Not till you're ready."

"Thank you."

Dad glances at the door. "I don't know if you're up for visitors, but Jason Solomona is out there waiting to see you. If you're ready."

"Yeah. I want to see Solo." I run a hand through my hair and touch the bandage on my cheek. I turn to Mom. "Mom, can you . . ."

"Of course, honey."

Dad leaves, and Mom grabs a handful of paper towels from the bathroom, wets them, and wipes my face. After fidgeting with my hair for a few minutes, she shrugs and smiles as if to say it's hopeless. She helps me adjust the bed to a sitting position, gives me a cherry-flavored antacid from her purse, and kisses my forehead again before leaving and closing the door behind her.

Solo peeks his head into the room and looks around. When his eyes land on me, they widen for just a second, and then he recovers himself and pushes open the door. He's carrying a brown shopping bag.

"Okay if I come in?" he asks.

"Yeah. But can you turn off some of the lights?"

Solo finds the switches and flips off one bank of fluorescents. "Better?"

"Yeah, thanks."

He pulls up one of the chairs, sets down the shopping bag, and puts his elbows on the bed. I flinch a little, and he withdraws.

"Sorry," he says, his face going pale.

"No, it's okay. I'm just twitchy today."

Gingerly, he leans against the bed again, and this time I don't flinch. He starts to say something, but I cut him off.

"Please don't ask how I'm feeling."

He digs into his pocket. "Actually, I was going to ask if you want a Starburst." He holds up a fistful of pink candies and flashes me his goofiest grin.

"Yeah," I say.

There's an uncomfortable silence as the two of us chew our Starbursts. Finally, I break it.

"Did Bec come with you?"

Solo starts to speak, then stops and shakes his head.

"What's wrong?"

"Last night, after they admitted you, she . . . she said she was sorry, and that she had to go."

"Have you talked to her today?"

"I've called her and texted her about a million times. She's not answering." He shrugs. "I don't know what's going on. Maybe it was all just too intense for her. I mean . . ." He trails off, looking embarrassed.

A cold, gray ache creeps into my head. *She's disgusted.* That's the thought that comes into my mind. I know it's probably wrong, but I think it anyway. *She knows what happened, and she's disgusted by me.*

"I don't want to talk about it." I say it suddenly, and more fiercely than I intended.

Solo's eyebrows go up. "Okay." He shifts in his chair, then glances around the room as if inspecting it. "I just came to make sure the hospital kitchen is meeting your culinary needs as a vegan."

I roll my eyes. "I don't think the hospital kitchen is meeting anyone's culinary needs."

Solo laughs, then reaches into his shopping bag and pulls out a stack of DVDs. "I have all the *Harry Potters*, the first four discs of *Battlestar Galactica*, and season seven of *Doctor Who*."

"What, no *Star Wars*?"

Solo sighs. "I wanted to bring the original, unaltered *Episode IV*, in which my namesake shoots first, as our Lord and savior intended."

"Why didn't you?"

"I only have it on VHS, and my dad's old VHS player broke halfway through the summer."

"Well, I've never watched *Doctor Who*."

Solo drops his jaw, then covers his mouth in mock concern, as though I've just told him I have a terminal disease. "We're going to get through this," he says, laying one big hand on my arm.

I know he's joking about me not having watched *Doctor Who*, but it sort of lands on me wrong—and all of I sudden I'm crying again. I pull my arm away and cover my face.

Solo doesn't touch me, but he leans in close. He speaks softly, but his voice isn't pitying or sad; it's just matter-of-fact. "I think this is going to happen for a while," he says. "Things making you cry for no reason. There's nothing wrong with it. My mom says crying is just your body expelling all the bad stuff. Like a sneeze. Like your soul sneezing."

And just like that, my sobs turn into laughter. It's a sort of horrible, hysterical laughter, but it's better than crying.

"Soul . . . Soul Sneeze . . . ," I say, gasping for air, "is the name of my new punk band."

We eat roughly a metric ton of Starbursts and watch five straight episodes of *Doctor Who*. Dad comes in after an hour and tells me he has to leave, but that he'll be back before dinner. I tell Mom she can go with him, but she insists on staying. She doesn't come in, though. She sits in the waiting room, "catching up on her magazine reading."

I text Bec, but she doesn't reply.

When dinner comes, Dad pops in to say hi, then leaves us alone again. Before he closes the door, he gives Solo this look that makes it completely obvious that he now thinks Solo is my boyfriend. I wonder silently if my parents will ever understand anything. Nurses come in twice to give me meds and check my vitals. Solo eats my Jell-O.

Finally, a nurse comes in and tells him he has ten more minutes before visiting hours are over. When the door shuts behind her, Solo turns to me, his eyes serious.

"I want to say something," he says.

I say, "Okay," but I'm not sure I want to hear it.

Solo glances at his lap and presses his lips together, like he does when he's playing video games, then looks up at me. "I'm sorry for what I said."

I frown, confused. "What you said about what?"

"Back at the Reagan Years." His voice is deeper than usual. "I told you that you—that you *invited* it. By the way you dress. Remember? I told you that you were asking for a fight. Inviting people to . . ." He clears his throat. "And I want you to know . . . that's bullshit. And it was not okay to say that."

I look at him. His face, usually cheerful—even goofy—is now grim. "Thank you," I say. "For saying that. And for being here."

Solo smiles. Then he reaches into the shopping bag at his feet. When he comes up again, he's holding a furry brown bundle. For a moment, I think he's brought an animal into the hospital—and then I realize what it is: his Chewbacca back-pack.

"I want you to have this," he says, but his grip on it seems to tighten.

I reach out and stroke the soft, plush fur, remembering how Solo made it sound like no big deal that he stopped wearing it; but he kept it. After all the harassment, he kept it.

"No way," I say, shaking my head. "That's your freak flag. I've already got one."

He frowns at me, then looks down at the plush Chewbacca face. His frown relaxes, and slowly, the corners of his mouth turn up in a relieved smile. He was ready to give it to me—but I think he really wanted to keep it.

"Solo," I say. He looks up. "How did you—I mean, you got there right when . . . How . . ."

"How did we know where to find you?" he asks.

I nod. "How did you even know something was happening?"

"Bec called me. She saw on the internet what happened at your dad's fund-raiser. She was kind of freaking out. Said you weren't answering your phone. She told me to come get her, so I did."

"And you came straight to me?"

Solo shakes his head. "We went to your house, but your parents said you had already left. We got really worried. I wanted to try Bec's house again; I figured you would go there."

"I did," I say. "But I went to Bullet Hole first."

"We checked there, too. We must have barely missed you. But, when you weren't there, Bec just seemed to know where to go." Solo swallows hard. "She was acting weird. I mean, I was worried, too—but she was freaking out, like she knew something bad was going to happen." He looks up at my IV pole. "She was right."

I stare down at the pale-green sheet covering me. How could she have known?

"Did you know she had a transgender sister?" I ask. Solo nods. "Maybe that has something to do with how she reacted."

Solo blinks at me as if he's processing the information. "Maybe," he says. We sit quietly for a minute, and then he reaches into his bag again. "Last Starburst?"

We split it, and Solo promises to come over and watch more *Doctor Who* with me once I'm home.

When he leaves five minutes later, Solo is wearing his backpack.

CHAPTER 31

I'M FINALLY DISCHARGED THURSDAY MORNING. Mom arranges for a substitute to take her classes so she can stay home with me. Each time she comes to check on me, she insists on throwing open the curtains to let in the sun, and then I have to get up to close them after she leaves; the light bothers my eyes. Finally, I snap at her, and she stops.

I'm afraid to watch TV or go on the internet. I don't want to hear what they're saying about me, and I don't want to know how badly my situation has impacted Dad's campaign. So instead, I finish season seven of *Doctor Who*, and then Solo brings the next two when he stops by after school with my Government homework. I ask about Bec, but he hasn't heard from her. He acts nonchalant about it—she's pulled this disappearing act before—but there's something in his eyes that tells me he thinks this time is different. And so do I.

That night it takes forever to fall asleep—and when I finally do, I have horrible nightmares. They're dark and heavy and vivid, but the details evaporate when I wake, and I'm left only with the looming sense that something terrible is going to happen. At one point I wake myself up shouting, and Dad comes in and gives me a sleeping pill.

On Friday, two detectives show up at my house, but I refuse to see them. Dad argues with me—even lays a whole guilt trip on me about preventing future incidents—but I just shut down and stare at the wall. Eventually, they go away.

By Saturday I'm able to come downstairs and eat breakfast with Mom and Dad. I want it to be normal, but it's not. Dad always watches the news in the morning, especially this close to an election. But today, the TV is off—for my benefit, I'm sure—and the silence is unbearable. On top of that, Mom and Dad are acting strangely, leaving a wide berth when they pass each other in the hallway. I hear them arguing at night.

I'm sure it's about me.

I can't fight the feeling that this is all my fault. That I caused this. That somehow, I provoked *him* to do this—I don't want to think of his name—by humiliating him in front of his friends, by rebreaking his arm. By refusing to just be normal.

My dad was right; I shouldn't have put my most personal thoughts out in public, where they could be read by anyone. I feel so stupid for not realizing what a risk that was—not just to me, but to him, and his campaign. I'm sure I've damaged his chances at reelection. I'm ashamed, too, that my parents have to keep taking care of me; I'm a burden to them now, a broken thing, a weight dragging them toward the edge of a cliff. And they can't bear to let go, so I pull them down with me.

Doctor Ann says guilt and shame are normal reactions to what I've been through. She encourages me to do my own research online and talk to my parents about it—but I'm not ready for that. The most important thing, she says, is to interrupt my thoughts when I'm feeling those things, and to identify that they're not true—that they're just a reaction to what happened. Post-traumatic stress.

It's hard to believe her.

I see Doctor Ann on Saturday, then again on Monday. I don't feel better, really, just *clearer*. In my head, I understand what's happening, and I can see the steps to getting through it. But in my guts, in my heart, I'm lost. Like I'm out in the middle of the ocean, swimming as hard as I can with no hope of land and no sign of progress. I see no shoreline, only an infinite, unbroken horizon.

And the dark, dark water beneath.

At dinner Tuesday night, the silence is too much. Dad shouldn't be home. He should be out at events and press conferences, and my mom should be with him. I'm not ready to face all that myself, not yet—but that shouldn't hold them back.

Dad eats slowly, saying nothing. Mom pushes cooked carrots around her plate with her fork. I have to do something, to say something, or things are only going to get worse. Finally, I clear my throat. They look up at me, surprised and expectant.

"What do the polls look like?" I ask.

Dad glances at Mom, then back at me. "Riley, that should

be the last thing on your mind right now."

"I'd rather not think about the first thing on my mind anymore."

Dad blinks, swallows.

I put down my fork. "I want to talk about something else, something real. I want to know."

Mom strokes her wineglass nervously with her thumb. "Honey, what's going on—it's not your fault."

"Just tell me," I snap. "I'm not a child. I can handle it." Then, more softly, "Please."

They exchange another glance. Finally, my dad looks me in the eye and speaks. "Gutierrez is up twelve points. The pundits are saying it's going to be tight."

I nod. I figured as much. Then, still looking Dad in the eye, I say, "Is it because of me?"

Dad's mouth drops open slightly, but he recovers quickly. "No, it's . . ." He shakes his head. "That's how these things can go. It's a conservative county. Any kind of story like this . . ." He trails off, looking at my mother for support. One part of me appreciates that he's trying to protect me—but another part is angry at him for thinking I'm too weak to face the truth.

Mom reaches for my hand, but I withdraw it. The hurt in her eyes just makes me angrier; she thinks I'm weak, too.

"You're more important to us than all of that," Mom says.

"Far more important," Dad echoes.

I nod, feeling heat start to build up behind my eyes.

Dad clears his throat. "I know you're still processing all of this. And I don't want to push you. But if you don't talk to that detective soon, they won't be able to—"

I stand up abruptly, cutting him off. "I'm not doing this right now."

Dad's face goes red. "You can't just give up like this."

"Oh," I say, my voice breaking, "and what about you? It's okay for you to give up?"

"What?" he says.

"You should be out campaigning, not sitting here, interrogating me about things you can't fix."

His face goes white, and when he replies, the words come out in choppy bursts. "Riley, whatever you think, I'm—I'm not giving up."

I clench my fists. "Well, I'm not, either."

Mom intervenes. "Stop it," she says, gripping my dad's arm so hard he winces. She looks at me, and there's a ferocity in her eyes I've never seen before. "Okay. You don't have to talk to the police. But you need to talk to *us*."

I look at the two of them sitting there, Dad confused, Mom scared. I think I ought to feel sad, or ashamed, but all I can feel is the heat in my face and the tension in my jaw. I take three long breaths. When I open my mouth to talk, the words won't come out, so I just shake my head.

Mom rises from her chair, walks over, and puts her arms around me. Dad gets up, too, and places a hand on my back. We stand there like that for a long time, not talking.

Finally, I push away. "I just need to be alone right now," I say. And then, pretending not to see the defeated look on my mother's face, I turn and head up to my room.

I put an old Trespassers William record on the turntable, lie back on my bed, and try to lose myself in the ocean of echoing guitars—but my brain won't be quiet. My dad is losing ground in the polls because of me. My best friend—girlfriend?—won't return my calls. And the guy who did this to me is walking around free, while I'm holed up in my room, hiding from reporters and the police, isolated from everyone. I consider calling Solo, but he'll only try to cheer me up, and that's not what I want right now. I wish I could blog—but that's out of the question. Even if my anonymity hadn't been stolen, it would only take one cruel message to break me into pieces. And I can't fall apart. Not again. So I turn off my phone, shove my laptop under the bed, and bury my face in my pillow.

I recognize what's happening—I'm isolating myself, just like Doctor Ann warned me I might. I'm withdrawing, closing myself off. I'm acting like a victim—and I hate that word. I hate it.

I have to do something.

But I don't have the courage to leave the room, let alone face my blog—and the thought of accidentally coming across some news article about what happened makes me physically ill. Still, I can't just lie here; I have to do *something*. So, more out of rage and desperation than a genuine desire to heal, I reach under my bed, retrieve my laptop, and fire it up. And, with a couple of carefully crafted Google searches, I start doing the research Doctor Ann prescribed.

I find dozens of websites about violence against trans and genderqueer people—but after half an hour of browsing, I end up back on QueerAlliance.org, reading personal stories written by survivors. Just like Doctor Ann said, many of them went through the same things I'm going through now: the numbness, the isolation, the nightmares. The guilt, the shame, the lack of appetite. It's weird; part of me is comforted by this information, but another part is angered by the thought that I went through this . . . *unthinkable* experience only to come out the other side as a stereotypical victim. A statistic who perfectly fits the profile.

And then I find a story dated June of this year—a month before I went to Pineview. It's about an eighteen-year-old trans man named Eduardo who was suffocated by his ex in an Orange County motel room. When I read the name of the motel, a shudder runs down my spine; it's three blocks down from the old hardware store where my dad used to take me when I was a kid. I've driven by it dozens—maybe *hundreds* of times.

I drove by it that night.

I put a hand on my head, feeling the tender spot where it struck first the windshield and then the hood of my mom's minivan. And that's when it dawns on me: I'm one of the *lucky* ones. Because I survived.

I'm surprised to feel a hot surge of anger rising in my throat. *I* survived—and yet, thanks to my famous father, my story has been all over the news. But what about Eduardo's story? How is it possible that a murder like this happened so close, and that I never heard about it on the news? Why wasn't this a headline?

There are dozens more, but the story that affects me most is about an eight-year-old trans girl in Ohio whose father beat her to death with a chair after she told him, "You know I'm really a girl inside, right?"

I have to wipe away tears to read on.

According to one site, over three hundred acts of violence have been committed against trans and genderqueer people this year in the US alone—and thirty of the victims were children and teenagers. I can only assume that Andie Gingham is one of them—that is, one of the thirty that were actually reported.

The thought that I might be number thirty-one sends a bolt of cold shooting through me.

But the feeling only lasts a moment, and then it's eclipsed once more by anger. A deep, slow-burning rage—at Jim Vickers and his accomplices, yes—but it's bigger than that. It includes Eduardo's ex. Andie Gingham's dad. The father of that eight-year-old girl. And, somehow, it includes me, too. For sitting here, unable—or unwilling—to do anything about it.

But what can I do? Me, who can't even face talking to my parents, let alone the police. I consider Mike/Michelle's invitation to speak at the Trans Health Con this weekend, and I shake my head. I don't have the courage to leave my room. How could I possibly stand in front of an audience of brave, out, genderqueer adults and claim to be some kind of "online community builder"? It's absurd.

But then I think about my blog and my fifty thousand followers—however unintentionally it came to be, it's an undeniable number. And even though it's only a virtual crowd, when I imagine those fifty thousand faces looking at me, I feel invisible bands begin to tighten around my chest. I remember vividly the *real* crowd of reporters outside the hotel that night—all those faces, all those microphones and cameras—and the pressure builds until I can't breathe. Until I just want to disappear.

My phone buzzes on the bedside table, and I flinch. The display shows Park Hills PD calling for the fourth time today; I never should have given that officer my cell number. Ignoring the call, I slide off the bed and go to the window. I peek out through the curtains and see a news van still idling on the curb across the street.

Just when I want to be left alone—isolated, Doctor Ann would say—I'm surrounded instead: by the police and the media and my parents, and by the overwhelming thoughts swarming around in my head. I can't go on like this. I need to talk to someone—someone other than Doctor Ann. And although Solo has been amazing to come see me every day, he's not the one I need. I need Bec. Now. And, since she won't return my calls, I'll have to go to her.

CHAPTER 32

THE CLOCK ON THE DASH reads 10:42 p.m. when I pull up to Bec's house, and all the lights are out. I try Bec's phone one more time. It goes straight to voice mail. It's way too late to knock on the door—so, using my phone as a flashlight, I walk around the side of the house, fumble with the latch on the gate, and make my way into the small, overgrown backyard. The lights are on in the back window, and there's a small gap in the curtains. I approach the glass and peer in.

It's Bec's room, all right, but it's a disheveled mess: bed unmade, dresser drawers hanging open, books piled on every surface. And there's Bec, sitting on the floor facing away from the window, staring at a framed photo surrounded by lit candles.

Gently, I tap on the glass, and she looks up in surprise. When our eyes meet, I take a step back; her face is drawn, her eyes hollow. Her hair is short and sticks up in clumps, as though she chopped it off with dull scissors. Finally, she crosses to the window and opens it.

"Hi," I say.

"Hi." Her voice comes out like a croak, as if she hasn't used it all day.

"Can I come in?"

She looks up at me, glances back at the door, and then sets about removing the screen from her window. I climb through, and she closes it behind me.

"Sorry if I scared you," I say. Bec shoves aside a pile of clothes and drops onto her bed. "But you weren't answering your phone, and I thought it was too late to ring the doorbell."

Bec shrugs. "Erik's at my dad's, and my mom took, like, three Ambien. She would've slept through it."

I lean up against the wall next to her desk. "You look worse than I do," I say. I hope to tease a smile out of her, but she just nods. "How come you haven't been answering my texts?"

Bec gestures vaguely at the door. "I dropped my phone in the toilet. I didn't want to talk to anyone." She licks her chapped lips and looks up at me. "How's your head?"

"It looks worse than it is." I move toward the bed and sit down next to her. I hope she'll take my hand, but she makes no move to touch me. I clear my throat. "I want to ask you about what happened that night."

As though she's been dreading this, Bec closes her eyes and nods.

"Did you know it was him? Vickers?"

"Yes."

"Did you tell the police?"

She nods again.

"Then why haven't they arrested him?"

She punches her thigh with a fist. "I *knew* it was him, but . . . that night, Solo and I hardly saw anything. Guys running. A truck pulling away. We couldn't see faces, let alone a license plate. When the detective took our statements at the hospital, he acted like we were wasting his time." Bec buries her face in her hands. "It's my fault," she says.

"What are you talking about?"

"All of it. It's my fault. That's why I couldn't talk to you."

My stomach twists, seeming to understand something my mind doesn't grasp yet.

When Bec speaks again, her voice is low, and she won't meet my eyes. "Erik hacked your computer. He found out about your blog."

My heart begins to pound. "What?"

"The night you came over to study. When he set up the Wi-Fi on your laptop, he stole your browser history."

I stare at her. "I don't understand. Are you telling me that Erik is the one who outed me? That he called the reporters?"

"No," Bec says. "It's more complicated than that." She lets out a long breath. "Erik had this fantasy of being on the football team. You saw him, working out with that video game. I guess he already knew who you were when you came to the door, because he'd overheard Vickers talking about you. So when I handed him your laptop that night, he saw a chance to get in good with the team. He hacked whatever he could and gave it to Vickers as some kind of bribe."

I stare down at the patchy brown carpet, trying to process

what I'm hearing. I remember spotting the two of them on the athletic field that day: Vickers, apparently teaching Erik how to throw. I remember Erik digging something out of his pocket and handing it to him.

"And then," Bec continues, "when we humiliated Vickers at the football game, I guess he just snapped. He had your blog, he knew your name. He must have Googled you, found out who your dad was. Read about the fund-raiser, and then made his plans to get back at you."

My mind is spinning, my face starting to tingle; Erik knew about my blog and gave the info to Vickers, who waited until the right moment to out me. The moment when it would cause the most damage.

"So . . . ," I begin, then pause. There's so much, it's hard to wrap my mind around it. "How do you know all this?" I ask.

"Erik told me," she says. But something in her eyes tells me it's not the whole truth.

"He admitted it to you?"

She nods.

"When did you find out?"

Bec starts to say something, then drops her gaze to her lap.

"*When?*" My voice sounds hard, and Bec seems to shrink from it. She glances up at the door, then back at me.

"The night you came over to study. Right after you left, I caught him looking at your blog. And I confronted him."

My chest tightens. "So you . . . you read it?" I ask.

Bec doesn't respond.

"Did you *read* it?"

She nods.

"*All* of it?"

She nods again, and suddenly I can't breathe.

"But I made him erase everything he stole," she says. "I thought it was gone, I swear—but he must have, I don't know, emailed it to himself before I caught him."

I put a hand on top of my head as if to hold myself down; the room has begun to tilt.

"But he didn't tell me the rest until—until *after* the . . . after it happened. I swear, Riley, I'm telling you the truth."

But I'm not listening; I can't listen. She read my blog. She knew everything, all along. Her invitation to the Q, our "dates," what I thought was flirting—was any of that even real?

My heart turns to lead in my chest.

"I'm sorry," she says. "I should've told you sooner. I didn't think—"

"So," I interrupt, my voice trembling. "I was just a project to you?"

Bec's head snaps up. "What do you mean?"

"You took pity on me." Heat rises to my face. "Thought you could 'fix' me."

"What? No. Riley, you know that's not how it was. I didn't—"

I stand up, cutting her off. "What do I know? That you invaded my privacy? That you lied to me?"

Bec opens her mouth as if to reply, but only shakes her head.

"And when it really counted, when I really needed you— you couldn't face it, so you ran away." I shake my head; now I'm the one who's disgusted. "You never liked me for me. You couldn't save your fucked-up sister, so you thought you'd try to save me instead."

Bec goes white.

I turn and stride to the closet. I dig my fingernails under the edge of the big rainbow decal on the closet door—Gabi's decal—and I tear at it, ripping it off in strips, shredding it. Something pops in my head—like a water balloon bursting— and I start to scream. My vision goes blurry. The sound of blood pumping through my ears is deafening. I push away from the closet door and stagger back toward Bec, yelling incoherently. My shins smash into the desk chair and I cry out. I stumble backward and kick the chair as hard as I can, sending paperback books flying.

And then Bec is on her feet, wrapping her arms around me, holding me. I thrash against her, slapping her back, trying to kick her, but she just holds me tighter, and my screams turn into wails. My legs give out, and I drop like a rag doll. Bec gets down next to me, not saying anything, just holding me. Just holding me.

There's a knock on the door, and a slurred, groggy voice yells, "Francesca? What's going on in there?"

"Nothing, Mom," Bec says. "I just had a bad dream. Go back to bed."

"Is that you yelling?"

"Go back to bed, Mom!"

Her mom mutters a few more incoherent protests, then withdraws. Bec holds me the whole time.

Gradually, my breathing slows. My heart rate goes down. I blink as Bec's face comes back into focus. She looks like herself again—her eyes are still hollow and her chopped hair still sticks up at random, but she's back in control.

"I have to go check on my mom," she says. "Stay here. I'll be right back." She stands and quietly leaves the room.

I cross to the bed, and my eyes find the framed picture Bec was staring at when I knocked on the window. It's a photo of a beautiful, dark-haired, fine-featured child about six years old, wearing a pair of patent leather Mary Janes. It's Gabi.

My phone vibrates in my pocket, and I check the display—it's Mom. They must have discovered I left. With a pang of guilt, I decline the call and text her back instead.

I'm okay. Had to see Bec. Home in an hour. Sorry.

Bec returns with a cold, wet cloth, and I use it to wipe my face as we both sit back down on her bed.

"Is she okay?" I ask.

"Yeah," Bec replies. "Are you?"

I look at her. "No. I'm pretty not-okay."

Bec nods, looks away.

"But I'm more okay than your hair."

She groans and runs a hand across her almost-buzzed scalp. "I'm so pissed I did that."

"I actually kind of like it," I say.

She rubs at it again. "I feel like a boy."

I smile. "I know what you mean. Sometimes."

Bec smiles back, that crooked smile, and warmth floods through me. I put the cold cloth against the back of my neck.

"I'm sorry I said that. About your sister. And about you."

Bec shrugs. "You were pissed off." There's a long silence as the two of us look at each other. Then she says, "When I saw the footage of you online, getting mobbed by reporters outside that hotel, I knew something was going to happen. I called Solo. We went looking for you."

"He told me," I say.

Bec's gaze drops to her lap, and she bites at her lip ring. "I didn't know Vickers was going to do what he did. But . . . I thought *you* might do something."

"Like Gabi."

"Yeah."

I glance at the photo of Bec's sister, and a lump forms in my throat. I haven't talked about why I ended up in Pineview since my first session with Doctor Ann. I swallow and look up at Bec. "I already did," I say. She cocks her head. "Over the summer, I chased a bottle of Xanax with a glass of my dad's favorite Irish whiskey."

"Why?"

"A lot of reasons, I guess." I look up at the ceiling. "I was into this guy, Derek. He was my friend, and then I made it weird, and he just . . . cut me off. I wasn't on meds yet, or in therapy or anything, and it kind of wrecked me. I didn't flush my phone, but I threw it pretty hard. Smashed the screen." I show her; she nods. "Anyway. I was getting ready for one of my dad's big events, like the fund-raiser last week." God, was that only last week? "Getting dressed up—it triggers my dysphoria. It was especially bad that night, and it snowballed into a full-on panic attack. And I just . . . I felt like it would never end. Like there was no other way out." Bec nods. I take a deep breath, and then I just keep talking. I tell Bec about Pineview. I tell her about Doctor Ann.

When I'm done, Bec starts to speak, but stops herself.

"What?" I ask.

"You never told me why you transferred."

"You don't want to hear that sob story."

Bec raises her eyebrows. "You owe me at least one, or we'll be out of balance."

I smile. "Fair enough." I lean back against the wall. "At Immaculate Heart, I had to take PE—I don't at Park Hills, I used my dad's pull to get it waived." I glance over at Bec. "I guess that makes me a hypocrite, huh?"

"No," she says. "It makes you smart."

"I guess. Anyway, I had to change in the locker room in front of other people. That's when I started having really bad anxiety. I couldn't eat. I lost a lot of weight. By the end of sophomore year I was having panic attacks two, three times a week."

"Wow," Bec says. I nod.

"Being undressed in front of other people . . . it's hard. Especially on days when I don't feel like the gender I was assigned at birth, you know?" Bec nods, and I wonder if she ever had this conversation with Gabi. "So I started wearing my gym clothes under my school uniform every day. You can imagine the harassment. One kid asked me if I was Mormon, and was I hiding my magic underwear. Catholic kids, you know? Obsessed with sex and religion." Bec smiles. "Anyway. One day—this was during the last week of sophomore year—I was changing in the locker room, and three of my classmates came in. They said school was almost out, and before summer vacation started, they wanted to see the magic underwear." I swallow hard. "It wasn't enough that I had to wear that fucking uniform every day. It wasn't enough that I changed right in front of them. They wanted to see my genitals." My voice breaks, and it's a few moments before I can go on. "I refused. So two of them pinned me against the lockers, while the other one pulled down my gym shorts so everyone could see. There were three other people in the locker room, but no one tried to stop it; they all just watched. One kid was about to take a picture when the coach finally came in and put a stop to it."

I expect Bec to act surprised, or to try to comfort me, but she doesn't, and I'm grateful. I don't want her pity right now—just her listening. And she seems to know that.

"At the time, I thought that was the worst thing that would ever happen to me."

I watch Bec's jaw tighten. She nods. She gets it. I look out the window at the big sycamore tree just beyond the back fence. The branches are swaying in the strong autumn wind, leaves detaching like skydivers jumping out of a plane.

"I thought if I changed schools, things would be better. I thought I could get away from people like that." I turn back to Bec. "But there are people like that everywhere. Just like there are people like me everywhere. Like Andie Gingham. Like your sister."

Bec's eyes drift to Gabi's photo. She shifts on the bed, runs a hand over her scalp.

I glance up at the shredded rainbow sticker on the closet door. I want to tell Bec everything that's happened to me: being stalked online, having my locker vandalized. Coming out to my parents. And, if I could tell anyone about what happened that night—how they held me down, how his stubble felt against my cheek—I would tell Bec. But now isn't the time. Right now, I just want her back. Us back.

"Riley," Bec says. I look up at her. "I'm sorry I didn't stay at the hospital. I'm sorry I left. I just—"

"No," I say. "You don't have to apologize. I didn't mean what I said, earlier. About you running away. You were there when it counted."

For a moment, I think Bec is going to cry; but she doesn't. She just takes my hand.

My parents are in the kitchen waiting for me when I get home. Mom rushes across the room to embrace me.

"Oh my God, Riley, we were so worried." She steps back, holding me at arm's length. Her hair is a tangled mess and her eyes are puffy. "Don't you *ever* do that again. You understand me?"

"I'm sorry, Mom. I won't." I glance at Dad, expecting to see his face red with anger, but he looks calm. "I just . . . I needed to see Bec. And I didn't want to talk to you about it first."

Dad walks over and puts an arm on Mom's shoulder. "Well, now I think it's time we did talk."

Mom makes tea and we sit around the kitchen table with her in the middle, gripping both our hands as though she's afraid the house might tip over and sink.

Dad looks at me. "You want to start?"

"Okay," I say. But then I just stare at the table, trying to think of what to say. Finally, I speak up. "I don't know what you think about me."

Mom inhales sharply and grips my hand even tighter. "We love you. You know we love you."

"I know," I say. "But that's not what I meant."

She glances at my dad. He looks intensely uncomfortable, and does his habitual throat clearing before he speaks up. "Well," he says. "We've only had a few days to process all this. And obviously, the circumstances weren't ideal when you told us."

"I know," I say.

Dad continues. "And, so much has happened since, we haven't really had time to deal with . . . with your gender identity stuff." His mouth tightens into a thin line.

"Okay," I say. "But you have to have some reaction, right?"

Dad blinks, then looks pleadingly at my mother.

"Well, honey," she says, "this is all very new to us. I mean, we understand gay and straight. And we know there are transgender people. But, until you said it out loud, neither of us had heard of 'gender fluid.'" She glances at him. "We had to look it up."

Dad grips his mug. "Honestly, there's so much information out there, and a lot of it contradicts itself. The pronouns and the . . . terminology, it's very complex, and . . ."

Mom cuts in. "But we love you no matter what, Riley. You're our child."

Dad looks at her, and then he nods. "Your mother's right." His eyes meet mine and he says, "But you're going to have to help us navigate this whole thing. We're old and set in our bipolar ways."

"Binary, Dad," I say.

He nods. "Right. Binary."

And then Mom sort of lunges forward and engulfs me in an awkward, suffocating hug—and after a moment, I hug her back. I expect my shoulders to start shaking, my eyes to start gushing tears, to have some profound catharsis—but apparently, I'm cried out for the night. Finally we release each other. Dad gives me a thin smile.

I say, "I think I'm ready to talk to the police now."

Dad raises his eyebrows. "Are you sure?"

"Yeah," I say. "But, will you guys . . . will you stay with me while I call?"

"Of course we will," he says.

The line connects on the third ring, and a man's voice asks whom I'd like to be connected with.

I say, "Officer Dinning, please."

CHAPTER 33

"THIS IS THE PART WHERE I don't ask you how you're feeling," Doctor Ann says, taking her usual seat.

"And this is the part where I tell you I don't know."

She makes an uncharacteristic throwaway gesture with one hand. "Make something up."

I frown; is this some new tactic to get me talking? "Make something up . . . you mean, lie?"

Doctor Ann glances at her watch. "Well, it's a fifty-minute session. If you're not going to talk about your feelings, you've got to say *something*."

I blink at her. "Something."

Doctor Ann laughs—and then I do, too. It's the first time I've laughed without crying since the assault. It's the first time I've thought of it as *the assault*. Today is Thursday; it's been over a week.

"What's going on over there?" Doctor Ann asks.

I fold my arms in front of my chest and look down at my feet. I know it's a defensive posture, but I need a little defense right now. "They arrested Jim Vickers," I say.

Doctor Ann raises her eyebrows. "When?"

"Yesterday."

She leans back in her chair. "So you spoke to the police."

I nod. "Tuesday night. I didn't want to go to the station, but with reporters still camped outside my house, we couldn't exactly have cop cars showing up—so the officers took one of their personal cars and came in regular clothes in the middle of the night."

"That was very accommodating of them," Doctor Ann says.

"Congressman perk," I say.

"Are you relieved?"

"A little. Not as much as I expected to be."

"I get that," she says. We look at each other for a moment, and I get the feeling she really *does* get it. Like, maybe she's been through something similar. But before I can ask, she goes on. "So you told them what happened, and they arrested him?"

"Not exactly. They said they'd question him, but they needed more than just my word to actually drag him away in handcuffs. They must have gotten something, though, because my dad made some calls this morning and found out he was in custody. My guess is one of his accomplices finally told the truth. Cole, maybe. Or the redheaded kid, Grady. I don't know. I answered all the cops' questions, but they've been super reluctant to tell me anything."

Doctor Ann shakes her head. "When the people involved are minors, they can't. Even when they want to."

"I know, they explained it to me about nine times. And what they did tell me was only after my dad leaned on them."

"Did you find out anything about your stalker?"

"Yes and no."

"What do you mean?"

"Well, after Vickers did what he did . . . I just assumed it had been him all along."

Doctor Ann nods. "I would have, too."

"But they checked all his stuff—his phone, his laptop—and they didn't find any evidence. So, it's possible he was sending me those messages from a friend's computer, or from the library or something—but it could be somebody else entirely. They're still looking."

She nods. "Are you angry? Are you disappointed?"

I look at Doctor Ann, amazed that she can read me so well. "Both, I think. The thing is, if Vickers wasn't the one sending the messages, it means he's in less trouble. Because stalking is a separate charge, and it would have helped prove that he was thinking about the . . . the assault beforehand." I almost don't say the word, and when I do, it sounds like gibberish to me.

"Do you ever find yourself asking *why*?"

I frown. "Why what? Why someone stalked me? Why Vickers did what he did?"

She nods. "Either. Both."

"I don't know. The cops told me Vickers's dad is a minister at a pretty intense church. So, maybe it has to do with that. Or maybe he was just getting back at me for breaking his arm, and he was drunk, and it went too far." I sniff, suddenly aware my nose is running. Doctor Ann hands me a tissue. I wipe my nose and look up at her. "I don't know. I don't know if I want to know, or if it even matters."

Doctor Ann looks like she's about to argue, maybe to correct something I've just said, but I interrupt her. "Can I get some water?"

"Of course," she says, and crosses to the cooler on the other side of the office. After a moment, she returns with a little plastic cup. I take a sip, and the cool water feels good on my throat.

"They're talking about this being a hate crime," I say. "It's kind of surreal. Like something from the news."

"Yeah," Doctor Ann says. "I bet it feels strange."

"Solo said they went all *CSI* on my locker. But, again, the police wouldn't tell us anything—even when my dad gave them his righteous elected-official act—because they're 'protecting the identity of minors.' Which is pretty ironic."

"And frustrating."

"Yeah. So, anyway. The first part of the interview was okay, but then it got hard."

"What was hard about it?"

"Giving my statement. They wanted to record me talking about the assault."

"Is there anything about that you want to share?"

I shake my head. "We've already been through all that, and it will just make me a mess."

"That's fair," she says. We look at each other for a moment, almost like opponents in a chess game. Then Doctor Ann says, "How's the anxiety been?"

And just like that, we've moved on.

"It's leveled out some," I say. "But it doesn't really go away. Like, there's this constant buzz in the background. My face pretty much starts tingling when I wake up, and doesn't really stop until I go to sleep. Maybe it keeps tingling while I'm asleep. I don't know."

"What else?"

"Bright lights bother me. Bec bought me these yellow sunglasses to wear indoors. She says they make me look like Bono."

Now, Doctor Ann does take the pad from her desk. She makes a note, and then sits back down. "I'm going to adjust your meds." Before I can protest, she gives me a stern look. "Just slightly. And temporarily. You need the relief."

"When you crank up my dosage, I feel foggy."

"You taking the bar exam or something?" She puts down the pad. "Let's try foggy for a month instead of buzzing. Just for a change. Okay?"

"Okay."

"How are you doing with your mom and dad?"

"We talked. Not about what happened that night—I mean, they were there when the police interviewed me—but we talked about me. About being gender fluid." I pause, but Doctor Ann doesn't say anything, so I go on. "Dad's being cool about it. But I think he might not believe it's a real thing. Or, maybe he thinks it's just a phase and I'm going to grow out of it."

"Does that bother you?"

I shrug. "I mean, he's a Catholic congressman. It might take him a while to wrap his brain around having a gender fluid kid. I'm giving him the benefit of the doubt."

At this, Doctor Ann smiles—but she recovers her clinical expression quickly.

"Have you talked about his campaign?"

"Yeah. He says he doesn't blame me, but I think he does, a little. But I think he forgives me, too." I stare down at the abstract pattern in the carpet. "I didn't know it was possible to blame someone and forgive them at the same time. But I think it is."

"And how about your mom?"

"I think my mom accepts it without really understanding it. After we talked . . . I got the feeling she's just relieved it's out in the open. But I don't know." I run my finger back and forth over one of the chair's brass buttons. The texture is soothing. "I think she's . . . disappointed. Mom likes to plan things—to pick out the colors and the flowers and the clothes. I think the idea that she can't take me shopping for a tux or a prom dress leaves her feeling kind of . . . cheated."

"You could let her take you shopping for both," Doctor Ann says.

I look up at her. "You know, as utterly unbearable as that sounds, I think she would love it."

Doctor Ann waves a hand. "No charge."

I laugh. That's the second time.

She gives me a faint smile. "Have you thought about when you might go back to school?"

I nod. "Tomorrow."

She raises her eyebrows. "You feel ready for that?"

"No. I'm tingling head to toe just thinking about it." But despite my nerves, my voice sounds clear, calm. It surprises me.

"But I can't hide forever."

"Another week isn't forever."

"I know. But I've already wasted so much time hiding. And I feel like the longer I wait, the harder it will be to go back. You know?"

Doctor Ann sits back in her chair and lets out a long, uncharacteristically dramatic sigh. "Well," she says. "You don't need my approval."

I frown. "I know. But I sort of want it."

She inhales through her nose and shakes her head. "Riley, I don't know what to say. You've been through a lot. I'd hate to see you push yourself too hard and have a setback. But everyone heals in different ways and at different speeds. And if you feel compelled—from the inside, not by someone else—then I think you should do it."

A shudder of relief runs through me. "Thanks," I say.

"Do you have a plan for how to get through the day?"

"Half a day," I say. "But, yeah, I have a plan."

"Why half a day?"

I smile. "I have a feeling I'm going off campus for lunch."

CHAPTER 34

"SCHOOL SORT OF SUCKED WITHOUT you," Solo says as we pull onto Imperial Highway. It's Friday morning—ten days after the assault—and I'm more than a little nervous about returning.

I smile at him. I almost say, "That's sweet," but it feels too girly. So instead, I just say, "Right on," in a terrible Matthew McConaughey voice. Solo gives me an odd look, like I've just said something in Klingon; apparently I overshot "not girly" and landed in "awkward." I guess some things don't change. I make a mental note to blog about it.

"So, I got a text this morning," Solo says. "Apparently the police showed up at Sierra Wells's house last night."

I whirl to face him. "Why? To question her about Vickers?"

"That was my first guess, too—but word has it she's the one who trashed your locker."

I gape at him. "*What?*"

"Yeah," he says. "Some freshmen said they saw her trying to jimmy the lock while everyone else was in class."

I stare blankly out the windshield, stunned. I picture the letters pasted in my locker.

POOR LITTLE RILEY

I put a hand to my mouth. "Oh God."

Solo turns to look at me. "What?"

"Sierra."

"What about her?"

I don't reply; it takes me a moment to process it all.

When Vickers found about my blog, of course he would have showed it to his girlfriend. I recall that first anonymous hate message—not "your a fag"; that didn't have the same threatening undertone as the others. No, the first one that hit me hard was: *go back to where u came from dyke r school doesn't need another faggot.*

I try to remember *when* I received it—only a day, or maybe two days after I embarrassed Sierra in front of her friends with my "you're really not my type" comment. Did she send that first message as payback?

Then the Andie Gingham story broke, and I got *c u at lunch. fuckin tranny.* That must have been her, too. And, after I emasculated her boyfriend by breaking his arm at the football game, she wrote: *poor. little. RILEY.* The same message the vandal had pasted inside my locker. If Sierra did the locker, then she sent the messages, too.

"Riley," Solo says, snapping me out of my trance. "What's going on?"

"Someone was stalking me on my blog," I say, only half aware of the words coming out of my mouth.

"What?" Solo says.

And then, as quickly as I can, I fill him in on the whole story, from the first anonymous hate mail to the final message pasted in my locker.

When I'm finished, I sink back into the seat, stunned, and more than a little scared.

"Oh shit," I say.

"I don't get it. Aren't you happy she's at least being questioned?"

"I am, but . . . if what she did to my locker was payback for humiliating her boyfriend, what will she do when she finds out I got him arrested?"

"I wouldn't worry about that," Solo says. His voice is low, almost a growl.

"What does that mean?"

"It means me and the rest of the guys on the team have your back. Anybody tries to fuck with you, they'll wish they were safe in prison."

I gape at Solo, at the sudden ferocity in his eyes.

He glances over at me. "What?"

"I've just never seen you go all papa bear like that. It's kind of hot."

Solo's cheeks redden, and he adjusts his grip on the steering wheel. He signals for a turn, and the hatchback shudders as he shifts into a low gear to climb the hill toward school.

"So, what are people saying?"

"Oh, there's the usual vomit of prejudiced nonsense," he says, recovering. "Most people are just confused or ignorant. Or both. Some of the results are funny, actually."

"Funny?"

"For example. The Fellowship of Christian Athletes got together and made temporary tattoos of that verse from Leviticus. You know, 'Man shall not lay within four cubits of another penis, lest he be smitten,' or whatever. They handed them out at lunch like black armbands. And then, in response, the theater gang made these stickers that said, 'Leviticus 19:28,' and plastered them all over the school.

"What's Leviticus 19:28?"

"It's the verse that forbids tattoos."

I laugh.

Solo continues. "So the bad news is, most people are grossly misinterpreting what's going on. But the good news is that there's open conversation about it."

We pull into a parking space at the far end of the lot, and Solo shuts off the car.

"So," he says, drumming his fingers idly on the steering wheel. "Bec's meeting us before?"

"Yeah."

"You're sure you want to do this?"

I glance up at the concrete walls of Park Hills High School and let out a long breath. "I'm sure."

Everyone looks up from their desks as Solo and I walk into AP English five minutes late. I stop, frozen in the moment as the door hisses shut behind me on its pneumatic hinge.

I've been absent from school for over a week, and during that time, my story has dominated the news; of course they're looking. My heart gives one frantic thump in my throat, and then settles into an elevated but steady rhythm as I move toward my desk. I glance at Sierra's usual desk—it's empty—and breathe a sigh of relief before moving down the aisle toward my own. When I've taken my seat, I look over at Solo for moral support. He obliges by rolling his eyes into the back of his head and giving me the finger. I grin in spite of myself.

Miss Crane continues her lesson, taking our entrance in stride; but when I sit down, I catch her looking at me. She smiles, but it's a sad smile, and I'm surprised to see not pity, but genuine understanding in her eyes. I wonder what she's been through.

She then proceeds to set the world record for Dropping Most Harry Potter References in a Fifty-Minute Period.

As I'm reaching for the door of Mr. Hibbard's room, a voice from behind stops me.

"Riley, wait up."

I turn around, and my jaw drops. It's Casey Reese—but it's not the pretty, long-haired girl I know from French. This Casey Reese has short, dyed-brown hair parted neatly on the side. She—*he*, I think—is wearing a bow tie, and looks like something out of a Banana Republic ad. But the eyes and the voice are unmistakably Casey's.

"Holy—" I say, clapping my hand to my mouth.

Casey's face splits in a wide, bright grin. "Surprised?"

"I'm sorry, that was so rude. I just—it took me a minute to—you look *fantastic.*"

"Thanks." Casey's smile dissolves into a more serious expression. "I heard what happened. I mean, everybody heard, but . . ." He shakes his head. "Sorry. This isn't going well, let's start over." He puts out his hand. "Hi, I'm Casey."

I smile and shake it. "Riley."

"Well, Riley," Casey says, "I'm a boy. And you gave me the courage to say that out loud."

I blink. My mouth has gone dry.

"You don't have to say anything," Casey says. "I just wanted you to know that . . . I wouldn't have come out if it weren't for you. So, thank you."

I glance around the hall. Two girls stare at us as they walk by. I don't even react. I look back at Casey.

"Are they giving you hell?" I ask.

He shrugs. "Not so much. I mean, yeah. But . . . so what? I am who I am, you know? And it feels good not to hide it anymore."

I nod. "I guess I haven't really gotten to that part yet."

Just then, the bell rings. Casey opens his mouth like he's going to say something else, something important, but instead, he just smiles.

"See you in French?" he asks.

"Absolutely," I say. And then I watch as Casey turns and walks off to class. Struts, really. His confidence is magnetic. I feel a swell of pride—and envy.

When then bell rings, I turn away from Mr. Hibbard's

room. I find a secluded spot in the back stairwell, pull out my phone, and place a call.

"Hi, Mike/Michelle? It's Riley."

After French, Solo "picks me up" outside Madame Bordelon's room. He's insisted on being my bodyguard as we cross the campus to meet Bec. I'm grateful, because the anxious buzzing in my head has been getting progressively worse all morning, and having him around helps. As we're passing the lockers, we turn the corner and I spot a short brunette girl walking toward us. She looks up, and I recognize her at once—it's Sierra Wells.

I stop, and she does, too. We stand there for a long moment, staring dumbly at each other. The buzzing in my head gets louder. My chest goes tight. Solo puts a protective hand on my shoulder.

Sierra looks from me to Solo and then back again, like she's sizing us up for a fight—and I'm caught completely by surprise when she actually speaks.

"I didn't have anything to do with what Jimmy did," she says, her tone daring me to argue. At first, I'm too stunned to respond—and then Solo takes a step forward.

"You did plenty," he says. "You should be in jail."

I surprise myself by reaching out to touch his arm with my tingling fingertips. "It's okay, Solo," I say. He looks at me, concerned, and I give him a reassuring nod. He takes a step back, and I turn to face Sierra.

Her expression is hard—not angry, but closed off. Withdrawn. Whatever vulnerability still exists in her, I got my last look at it that day in Miss Crane's classroom when I walked in on her crying. Now, her shield is up, and I doubt if any of my words will get through. But what I have to say isn't for her, anyway. It's for me.

I swallow, and fight to keep my voice even. "I'm not going to stop being who I am just because you don't like it." Sierra glances around uncomfortably, as if she doesn't want to be seen having a conversation with me. I clear my throat—Congressman Cavanaugh style—and she turns her attention to me again. "And I'm not going to stop talking about it just because you don't understand it." Knees shaking, I take a small step toward her. "I'm only going to talk *louder.*"

I raise my voice on this last word, and Sierra glares at me. Just when I think she's about to retort, her bottom lip quivers, and her face softens. She looks down at her feet and whispers something—it could be "I'm sorry," but her voice is too quiet to be sure—and then she hitches her bag up on her shoulder and walks away.

As soon as she turns the corner, I have to steady myself by grabbing Solo's massive arm.

"You okay?" he says.

"I will be," I reply.

Bec is waiting for us behind the language arts wing, and when I see her, I throw my arms around her and bury my face in her neck. The collar of her denim jacket is rough and real against my cheek.

"What happened?" she asks. Bec holds my hand while Solo fills her in on the encounter with Sierra.

"You know," Bec says, shaking her head, "all this time, I

thought it was me. But it turns out you're the one. You're the one who has it."

I frown. "Has what?"

"The overdeveloped sense of drama."

I smile.

"Put your glasses back on, Bono," Bec says. "We have an entrance to make."

My heart rate seems to accelerate with every step we take toward the cafeteria, and by the time we're standing at the top of the stairs, the blood is pounding in my ears and my vision has gone full-tunnel.

"Are you all right?" Bec asks.

"No," I say, breathing in shallow gasps. "I'm having a— full-on—panic attack."

"Should we go back?"

I shake my head. "No. We walk—all the way through. No matter—what."

Bec looks at Solo, then back at me. "Okay," she says.

And something seems to snap inside me, like a spell breaking. Like that feeling when your ears pop as the plane is landing—and suddenly you can hear again.

I blink. The tunnel vision is gone. My heart is beating a thousand times a second, my breath still coming in shallow gulps, but I don't care. I take one step, then another. Then another.

And then we're in the Gauntlet, all three of us, walking right down the center of the aisle. I glance over at a table full of kids eating while they study, and make eye contact with a tall, skinny guy in a red T-shirt. He smiles and nods, but there's no special recognition in it; he's just being polite. We pass the band kids, but no one looks up. As we approach the football table, someone calls out to Solo. He waves in response. Vickers isn't here—he's still in custody—and there's no sign of Sierra, either. Or Cole, or any of that crew.

I stop in the dead center of the cafeteria and look around. Some heads turn in my direction, and maybe half a dozen people lean over and whisper to their friends. One guy looks at me and shakes his head in disgust, then goes back to eating. A group of cheerleaders breaks out in a chorus of giggles that I'm pretty sure is because of me. But for the most part, nothing happens.

A hush does not fall over the crowd.

No one yells "faggot," or "dyke," or throws food.

On the other hand, no one shouts my name in triumph, either. There is no slow golf clap building up to a standing ovation.

It's just a bunch of people eating lunch.

I laugh out loud, and Bec turns to look at me, her face drawn with concern.

"You all right?" she asks.

"Yeah," I say. "I was just thinking—if I have to eat one more dry-ass cafeteria burrito, I might have a complete nervous breakdown."

Bec nods. "So, On the Vedge?"

"Definitely."

And before I know it, we're out of the cafeteria and scrambling down the slope to the parking lot.

"I need meat," Solo says. "Let's go to the Reagan Years."

"You want me to fall into a dairy-induced coma?" I reply.

"You like their fries."

"A teen of indeterminate gender cannot live by fries alone."

"Wait," Solo says. "So we can joke about this now?"

I shake my head. "*I* can joke about this. You must remain neutral and respectful at all times."

Bec snorts.

"That's totally unfair," Solo says. "You're a rich white kid, why can't I make fun of you?"

"I don't make the rules, Solo. I just represent." I pound my chest with a fist.

Solo laughs. "So be it."

CHAPTER 35

DAD COMES HOME EARLY, citing a long day of campaigning ahead of him tomorrow—he looks absolutely beat. My mom, who took the day off to go event-hopping with him, looks pretty wiped out herself. I *know* she's tired when she announces that Shelly will be dropping off Thai food at six.

Dinner conversation is light, and I only pick at my vegetable *pad see ew*; I'm too amped up to eat. Finally, I push the Styrofoam container away.

"Mom, Dad?" They look up at me. I take a deep breath. "There's something I want to do. But, it's kind of big, and I don't want to do it unless you're okay with it."

They exchange interested looks.

"All right," Dad says. "Tell us."

So I do. I tell them about Mike/Michelle's invitation to speak on the panel at Trans Health Con tomorrow, and how

Casey's coming out today inspired me to do more than just blog about what I've been through.

When I'm done, Dad loosens his tie and clears his throat.

"Riley," he says, "I don't know about this. You'd be obliterating your privacy."

I meet his eye. "Dad, I've spent the last week holed up in my room, avoiding the TV, hardly even going on the internet. We've disconnected our home phone. Reporters stake out the house. You have to sneak out through the side yard and get picked up in a rental car. Our 'privacy' is sort of over." He exchanges a dark look with my mom. I continue before they can interrupt. "You always say the best leaders figure out how to turn a bad situation to their advantage. When life gives you gators, you make Gatorade. Remember?"

I watch his face for some sign—and after a moment, I'd swear he's trying to suppress a smile. I think I may have won him over. My mom's face, on the other hand, is tight with concern, so I turn my attention to her. "I feel like if I can talk about it—about coming out, and my situation . . . maybe it will help me process all of this. And give it a positive meaning, instead of just being a sad story about something that happened to me."

Mom lets out a long sigh, reaches up like she's going to chew her cuticle, then folds her hands.

I go on. "I think about what Bec will say if I just hide from all this. And my friends at the Q. Andie Gingham. Casey Reese. The fifty thousand people who follow my blog."

Dad says, "I know you feel accountable to your community. And that's admirable. But you don't owe it to them. You don't owe it to anyone."

I look up at him. "I owe it to me."

Finally, Mom speaks, her voice heavy with worry. "It's just so *soon*."

I shake my head. "The timing is right. The election, the assault, it's all still in the news. I have this little window of time when I can talk into a big microphone. This is my chance to speak up for other people like me."

Mom looks at me. Her eyes are getting moist. Dad puts his hand on hers and says, "Sharon? What do you think?"

She shakes her head. "You are your father's child, Riley."

On Saturday morning—the day of the conference—I stand in front of my closet, staring at the palette of faded black and blue clothes hanging inside. The only brightly colored thing in here is a yellow T-shirt I've never worn, crammed way in the back. For the first time, I understand what my mother has been complaining about since I was a kid: my wardrobe has all the color of a week-old bruise.

Mom is sitting on the couch in the living room reading one of her guilty pleasures, a bodice-ripper romance novel. When I enter the room, she looks up from her book, embarrassed like a kid caught watching an R-rated movie.

"You startled me," she says, closing her book. "Is everything okay?"

"Yeah," I say. "Everything's good. I was just wondering... I was wondering if you'd take me shopping?"

I've never seen my mother get into a car so quickly in my life.

★ ★ ★

When we walk out of Nordstrom two hours later, both of us are smiling like we've won the lottery. The outfit I end up with is, as my mother put it, very *me*: a simple white dress shirt with a blue tie—darker than my dad's cornflower blue, but not by much. Below that, I chose a dark green tartan fabric with thin blue lines running through the plaid. It hangs just above the knee and lands somewhere in the middle of the skirt/kilt continuum. On my feet: a brand-new pair of blue sixteen-hole Doc Martens. The outfit is part punk rock, part Catholic schoolgirl, part prep-school lacrosse guy.

I love it. I absolutely adore it. I want to marry it and make babies with it.

Solo and Bec are late picking me up for the conference.

"I couldn't find Bullet Head," Solo says.

"You've been there," Bec says. "And it's Bullet *Hole*."

Solo throws up his hands. "Well, that's why. I was looking for a sign with a head on it."

"The sign does have a head on it, you nincompoop. A head with a *bullet hole* in it."

Solo frowns. "Did you just use the word 'nincompoop'?"

"I'm reviving the Dickensian insult movement."

"There is no Dickensian insult movement."

"Then I'm starting one."

"Hey, guys," I say, "I hate to interrupt. But, Bec, could you please let me ride shotgun? I don't want to puke in the Solomobile." My stomach is already churning at the thought of walking into the conference. And, truth be told, the tingling from this morning hasn't really gone away. On top of that, despite my upped dosage, the buzzing in the back of my head keeps getting louder. In short: I'm a wreck.

Solo reaches across Bec's lap to unlock her door. He fixes her with a triumphant glare. "Be gone, thou scruffy-looking nerf herder."

Bec gives him a sour look. "That's not even . . . who *are* you?" Carefully, she opens the battered car door.

She's evened out her choppy hair into a smooth buzz cut that actually looks good on her. She's got her jean jacket on over a T-shirt that features a glittery, prancing unicorn; I'm not sure if she's wearing it out of a sense of irony, or if it's her attempt to balance out her new hairdo with something more feminine.

When she gets out of the car, she glances at me, and then does a double take.

"Wow," she says. "You look . . . extremely hot."

I blush with the fire of a thousand suns.

The parking lot is packed when we arrive a few minutes past two o'clock, so Solo drops us off in front and says he'll meet us inside. Bec and I turn our faces down against the strong autumn wind and walk side by side toward the entrance.

The convention center is a massive, looming glass structure the size of a football stadium. The closer we get to the front doors, the shallower my breath becomes; I can't stop imagining all the people inside. All those eyes looking at me. The tingling in my hands spreads up my arms. I take deep Doctor Ann breaths—I have to fight this. I need to be at my best today. It's important.

But the breaths don't help. The tingling radiates through my body, and tunnel vision starts to close in; I'm losing control. My feet go numb. I catch my toe on a seam in the concrete and stumble.

Bec catches me before I can fall, grabbing me by the shoulders with surprising strength, holding me steady. She leads me toward a ring of trees off to one side; there's a green metal bench in the center. My heart is pounding in my chest, my vision blurred.

Bec doesn't ask if I'm okay. She doesn't tell me there's nothing to be afraid of. She just guides me to the bench, puts a hand on my back, and says, "Breathe." She takes my hands in hers and looks into my eyes, but I can't seem to focus on her. The wind picks up and parts the canopy of leaves overhead. For a split second, the sun peeks through, flashing in my eyes, bright and angry. Like a camera flash. Like a sodium lamp.

Like the headlight of a truck.

And all at once I'm there again. I feel their hands holding me down, feel the pressure against my back.

Somewhere in the distance, Bec's voice says, "Stay with me."

But I can't. I can't stay. I have to go. I withdraw. My face is numb. My face is numb. The world shrinks to a pinprick.

Far away, I feel Bec grip my shoulders. She pulls me into her arms.

I feel her hands on my back, holding me, and I start to thrash, but she only hugs me tighter. I struggle for a moment—but when I know she isn't going to let go, I stop. I feel my body go slack.

She holds me. Not forcing; containing. Stilling.

My heartbeat slows. My breathing becomes more even. My face is pressed against Bec's shoulder. It's wet.

After a long time, she pulls away and looks at me. Her face slowly comes into focus: elfin ears, high cheekbones, strong nose—and those eyes. Those lightsaber-blue eyes. She takes my hand again, brushes the tips of my fingers with her own.

The tingling is gone.

I feel a sensation in my stomach—not the uncomfortable twisting from before, but the fluttering of butterfly wings. Bec's face is strong, set. There's concern in her eyes, but no panic. The butterflies in my stomach rise. I lean closer. My eyes drift down to her mouth, her thin lips set in a straight line. The metal ring in her lower lip twitches.

"Riley, it's too soon."

"It's okay," I whisper.

And I lean in.

I'm only an inch away when she stops me with a hand on my chest, and I feel my heart dive into my stomach. Bec sees the expression on my face and shakes her head.

"It's not like that," she says.

Shame and confusion well up inside me.

"I'm not stopping you because I don't want us to kiss," she says.

I want to reply, but no words come.

"I'm stopping you because I want it to be like *this*."

She takes my hand, places it over her heart. Hers is beating fast too, and I can feel her breath quicken at my touch. And then she smiles that crooked half smile, grips my shirt in her fist, and pulls me into a kiss.

Her lips are firm. The metal of her lip ring feels cold and solid against my skin. She puts her hand on the side of my face, brushing her thumb across my cheek. A swirling dizziness replaces the tingling in my head, then spreads through the rest of me. And then, it's as if a bank of stadium lights comes on behind my eyelids—but it's a good brightness. A warm brightness. And I don't flinch from it.

There's a soft sound, and our lips come apart. Bec leans her forehead against mine.

"I've been wanting to do that for a long time," she says.

I keep my eyes closed. I don't want that brightness to go away. "I thought you liked the scruffy lumberjack type. Like your drummer."

Bec laughs. "Don't be stupid. I don't have a type. I have standards."

I open my eyes and look into hers. "And I meet them?"

"You *are* them."

I start to reply, but she puts a finger to my lips. "We can talk about all this later. Right now, your public awaits."

CHAPTER 36

MIKE/MICHELLE AND KANADA ARE WAITING for us outside the conference hall. Kanada actually lifts me off my feet when she embraces me, and Mike/Michelle follows with a more subdued hug. Solo and Bec wish me good luck, then head in to find seats.

When the door has closed behind them, Mike/Michelle turns to me, her expression serious. "Riley, listen, there's—"

"Don't worry about me," I interrupt. "I'm okay. I'm ready."

"I don't doubt you for a moment," she says. "But you need to know that the room is packed with reporters and photographers."

"I know," I say, "I invited them."

Mike/Michelle frowns. For a moment, I think she's going to be angry—but then she says, "You couldn't possibly have called every news station in the greater Los Angeles area all by yourself."

I shrug. "Didn't have to. I figured they'd all be checking my blog—so I just posted the time and the address."

Kanada throws back her head and laughs. "My, my," she says. "Somebody just out-Mike/Michelled Mike/Michelle."

I smile. "Sorry for the surprise."

"Don't apologize," Mike/Michelle says. "We'll take all the attention we can get." Her smile falters, and she grips my arm gently. "I'll do my best to keep it civilized in there. But once the Q and A starts, I won't be able to control them."

I remember the storm of reporters outside the hotel last week—was it only last week? The cameras flashing, the din of raised voices, the press of arms and elbows, the microphones being thrust at me as I tried to push my way through. I feel my heart beat in my throat again.

I look from Kanada to Mike/Michelle, and then I walk to the doors and push them open.

I'm staring into the biggest conference hall I've ever seen in my life. You could park a 747 in here—and yet, a claustrophobic dread settles in on me as five hundred people turn in their seats like attendees at a celebrity wedding. There's a pause as reporters and conference-goers alike try to identify me. Finally, someone yells, "Alix!"

And then the flashes start going off.

Kanada takes me by one arm, Mike/Michelle by the other. Reporters call out questions as we make our way down the aisle—but there are legitimate attendees in the crowd too, shouting encouragement. I spot one conference-goer with dyed-green hair holding up a sign that reads "We Love You, Alix!" Another throws a lei of plastic flowers in my direction as I walk past.

The whole gang from the Q is here—even Morgan, who's still wearing that same green flight jacket. I spot Casey Reese, too, standing just across the aisle. He makes a point of gesturing to his hair, which he's spiked into a fauxhawk, and gives me two thumbs up; I smile at him.

Bec and Solo are seated about five rows from the front. Bec waves, but Solo looks concerned, half standing as though he might plunge into the aisle and start clearing the crowd—but Bec pulls him back into his seat.

There's a stage at the front of the room with a long banquet table and a lectern packed with microphones. I take my place between the two panelists already seated at the table—a tall man in a loud green shirt and an older woman with a wispy gray ponytail. Kanada finds a seat in the front row, and Mike/Michelle takes the podium.

"Good afternoon, everyone, and welcome to 'Building LGBTQ Communities Online.' Today we're going to explore—" But she's interrupted as the first reporters sound off.

"Riley, how do you think your coming-out will affect your father's campaign?"

"Do you feel responsible for the—"

Mike/Michelle pounds a fist on the lectern and it booms through the sound system with a squeal of feedback. "Folks, this is a panel, not a press conference. I would ask you to kindly hold your questions until the end."

As the panel goes on, I struggle to keep my breathing under control. Every time a flash goes off, I jump a little in my chair; I wish I'd thought to ask Doctor Ann for an extra Xanax.

Mike/Michelle mediates, and I'm grateful that she poses most of the questions to the other two panelists: The man in the neon shirt is a professional lobbyist, and the older woman runs the biggest gay and lesbian newsletter in the United States. I field a few of the questions, trying to answer as best as I can, but I feel like a child next to these two older, more qualified experts. But, eventually, my turn comes.

"How did you approach building your own online community?" Mike/Michelle asks, and looks at me as if I have some kind of expertise to offer.

"Um, it sort of happened by accident," I say. I'm totally serious, but it gets a big laugh, reminding me vaguely of my "gymnastics scholarship" moment at Dad's fund-raiser. "My doctor told me to start an anonymous blog as part of therapy. And then the Andie Gingham story broke, so mostly it was out of my hands. I guess I just tried to be real, and give the advice I'd want someone to give me." Mike/Michelle gives me a tender smile, and then the other two panelists cut in with a bunch of jargon about SEO and other things I don't really understand.

With about ten minutes left—I'm watching the clock on my phone, counting down the minutes—Mike/Michelle steers the conversation off-topic. She looks down at her cards, seems to consider, and then sets them aside and looks at me.

"What would you say to someone who claims that nonbinary gender identities aren't real? What do you think of people who say: man or woman, that's all there is, pick one?"

I glance into the audience. A few flashes go off. "I don't know," I say. "People are complicated. And messy. Seems too convenient that we'd all fit inside some multiple-choice question."

Finally, Mike/Michelle invites us to make our closing statements. The newsletter woman goes first, then the lobbyist in the neon shirt—and then it's my turn. Hands shaking, I unfold a printout of something I wrote late last night. I shouldn't be so nervous—it's basically a blog post—but the thought of reading it out loud makes my face tingle. As I read, I avoid making eye contact, and I stumble over my words quite a bit—but I think it comes off okay.

"I wish I had some all-encompassing wisdom to give you. Or to give myself. You know? Because I've been through a lot, and it hurts. I want everything I've been through to make sense. I want the pain to have meaning. I want it to change something." I look out into the crowd and find Bec. Her eyes are wide and serious, and she never takes them off me. "But the truth is, feelings don't change anything. To change something, you have to say things out loud. Do things. Take chances. Take a stand." I pause, and when I clear my throat, it echoes through the PA. "So, this is the stand I'm taking: I'm not going to hide anymore."

The room is quiet for a second, and then the crowd starts to applaud. I have to wipe at my eyes with my sleeve.

When Mike/Michelle finally opens the panel to questions from the audience, the room explodes in cacophony. The media, who have managed to keep their silence for the last thirty minutes, all start yelling questions at once. Mike/Michelle pounds on the lectern like a courtroom judge, but they ignore her.

In the midst of all the shouting, one of the doors in the back of the hall opens partway, and a man slips in. He's tall, and wears a blue baseball cap over dark aviator sunglasses. Avoiding the center aisle, he makes his way down the side of the big room and finds an empty seat at the end of the sixth or seventh row. I look closer and see that there's gold writing on his blue cap; it's the University of Notre Dame logo.

It's my dad.

My heart swells in my chest, and I can't stop tears from leaking down the sides of my face. I wipe them away quickly and smile at him. He nods in reply, then he sinks down in his chair to disguise his height.

I glance around to see if anyone else has noticed his arrival, but if they have, they don't appear to recognize him. Mike/Michelle walks over to my chair and leans down to talk in my ear.

"We should just end it now and escort you out of here. The Q and A is a joke. They're not going to stop yelling."

I shake my head. "Let me talk to them."

To my surprise, Mike/Michelle nods and steps aside. I stand up and make my way to the podium.

At first, the noise swells, and a fireworks show of flashes pops across my vision. I hold up my hand to shield my eyes.

"Hey," I say into the cluster of microphones. "Hey, can everybody quiet down?"

Slowly, the din of shouting ebbs. I glance at Mike/Michelle, and she gestures for me to go on. I turn and look out at the hundreds of faces gathered in the hangar-sized hall. Here and there, a flash goes off. I grip the sides of the lectern. I look down at Morgan and the group of Q members seated at the front of the house. My eyes move to Solo's massive presence a few chairs behind. To Bec, smiling that half-smirk smile, her blue eyes burning up at me from the fifth row. I look at my father, hunched down in his chair, watching me intently. He lifts his hand so that it's level with his chest, then extends his pinkie and index fingers, making rock 'n' roll devil horns. I smile at him. Then I take a long, deep Doctor Ann breath, and close my eyes.

To my surprise, it's not a black void that appears behind my eyelids, but a familiar, comforting light. I picture a blackboard suspended in it. I dip my brush into the surrounding light and begin to paint, erasing the cold blackness bit by bit, replacing it with warm, bright light. I get all the way to the far edge, until there's only a sliver of black remaining—

And I reach up with my brush and paint it white.

AUTHOR'S NOTE

I was on my way to dinner with friends, crammed into the backseat of a car not quite as battered as the Solomobile, when one of our group—let's call her Jane—brought up a court case pending in my county. A transgender girl (assigned male at birth, but identifying as female) was suing the school district for the right to use the girls' locker room at her high school. Jane gave us the gist of the story—and then she said, "It's probably just a pervy boy trying to see some boobs."

I waited for one of my friends to object—or, at the very least, to defend the trans girl—but no one did.

I woke up the next morning thinking about the girl—and the morning after that, too. So I sat down to start writing, and what came out was Riley's opening blog post:

The first thing you're going to want to know about me is: Am I a boy, or am I a girl?

As soon as I typed the question, I realized I didn't know the answer. So, in order to buy some time while I figured it out, I put off making the decision about my main character's birth-assigned gender and just kept writing. I assumed it would come to me eventually—and besides, I didn't think I could write more than fifty pages before the question of pronouns forced me into a corner.

But then something unexpected happened. I got to know Riley not as a "boy" character or a "girl" character or a "transgender" character, but as a human being—and I knew that this was the experience I wanted my readers to have, too. So I discovered, rather than decided, that Riley was gender fluid, and that maybe I didn't need to reveal—or even to know—Riley's birth-assigned gender to tell the story.

I had serious doubts, though—not only about the plausibility of sustaining a story with such a big "secret," but about my ability to authentically write a character who was struggling with gender identity. Still, the compulsion to write this story was overwhelming. And when I handed in the first fifty pages to my writing group, they enthusiastically urged me to continue—but first, they wanted to know if being gender fluid was "a real thing."

That's when I knew I *had* to write this book.

Symptoms of Being Human took more than a year to research, write, and revise. I had a few key one-on-one conversations, and I read a lot—mostly firsthand accounts by trans and gender nonbinary people, but academic studies as well. Some of what I learned shocked me: 64 percent of transgender and nonbinary people in the US experience sexual violence in their life—12 percent before they graduate high school. Forty-one percent will attempt suicide. Genderqueer and transgender people are four times as likely to live below the poverty line.

Riley goes through a lot in *Symptoms*, but is blessed with understanding parents, supportive friends, a professional therapist, and a big network of online and IRL people dealing with the same issues. Very few trans or genderqueer teens are so lucky, and almost none have access to the kind of resources or media platform Riley does.

If you're struggling with gender identity, anxiety, or depression, you are not alone. Please make use of the resources on the next page. They want to help.

RESOURCES

TRANS LIFELINE

translifeline.org

US: 1-877-565-8860

Canada: 1-877-330-6366

THE TREVOR PROJECT

thetrevorproject.org

1-866-488-7386

NATIONAL CENTER FOR TRANSGENDER EQUALITY

transequality.org

TRANSGENDER LAW CENTER

transgenderlawcenter.org

ANXIETYBC

youth.anxietybc.com

ANXIETY AND DEPRESSION ASSOCIATION OF AMERICA

adaa.org

ACKNOWLEDGMENTS

THANK YOU:

To Ami for lighting even the darkest of places so that I could see to keep writing.

To Rachel Ekstrom for delivering my dream, and then staying to help me unpack it. To Kristin Rens for her generous and unrelenting dedication to making this a better book and me a better writer. To Mike/Michelle Dennis for her time, her commitment, and for reminding me who Riley really is.

To Kelsey Murphy, Caroline Sun, Nellie Kurtzman, Alexei Esikoff, Alessandra Balzer, Donna Bray, and everyone at B+B/HarperCollins for making this book possible. To Sarah Kaufman for the perfect cover.

To Don Houts, MD; Diane Chen, PhD; Todd Harmonson; and Melanie Schlotterbeck, CMP, for helping me get the details right. To Sean Francis for making Fullerton real, and to

Anna-Lynne Williams and Dean Dinning for the soundtrack.

To my mentors, Cameron Thor, Barbara Deutsch, Father Coughlin, and Graysen Harnwell for pushing. To the teachers who got to me: Julie Crain, Heidi Burns, George Baratta, Norman Cohen, Vicki Silva, Pam Ezell, Everett Lewis, and Mark Axelrod.

To Riki, for teaching me to love books (and to not split infinitives or use prepositions to end sentences with). To my D&D crew for believing, and especially to Dan, for taking the plunge with me. To Lissa Price, for her unselfish guidance and generosity. To Brian Perry and Derek Rogers, for making me a better writer. To Tara Sonin, for finding me and insisting that I could. To my brothers, Corey and David, for all that time on the bus and in my heart. To Scott Satenspiel, for being *really good* (flaps arms) and always there. To Corey, Adam, and Zander, for unreasonable support. To Jasmine & Pete, for giving me a home base in NYC.

To J. K. Rowling and Stephen King, without whose work I might never have sat down at the keyboard again after so much time away.

To the LGBTQIA community for their bravery, love, and support.

And to you, dear reader, for giving me my dream job. I'll see you at work tomorrow.